THE LANCASHIRE LEOPARD

A Selection of Recent Titles by J M Gregson from Severn House

Lambert and Hook Mysteries

GIRL GONE MISSING
TO KILL A WIFE
AN UNSUITABLE DEATH

Detective Inspector Peach Mysteries

MISSING, PRESUMED DEAD
A TURBULENT PRIEST
WHO SAW HIM DIE?

THE LANCASHIRE LEOPARD

J. M. Gregson

severn House

Gre

This first world edition published in Great Britain 2001 by
SEVERN HOUSE PUBLISHERS LTD of
9–15 High Street, Sutton, Surrey SM1 1DF.
This first world edition published in the USA 2001 by
SEVERN HOUSE PUBLISHERS INC of
595 Madison Avenue, New York, N.Y. 10022.

British Library Cataloguing in Publication Data

Gregson, J. M. (James Michael)
   The Lancashire leopard
   1.   Police - Fiction
   2.   Detective and mystery stories
   I.   Title
   823.9'14 [F]

   ISBN 0-7278-5638-3

Typeset by Palimpsest Book Production Ltd.,
Polmont, Stirlingshire, Scotland.
Printed and bound in Great Britain by
MPG Books Ltd., Bodmin, Cornwall.

To John and Julie,
leaders of the
New Zealand Fan Club

Author's Note

The events and characters in this book are entirely fictional. Forensic psychology, however, is real enough and increasingly used in cases of serial rape and/or murder. For those with an interest in this field, the best introduction to the subject is David Canter's *Criminal Shadows* (HarperCollins, 1994), while Diane Scully's *Understanding Sexual Violence: A Study of Convicted Rapists* (Boston: Unwin Hyman) examines the wide-ranging criminal experience of rapists.

One

There was snow upon the ground. A soft carpet, an inch of sound-muffling whiteness. The flakes fell softly and slowly, brilliantly white for a second against the street lights, then almost invisible as they gradually thickened the covering upon the narrow streets and slate roofs of the nineteenth-century town. The terraces, which were normally so grim and functional, glittered with a fragile and transient beauty.

Once Christmas was over, the weather had turned cold as usual, just as the children, who would have relished the snow, were about to return to school. At seven thirty on the evening of January 5th, most of the older residents of Brunton shut their doors gloomily against the snow and shook their heads over the trouble it would bring in the morning. The town was preparing to drop into its habitual resentful but resilient mood. Those soft southerners wouldn't have to put up with weather like this – it was probably just drizzling in London; but Brunton folk were tough: they could handle snow, frost and worse.

Most of the young who lived here were free of this siege mentality. They felt it was up to them to take a wider and less parochial view than the older generation. Hannah Woodgate, hurrying along with fun-fur collar turned up against the snow, was now nineteen but still near enough to childhood to feel she still wanted to enjoy this weather. She looked over her shoulder up the short street, found that she was unobserved, and broke into a joyful little run. She slid for

1

two yards along the tarmac, feeling the soft snow build beneath the soles of her boots. It was only with difficulty that she resisted the impulse to go back and slide again over the same ground, building the incline into one of the glassy slides of her childhood.

Daft ha'porth! she said to herself. It was a way of perpetuating the memory of the grandfather who had died at this time last year. He had always called her that, though young Hannah had arrived long after the days when you could buy a halfpennyworth of anything. Hannah thought of Gramps with great affection in that moment. But by the time she reached the end of the street she was ready for another, more ambitious glissade, whose abrupt conclusion almost precipitated her into the gutter.

She was saved by a hand from her friend Anne, who'd appeared right on cue, and they fell laughing into each other's arms. It was the first time they had seen each other since Boxing Day, so they had much gossip to exchange as they turned their steps towards King George's Hall and the Saturday night dancing. As they moved into the centre of the town, the lights grew brighter and other groups joined them, all hurrying like ants towards the centre of activity. It was a scene which Lowry might have cared to paint, though it was given unwonted glamour by the brilliant whiteness of the falling snow and the glitter added to it upon the ground by the softened light of the lamps.

As always, Hannah enjoyed the enclosed world of the disco, where the realities of life outside were temporarily forgotten. Anne had a boyfriend with her, whereas Hannah would not see her Tom until she returned to university next week. She thought of Tom for a moment, drinking with his fellows, trying to look as if he had done it for years and could handle it, offering her his opinions of the books she was studying and the ways of the university with all the lofty experience of a man a year ahead of her in his studies. Tom might think himself a man when he was at the bar, but he was a mere child when it came to bra-straps! Daft ha'porth, she thought affectionately. She'd be happy to see him again next week, to hear his fashionably disenchanted account of his family Christmas in Surrey.

The evening passed surprisingly quickly. The lights, the rhythm, above all the noise, created a temporary world which was larger than life but also divorced from life, one which was intensely enjoyable but which would end with the last note of the music and the transition to the real world outside. There was a minor crisis when Hannah was offered pot in the Ladies. A few spliffs might do no real harm, might even be largely ignored by the police nowadays, but her New Year resolution was that she would have nothing more to do with drugs in any form, and that included even the smallest of spliffs.

It was an embarrassing rather than a fearful moment. Her refusal was accepted with a shrug as the girl transferred her attentions to people who would be glad of the stuff. Hannah was relieved to get back to the dance floor. Brunton was her town, and she had grown up with most of the people around her on the dance floor; many of them had attended the comprehensive school together.

She danced for ten minutes with Jason Wright, who had been her boyfriend when she was in the sixth form, who still fancied her, she knew. She was as friendly as she could be without encouraging him to think that the ashes of their relationship might be rekindled. It seemed to her to work quite well. The last hour passed in a pleasurable frenzy of brash rhythms and energetic dancing, with laughs of recognition interspersed with frenzied explosions of activity.

They called their goodnights to each other at the front of the hall. Once these cheerful shouts were over and they moved away from the tall stone building, the town seemed unnaturally quiet beneath its blanket of whiteness. She had agreed earlier in the evening that she would share a taxi with three of her friends, but they had lost contact with each other during that last, intense hour and she could not find them in the crowd around the doors. Perhaps they had already gone, while she was changing back into her boots in the cloakroom, or perhaps assignations made during the evening had led to a hasty reorganisation of plans. These things happened at King George's on a Saturday night.

Hannah didn't mind. She could walk most of the way home with Anna and Robin, without being a gooseberry, for the three had known each other for years. And what a night it was for walking! It had stopped snowing now. The even carpet was two inches deep, beginning to glitter with the sharp frost which would crust it by morning. The navy sky was spattered with a million points of light. Once out of the main thoroughfares of the centre of the town and into the unsullied white of the side streets, the trio ran and slid more joyfully than Hannah had four hours earlier, with any inhibitions removed by alcohol and the crisp, clear cold about them.

The three of them stood talking excitedly for several minutes at the point where their ways diverged, reluctant to let a magic moment go, watching their words wreathe into funnels of steam as they spoke. It was only when a light went on and the curtains were drawn back in the corner house beside them that they realised guiltily how late it was and how loudly they had been speaking. Their hasty leave-taking dissolved into gales of giggles as they glanced up at the shadow behind the lighted curtains. Then they turned away from each other and went their respective ways.

Within twenty yards, Hannah became aware for the first time since they had come out of the hall of just how piercingly cold it was. Still, it was less than half a mile now to her home. She pictured her mother, lying in bed, waiting for the soft scratch of her daughter's key in the lock, waiting for the moment when she could sigh contentedly and drop into sleep. "Don't wait up for me!" Hannah had said, as usual. Yet she would be willing to bet that her mother would not sleep soundly until her brood was complete and safe within the walls of her house. For the first time in her life, Hannah Woodgate felt glad of that, though she could not have said why.

She was not afraid of the dark. As the eldest of four children, she had spent much of her adolescence telling the younger ones that there was nothing to fear, and in this respect bravado had become a habit with her. She crossed from shadow into light as she went down her first street alone, but that was to get the full effect of the panoply of moon and stars above her. She slowed for a moment, staring up and considering the remoteness of those pricks of light in that vast darkness, of the smallness of her own tiny spot within the universe. Then she hurried on.

There was going to be a hard frost on top of this snow, there was no doubt about that. As she passed the allotments on her left, a frost-encrusted row of Brussels sprouts glittered like beacons in the light of the moon. Her father had spent many of his happiest hours here as she grew up, and she had often been sent to fetch him for his meals, when he became too absorbed to remember the time.

It was as she hurried past the allotments that she became aware of the presence behind her.

She was not sure how she knew that there was someone there. She could scarcely have heard him, for the snow mantled every sound. Nor could she have said why she knew immediately that this presence was male. Perhaps she had caught some tiny movement of a shadow, for her eyes were now well accustomed to the night, and the moonlight across the acres of snow on her left made it seem very light here. She knew that the presence itself was what mattered, that her queries as to how she had become aware of it were made only to keep her fear at bay.

She wanted to turn and confront him, to have her fear made absurd by a familiar, friendly apparition. Yet she knew she could not turn round. And in that moment she became aware of the depth of her terror.

It was greater than any fear she had known before. Greater than that of her childish nightmares; greater than that of the

5

moment when she had seen her small brother slip beneath the wheel of a motorcycle. This terror was seizing her whole body, making it impossible for her to co-ordinate the familiar, automatic movements that were necessary if she was to run.

She had to force herself to thrust first her right leg forward, then her left. It was as if she were rediscovering movement after a long immobilisation after an accident. It was no more than three hundred yards from here to her house. She could escape, if only she could run. She took the short cut, along the back of the terraced houses, past the row of garages where once there had been outside privies.

And now she could hear the pursuit behind her. The man must be close. She felt the movement coming back into those reluctant limbs of hers. She sucked in a great gulp of air and tried to scream, but nothing would come. She reached the corner, and cursed the snow; with her arms flailing like a clown's, she strove to keep her balance for the turn. It was a straight run for home from here.

It was that turn which was her downfall. The soles of Hannah Woodgate's winter boots were smoother than those of the sturdy wellington boots worn by her pursuer. She slipped, was almost down, touched the floor with a desperate right hand, and recovered.

But her pursuer did not slip. He flung his arms round his quarry, with a low, exultant, animal growl. He crushed her for a moment against him, feeling the brief thrill of the supple young flesh beneath the winter clothes. Then his hands were at her throat, thrusting her down into the snow, watching the anguish in those bright eyes as they died in the moonlight.

He held her for a long moment after all movement had left the flailing limbs, as if there might be some trick still left in this lithe young body, as if he could not believe that so much young life had been stilled so quickly. Slowly, experimentally, he released the vice of his grip. Then he stood for a moment over his victim on the ground.

So still; so quiet; so innocent. For ever, now.

Weeks ago, someone had dumped a van by the allotments. Long before Christmas, anything useful or valuable had been stripped from it. The back two wheels, the only ones with decent tyres, had been removed, so that the vehicle reared its nose crazily into the air, like some extinct monster. Now the hulk had one final use. It became the temporary tomb of nineteen-year-old Hannah Woodgate. Her killer shut the damaged rear doors as closely as he could upon the body.

Then he was away, as silently as he had come, swift as a snow leopard over this white land, his excitement keeping the warmth coursing through his body on this coldest night of the infant year.

Two hundred yards away, Mrs Woodgate, drowsy with unaccustomed sherry, listened to her husband's soft snoring, and wondered if she had missed the sound of Hannah's key in the lock.

Two

D etective Inspector Percy Peach was beginning to enjoy himself.

The neanderthal youth in front of him said truculently, "I don't talk to the filth. Didn't you hear me the first time, cloth-ears?"

DI Peach allowed a delighted grin to light up his round face. Its breadth seemed to be accentuated by the lack of hair on his shining bald pate; after a few seconds, this smile seemed to have a life of its own, extending beyond the features which had produced it. A Cheshire Cat of a smile Peach had, visible in the minds of his victims long after its owner had departed. He spoke confidentially into the cassette recorder which turned silently on the square table at his elbow. "Mr Dodd refused to speak. At first." He lifted his head to the sullen figure opposite him. "I suppose they did tell you how it might prejudice your defence if you withheld information which might later be used in court? Yes, of course they did. I expect you just didn't understand. Pity, that."

The first, minimal doubt stole across the massive pink face opposite him. The stubby, grime-encrusted fingers of the man's right hand pulled unconsciously at the left forearm, agitating the tattoo of the naked woman on which they rested. Her buttocks writhed suggestively under the pressure and Peach affected a little shock. "Mr Dodd produced a show of mild pornography in an attempt to divert DI Peach and DC Murphy. The officers refused to become inflamed."

"'Ere, what you . . . ? I 'adn't never—" Dodd stopped abruptly, then stared accusingly at the tattoo. He knew that despite his best intentions, he had been provoked into speech by this odious little opponent.

"Be better if you 'adn't never 'it the bloke, wouldn't it, Cecil?" said Peach truculently.

"Don't you bloody Cecil me!" said Dodd viciously. "I'm Wayne, and just you bloody remember—"

"Cecil Albert Wayne Dodd, it says on your charge sheet," said Peach, enunciating each name with relish. "Go down well in court, that will. Give the gallery a bit of a giggle on a wet Monday morning. Make a good headline for the *Evening Dispatch*, I shouldn't wonder. They'll probably use the Cecil in prison, you know, when you're sent down. They can always use a few cheap laughs in Strangeways."

"I ain't done nothing." Dodd glowered menacingly from beneath his jutting eyebrows.

Peach's pleasure visibly increased. "Double negative, that is, Cecil. Really, you're saying you did something. Wonder if that could be construed as an admission in court, DC Murphy?"

"Oh, I should think so, sir. Especially if you get one of those clever prosecuting counsels the Crown seems to use nowadays." DC Brendan Murphy might be the newest recruit at Brunton CID, but he knew his supporting role in this little cabaret.

"Pity that, really. Because I'm inclined to think that Cecil here meant to imply that he had not really done anything criminal. Still, the law will take its course, I expect. I've always said it's weighted against the really thick boys who won't take advice, but I suppose some people would argue that that's a good—"

"You're trying to fit me up, you bastard! All I said was that I 'adn't never 'it no one, and you're trying to—"

"Not trying anything, Cecil. I did think of trying to make you look a bit of a prat when I came in, but then I decided that you could do that for yourself, without any assistance from me. I believe in fostering individual enterprise, wherever possible, and—"

"'E 'ad it coming to 'im, the bastard!" said Dodd, desperately trying to interrupt the flow of words from his tormentor.

Peach looked puzzled, then allowed joy to suffuse his face again in slow motion, the pace of the whole exercise being designed to suit Dodd's dull brain. "You're telling me you hit him, now? Well, there's a change of tack, and no mistake." He turned to the man beside him. "This is progress, DC Murphy. This is what I mean by a man helping police with their enquiries. A model prisoner this is. We shall have a full confession before the hour's gone, you mark my words."

The gorilla, thoroughly alarmed by that word "confession", lurched into speech. "'Ere, what you making me say? I ain't confessing to nothing! All I said was I 'it 'im when 'e asked for it."

He hadn't said that at all, thought Brendan Murphy. Well, not until now. That was the trouble with Percy Peach. By one method or another, he led you into indiscretions – sometimes even when the two of you were on the same side. DC Murphy leant forward eagerly to seize his piece of the action. "So you're now telling us that you hit him, Mr Dodd?"

The gorilla looked thoroughly puzzled now. "I just said so, didn't I? When Wayne Dodd 'its 'em, they stays 'it."

Peach beamed his approval. "Indeed they do. Even when Cecil Albert Wayne Dodd hits them, it seems. Good thing, that. Having a good thump on you, I mean. A bloke called Cecil might need to be able to defend himself, where you're going." He looked assessingly at the huge fists, now clenched tight two feet in front of him on the square table and plainly longing to hit him.

He looked into the hatred of the brown eyes opposite him. "Don't even think about it, Wayne! Assaulting a police officer would complete the set for you. Go down well in the

Crown Court, that would." He reached forward slowly with his ball pen, indicating a point on the huge knuckles of the right hand as precisely as if he had been unfurling the petals of a chrysanthemum. "Skinned your knuckles there, Wayne. Hit him pretty hard, didn't you?"

There was a tiny hint of admiration in the tone, just enough to lure this floundering fish into the Peach net. "Wayne Dodd don't need no knuckle-dusters, mister. I told you, 'e asked for it. And when I 'it 'em, they stays 'it. He 'ad a swing at me, so I laid into 'im, then. Stretched 'im out good and proper at me feet, didn't I, before your lot ever come."

Peach leaned forward earnestly. "How many times did you hit him, Wayne?"

The slightly bloodshot eyes narrowed, aware now that he had been tricked, wondering at exactly what point in the proceedings he had capitulated. "Six or seven. Maybe ten. I told you, 'e asked for it."

"And he got it. He's still lying in hospital. Wasting the time of doctors and nurses, who could be attending to more deserving cases."

There was a discreet knock at the door. Detective Sergeant Lucy Blake entered, moving as unobtrusively as her gently pneumatic contours allowed. "They've found that missing girl," she whispered into Peach's ear.

"Dead?"

She nodded. "Since last night, it seems."

Peach was on his feet in an instant. He did not even accord Wayne Dodd the status of a final nod from the door. He had known from the start that the scum in hospital would never bring charges against the scum in the interview room.

He gave his advice to the custody sergeant as he passed the desk at a brisk walk. "Get a statement from Cecil Dodd in there, in case we should need it on a future occasion. Then give him a caution for ABH and pitch him out of here: he makes the nick look untidy."

It was time to cease amusing himself. There was real crime demanding the attention of DI Peach.

That Sunday morning was bright but bitterly cold. But the weather had not dispersed the bystanders who gather like vultures around the scene of any sensational crime. There was nothing for them to see: the van was already invisible behind screens, the white plastic tapes kept the public a good thirty yards away from what limited activity there was around the body.

The police surgeon had already completed the absurd formality of certifying that the ice-cold thing that had been found in the back of the van at 09.47 hours was indeed a corpse. He had been and gone within ten minutes, causing a little stir of excitement among the ragged circle of onlookers, two thirds of them children, who had assembled at the end of the short street by the allotments. There would be no further activity visible to them until the "meat wagon" eventually took the body away in its plastic shell for the post-mortem examination. Yet the number of onlookers increased steadily through the morning.

There were already two police cars there when Peach arrived with Lucy Blake. "Typical bloody police," said a sour, anonymous voice behind them as they pushed through the crowd of observers. "Place is swarming with the buggers now. It took one of our kids to find the body in that van. Where were they last night, when they might have done the poor girl some good?" A mutter of agreement followed, from a crowd anxious for anything which might warm them. Resentment was better than nothing. Better than the feeling of blank, helpless outrage which always followed a crime like this.

Peach watched the police photographer completing his pictures of the corpse as it lay on the sloping floor of the van. The girl looked absurdly young and tender, innocent as a child in her death. Her fur collar was turned up around her neck; she had one arm thrown awkwardly above her head, as if in a final supplication to a world which had not heard her distress. But that was no doubt just how she had landed when she had been thrown, dead but still warm and floppy, into the concealment of the van. The eyes were open. As he bent over the unlined, surprised face, Peach saw the pin-point haemorrhages in the whites of them which almost certainly indicated strangulation.

A young DC who had been recently assigned to the Brunton CID section, Tony Pickard, stood awkwardly on the fringe of the group, apprehensive of Percy Peach and yet wishing to be acknowledged as one of his team. But it was DS Blake who said to him, "Is there any indication yet of where she died?"

Pickard was eager to show his industry. "No. But I'd be pretty sure it wasn't within fifty yards of the van. It was a uniformed lad who reported the body – I think some kids alerted him to it – but I was here within five minutes. There wasn't much disturbance of the snow in the immediate area, then. I had a good look round, but I couldn't see any signs of a struggle."

"Which would have been what, lad?" Peach, rising and turning quickly from his contemplation of the body, caught Pickard off guard.

"Well, signs of a scuffle in the snow, sir. The marks of a body, perhaps, if he pressed her to the ground as he killed her."

"Fair enough, Sherlock. So long as you don't start telling me about the deeper footsteps of a man carrying a body – I don't believe you could distinguish that, you see, in two inches of frosted snow."

"No, sir. I did search for just that, as a matter of fact, but what footsteps there were all looked much the same, I'm afraid. Standard welly prints were the norm." He looked down at his own stout size ten police-issue wellington boots ruefully.

"And anywhere further afield than a thirty-yard radius will have been contaminated by this lot, no doubt." Peach looked with distaste at the ring of onlookers beyond the tapes. "Nevertheless, you can make yourself useful by scouting around a bit. Public won't take much notice of you if you melt quietly away and start looking. Advantage of plain clothes, that." He looked at Tony Pickard's rather garish red anorak and ski trousers with some distaste: these were not clothes designed to be obscure. But the young man moved eagerly away beyond the public to begin his search.

"My guess is that she died within a hundred yards of this van," Peach said in a low voice to Lucy Blake. "You wouldn't want to carry a dead weight very far over freezing snow. Even a slender girl like this would take a bit of carrying, once she was dead. More important, chummy wouldn't want to run the risk of being seen with a body for any longer than he needed to."

"You're assuming this is the work of one man?" said DS Blake.

Peach smiled grimly. "Yes, I'm assuming just that, until we find any evidence to the contrary. But that doesn't mean I'm ruling out a gang-bang. Or even a woman. Or even Santa Claus and his bloody reindeer. Just in case anyone from the press asks you about it."

The pathologist arrived, picking his entry carefully over the narrow track of frozen snow they all had to use to protect the rest of the site, almost slipping over as the plastic bags they had to wear over their footwear betrayed him on the packed snow that was turning to ice. He conducted a cursory examination of the corpse on the site, taking the air temperature in the van with an electronic thermometer, slipping a clinical thermometer inside the girl's ear to record a temperature reading from the site without disturbing the girl's clothing.

He glanced at the grim-faced Peach. "Do we know who she is?"

"Yes. She'll be formally identified later, but we know. She's called Hannah Woodgate. She lived over there – about two hundred yards over there." He waved with the back of

14

his hand, as if he wished he could make the gesture into a blow. Peach felt a blind fury at this killing which seemed already so pointless, a fierce frustration even at this early stage that the killer should still be so anonymous.

The pathologist was more even in his tone, less personally affronted by this death. "Well, I can only confirm things you'll feel you already know. She's been dead many hours now – almost certainly since last night. And she very likely died from asphyxiation. From the looks of these bruises on her neck, whoever did it wore thick gloves, and pressed very hard with both thumbs on each side of her throat. It will be scant consolation to her family, but I'd say that she died very quickly; that she suffered very little."

But how do you measure suffering? thought Peach. How do you assess its intensity? How fierce was the anguish the girl suffered in those final few seconds, knowing that she was dying, so pointlessly, so close to home. He wondered whether she had known her killer. And in that moment he felt the thickness of the blank wall of ignorance which separated him from this slim figure in the van. He said harshly, "We'll need all the help you can give us, when you get her on the table and cut her up."

The post-mortem examination: another savage indignity for this seemingly flawless young body. Another horrid imagining for the parents and siblings who would already be finding this death too much to bear. He watched the two constables from the Scenes of Crime team, who were examining the interior of the ruined van in minute detail, working with tweezers to gather any wisp of hair or thread of clothing that the murderer might unwittingly have left behind. "Gather the lot and bag it, whether it looks useful or not," he said unnecessarily – these men knew their job better than he did. "This is all we've bloody got, you know."

By half past four on that afternoon of the sixth of January, it was completely dark. The body had gone for its post-mortem examination, the van had been lifted on to a trailer and taken

15

away to the car park behind the new police headquarters in Oldford. The crowd of frozen onlookers melted slowly away, preparing to review their brief contact with melodrama in the warmth of their own homes.

The killer of Hannah Woodgate sat very still beside his new hi-fi stack as he listened to the news from Radio Lancashire. The summary gave the girl's name now, and a little of her family background. It provided a local context and an identity for a victim who had been anonymous in the earlier reports.

There was nothing he found alarming. The impersonal voice of the announcer did not say that the police were anxious to interview anyone in particular.

They knew nothing.

But the murderer had studied these things long enough now to know that Monday morning's newspapers would be more interesting and colourful in their accounts of his crime. Their reporters would be digging hard at this very moment, just as the police would be resisting their overtures, trying to reveal as little as possible about this death.

Trying to conceal the full, appalling extent of their bafflement.

Hannah Woodgate's killer smiled on that thought. He looked forward to what the newspapers would say. He would buy them all tomorrow. Not all in one place, of course: that would arouse suspicion. He would buy not more than two at any one outlet. He quite enjoyed the planning that went with this.

And he was certain of one thing which both broadsheets and tabloids would carry, though it had not yet been mentioned in the radio and television reports. By tomorrow morning, with no killer in sight, they would be speculating that this was not one of those silly family killings which took place so often at this time of year. Nor even an isolated death.

He was confident that the newspapers would place this as one of a chain of killings, the third one to go undetected.

The third in the chain of deaths associated with the man the papers had tagged "the Lancashire Leopard".

He rather liked that label. He fell to wondering how many more deaths the Leopard might achieve.

Three

S uperintendent Thomas Bulstrode Tucker was not sorry to get back to work.

Most police officers work either Christmas or New Year, with much jockeying for position beforehand according to individual requirements. Tucker expected his staff to work one or the other of the holidays, but felt he was now near enough to retirement to ignore the setting of examples. Do as I say, not as I do: that was the attitude of the man who commanded the Oldford CID section.

Tucker had taken both the holidays, and bridged the gap between them with three days of his annual leave. He had not been seen in Brunton Police Station since Christmas Eve, an absence which could only benefit the CID unit he directed, according to DI Peach. As the senior inspector in a smallish CID section, Peach carried the man he called Tommy Bloody Tucker on his broad shoulders, and as a result took certain liberties in their relationship.

"It's good to have you back, sir. The unit has missed your example and direction."

Tucker, who was not impervious to the irony which has such a large role in English speech, peered suspiciously at his blank-faced inspector. He had been attempting a breezy zest and dispatch on his return after such a long break. Now he said, "I expect you've all had an easy time of it over the holiday period. I hope you haven't allowed discipline to slip, Peach. I hope there hasn't been any slacking in my absence."

The Lancashire Leopard

"Slacking?" Peach looked puzzled, as if the idea of slacking in the police was a new and difficult concept for him. "We've been pretty hard at it, on the whole, sir. And the criminal fraternity has done its part, while you've been away. Quite a lot of wife-beating over Christmas, as usual. Festive spirit, I expect. And as a sign of our emancipated times, two husbands roughed up by their wives. Not a thing you'd even be able to comprehend, from your own loving relationship with your spouse, sir. One of your many strengths, that is; I always think that it's that rock-like certainty at home which enables you to bring a perspective into the station which many—"

"Just leave Barbara out of this, will you, Peach? I don't wish my domestic life to be discussed in the station, as I seem to tell you repeatedly." Tucker's dragon of a wife was a perpetual source of interest to Peach, who had seen at a glance this morning how his chief was regretting his prolonged bout of domestic intimacy over the holiday period.

"As you wish, sir. I can see that you do not wish to wave your perennial domestic bliss in the faces of those of us who have been less fortunate in the lottery of the marriage market. You have always been very considerate in that way."

Tucker again peered suspiciously at the earnest face over his gold-rimmed glasses. Peach was always at his worst when he exercised his extensive vocabulary. He said petulantly, "Yes. Well, it's not my fault if some people can't make their marriages work." Peach's wife had left him several years previously, in an atmosphere of mutual acrimony which Peach had carefully preserved over the ensuing period.

"No, sir. Indeed it isn't. Those of us who live in a state of quasi-monastic celibacy have much to envy." He allowed a picture of the formidable Barbara Tucker in bra and pants, pursuing her fearful husband across their spacious bedroom, to swim across his vision. It was one of his favourite fantasies; Peach told his colleagues that the horrors of

19

Stephen King were much overrated by comparison with this lurid apparition.

Tucker attempted to strike back, lurching into the vernacular which did not come easily to him. "Yes, well it's not my fault if you're not getting your end away, DI Peach. It's not part of the police employment package to provide spare totty for inspectors, you know, even in these enlightened days." He allowed himself a nasty laugh at that thought.

He still doesn't know about Lucy Blake, thought Peach. Oh, thank you, God! He still hasn't heard about me and luscious Lucy, though it's stale station gossip by now with the rest of CID. Par for the course, that is, with Tucker. In life, as on the golf course, this prat remains a twenty-five handicap hacker. Thank you, Lord, I owe you one!

Aloud, Peach said, "Well, those of us without the comfort of warm sheets and pretty backsides to cuddle have been getting on with the crime, sir. Sexual frustration concentrates the mind wonderfully, someone said – Saint Augustine, I think it was. We've cleared up all the minor stuff without too much trouble. There was one incident which might concern you, sir. Press Officer's outside now, as a matter of fact. Waiting to see you, when we've finished our little chat.

"Incident?" Tucker was looking at him doubtfully over the glasses again.

He hasn't heard, thought Peach. Doesn't the idle sod even get the radio or television news? As if in answer, Tucker said apologetically, "We were at my wife's sister's over in Leeds all day yesterday, so I didn't—"

"Murder, sir. One we didn't want on our patch, to be frank. I expect you'll need to mount one of your media conferences, to tell the world what we're doing about it. Looks rather like another killing by this bloke they're calling 'the Lancashire Leopard'."

He left Thomas Bulstrode Tucker looking like a particularly surprised dead cod on the Brunton fish market.

*　　*　　*

Peach offered to accompany Lucy Blake on her journey to see the parents of the dead girl, but she refused the offer. She knew a more private and gentler side of the man, but she could do without his abrasive presence at her side in a task like this. She took DC Brendan Murphy with her instead.

The woman who opened the door to them at eleven o'clock on that Monday morning looked as if she had been through the full gamut of grief in twenty-four hours. She was only in her late forties, but she looked nearer sixty now, though her grief gave a painful and timeless dignity to her ravaged face. Her surviving daughter had been combing her mother's dishevelled hair when the bell rang and Mary Woodgate insisted on going to the door. The tidy greying hair gave a curiously formal framework to the lined face, with its eyes deep in sockets grey from crying. When DS Blake produced her warrant card, she said dully, "We've seen the police. The girl in uniform was here yesterday."

"Yes, Mrs Woodgate, I know that. I'm from CID. We need to ask you some questions, I'm afraid, if you can bear it."

"Won't it wait?" The question came in a man's voice, harsh and abrupt, from a face scarcely visible in the shadows of the hall. But then the speaker came forward and put a hand gently on each of his wife's shoulders, his own weariness being thrust aside in the need to protect his partner.

"I'm afraid it won't, Mr Woodgate. Not if we want to find out who did this awful thing. Time is important, you see."

Mary Woodgate nodded. This bright woman with the open face and the auburn hair was only a few years older than the daughter she had lost. Why Hannah? The selfish, inevitable question banged again at her heart. Why was this girl standing here so pretty and so healthy when poor Hannah lay dead and cold on a slab? She said, "You'd best come in."

She led them into a room where television pictures danced bright and meaningless without their sound accompaniment.

21

There were two sofas and two armchairs, a table with unread papers, and scattered tea cups which Brian Woodgate hastily collected and removed, as though the preservation of domestic tidiness was part of the therapy of recovery. He came and sat upright beside his wife on the sofa opposite the two detectives, his hand stealing shyly across to rest on top of his wife's wrist. He looked as if he thought these unique circumstances allowed a contact he didn't usually permit himself in public.

"She was a good girl, our Hannah," said Mary Woodgate, pronouncing the words with great care, as if elocution might bring back her daughter and end the nightmare which was turning into reality.

They were always good girls, thought Lucy. Usually events proved them to be more than usually flawed, but this seemed a close and caring family, and perhaps this time the phrase might be justified. Curiously enough, that notion didn't cheer her: bad girls usually had bad contacts, and their killings were usually easier to solve. She said softly to the mother who was still in shock, "I'm sure she was, love. And we need to get the man who did this. I know it can't help Hannah now, but it might save other girls from dying as she did."

Brian Woodgate said unexpectedly, "We didn't realise she hadn't come home until this morning. I identified her, you know. She looked lovely in that cold place. Almost . . . almost as though she was just asleep." His voice broke on the thought; his wife clasped the hand he had put on her wrist in both of hers.

Lucy tried to be brisk, lest they should descend again into their grief. "Yes. She was a very good-looking girl, was Hannah." She made herself use the name for the first time, trying not to look at the photograph of the laughing girl with her hair flying in the summer breeze which stood on the sideboard behind her parents.

Mary Woodgate said, as abruptly as if she were shutting a book, "And now she's gone. Who would want to do it, Sergeant . . . I'm sorry, I've forgotten your name, love."

"It's Lucy. And this is Brendan."

Mary Woodgate looked at the DC as if she was seeing him for the first time. "That's an Irish name."

"Yes. And I couldn't have a more Irish second name than Murphy, could I? Even though I've lived all my life in Lancashire. But my father's Irish, you see. And my mother's family. I think I've seen you and the family at church on a Sunday, haven't I, Mrs Woodgate?"

She looked full into his face then, noting the fresh complexion, the large brown eyes, the slightly unruly brown hair. Why couldn't Hannah have fallen for someone like this handsome lad, in her own town? She would surely have been safe with a policeman. She said, "That would be at Saint Alban's, wouldn't it? Not that the church matters so much, nowadays. We're all Christians, they say, and that's how it should be."

Brendan Murphy said gently, "It was at Saint Alban's, yes. Mrs Woodgate, we need you to tell us about all the people Hannah knew. That's the way we work, you see, when something like this happens."

"Yes, I can see you'd need to know that. And poor Hannah can't tell you herself, can she?" Then the shock-frozen face melted suddenly into alarm. "But no one she knew would have killed her. Not our Hannah."

Brendan said, "Perhaps not. Probably not. But that's the way we work, you see. The way we have to work. Usually the victim in a case like this has some knowledge of the killer, even if they weren't very close to each other."

It was true enough, but Lucy Blake wondered even as he said the words whether this might be the exception. For a young man, Brendan was surprisingly good in this situation. She let him handle the questioning as they went carefully through the list of boys the dead girl had known. Hannah had spent eighteen years in the town before she went off to university, had passed through seven years in the local

23

comprehensive school, so there were a good many names, all of which would in due course need to be laboriously checked out.

Brian Woodgate eventually brought in the three younger children, and they added half-a-dozen names that their parents had either forgotten or been unaware of. Lucy noted these within the list as a priority: often it was the men whom a daughter had concealed from her parents who were the best leads in a criminal investigation.

The two boys of twelve and thirteen had been close to their elder sister, who had baby-sat them many times and guided them towards adolescence. They were shocked by their grief into an uncharacteristic silence, and could contribute little. It was sixteen-year-old Kath who responded when they touched upon the delicate matter of whether anyone might have had a grievance against this shining dead girl. "Jason," she said. "Jason Wright. Hannah went out with him for over a year when they were in the sixth form. She ended it before she went off to university, but Jason wouldn't accept it. He came round after her every time she was home. And when he found she'd got herself a new boyfriend at the university, he was really upset."

They took his address, and the name of the university boyfriend as well. This lad down in Surrey would need to be checked out, as would a whole list of university acquaintances, if local enquiries did not produce something quickly. The local boyfriend who had been ditched was promising, but only if this was a one-off killing, rather than one of a series of apparently motiveless murders by this man who was no doubt now glorying in his billing as "the Lancashire Leopard".

They made their clumsy goodbyes, assuring the family that they would be in touch as soon as they had any news – giving them the impression, Lucy was sure, that a solution was just around the corner, that a killing like this was well within the compass of CID competence. Yet she felt in her heart that this pointless death was going to be difficult to solve. A phrase came back to her from her A-level studies a decade earlier: "motiveless malevolence". That was Iago in *Othello*, wasn't it? Anyway, it was malevolence without motive that modern police forces found most difficult to pin down, however sophisticated their equipment, however extensive their resources.

Brian Woodgate followed them into the hall. He shut the door carefully behind him before he said, "She looked so peaceful when they showed her to me. Was she – you know . . . ?"

"Hannah wasn't raped, Mr Woodgate. We'll need the post-mortem findings to be absolutely certain, but as far as we could see there was no sign of any sexual interference." Lucy Blake was happy to reassure him, to offer that tiny consolation to this shattered family. And as a woman, she rejoiced that the girl had not suffered this final violation. But the detective in her knew that it would have been a help to the investigation. There would now be no traces of semen, no DNA to test against a suspect to clinch an early arrest.

Brendan Murphy was shutting the gate when the youngest boy, twelve-year-old Tim, came trotting round the side of the house. His face ran with fresh tears; he was still a child in his grief, without the adult defences of simulation and concealment. He stopped abruptly halfway down the path, as if he could not find words for what he had run here so urgently to say.

Then he blurted out to them, "Get the man who killed our Hannah! Get him quickly, please!" and disappeared as suddenly as he had arrived.

Four

Monday, January 7th

A t midday, Superintendent Tucker held the media conference which Peach had forecast.

Tucker was at his best in such exercises. He put on his
immaculately pressed uniform – he might be CID, but the
punters preferred the reassurance of a uniform in the TV
pictures – and presented the caring face of the police to
the public.

He knew little more about the killing than Peach had given
him, but he was urbane and confident. That is what the public
wanted to see. The hardened journalists might see through
him, might read between the lines and see how little was
there, but Tucker had the air of a patient father calming
overexcited children. All would be well, his bearing told
them, if they would just calm down and allow the police
machine to operate smoothly.

He had established a cordial relationship with Sally
Etherington, the young television interviewer from Granada,
in her days with Radio Lancashire, and he exploited that
relationship now. He farmed what she had devised as
penetrating questions expertly, with a smile which stayed
just on the right side of condescension. His hair was
now nearly white, but still plentiful; framing his regular,
experienced features, it helped to give his statements an
appropriate gravitas.

"Would you say that you are near to an arrest, Superintendent Tucker?"

"No. I want to be perfectly honest with you about that.

26

But with a murder of this kind, one would not expect an immediate arrest."

"Do you have a list of suspects?"

"Indeed we do. We should be failing in our duty if we did not. Even as I speak to you now, my experienced team of detectives are at work on narrowing the field. The public have a glamorous view of detection – partly as a result of the fictional series they see on television, I'm afraid – but much police work depends on the repetitive, even boring routine of elimination. It is often tedious work for the many officers involved, but it produces results. And results are what we policemen live by." He gave his interviewer and the camera his most dazzling smile. Without that cynical fellow Peach to puncture his pronouncements, he could be highly effective, he thought to himself.

"Would you care to say whether you have anyone helping police with their enquiries yet?"

The press's flash bulbs went off as he weighed his reply with a grave face. Then he afforded them his most avuncular smile. "That phrase has acquired a particular overtone through its use in the media, you know. It has often been taken to mean that we have arrested and are interrogating a prime suspect in a case. But it should really mean just what it says. Many people are at present helping us with our enquiries. Indeed, I may say here that the response from the Brunton public has been most encouraging. The great mass of people around here are respectable, law-abiding folk. They are as anxious as we are that the man who did this dreadful thing should be put where he can do no further harm."

It was the bromide that he had prepared in his office before he went out to face the cameras and the flash-bulbs, knowing that there would be an opportunity for it. But he delivered it well, and his ringing sincerity brought nodding agreement from the Granada interviewer, who knew as well as he did that the public always enjoyed a compliment. People lay back like contented cats to have their bellies rubbed: it was a well-known television axiom.

The yawns of the cynical hacks in front of them were fortunately not on camera. It was a good note on which to wind down a television item. Sally Etherington offered him her last, inevitable query. "You say we should not expect an immediate arrest, Superintendent Tucker. Can you give us any indication of how quickly you hope to solve this crime?"

The CID chief leaned forward earnestly. "I won't attempt to deceive you, Sally. This is far too serious a matter for any fudging. So I won't pretend that we know who did this before we do. With many murders, we can arrest someone within hours, and we do. These are not the cases which get heavy coverage from the media, so that our successes tend to pass people by." He allowed himself a small, philosophical smile at the unfairness of the world. "Other killings, such as this one, are more complex. In such cases, murder investigations are not sprints, but marathons. But I venture to say, successful marathons, in our case." Tucker jutted his determined chin at the camera for its last shot.

He relaxed a little as the television machinery ceased to whirr. He was less at home with the rough and tumble of journalistic exchange, but he knew that what most people, including his superiors, would see was the television slot. That had gone well, and the crime reporters could only print what he gave them. As the flash bulbs flickered again, he gave them his professional smile, friendly but concerned; approachable, yet never letting people forget that crime was a serious business. His face would come out well in the evening papers: he had practised this smile for too long for it to let him down now.

The old hands in front of him tried to establish how little the police knew by concentrating upon the Woodgate family and their loss. Tucker turned their queries aside smoothly with a plea that the privacy of grief should be respected. "We have had to station a constable outside the house around the clock to make sure that the Woodgates are not pestered with questions about their daughter and their feelings. I understand that you have a job to do, but it must be done without harassing a grieving family. Mr and Mrs Woodgate and their three younger children must be allowed to take up the reins of life as best they can, without press interference. The officers who have been ensuring their privacy could have been employed in the hunt for Hannah's killer, had they not been needed to protect her family. That is quite a thought, is it not?"

T. B. Tucker was rather proud of the way that came out. Pity it hadn't been in the television interview, but he did see the Radio Lancashire microphone in front of him. They were always so short of news material that it was sure to be quoted there, and with any luck transferred to the national radio bulletins. An attack on the press was always a safe tactic. With a bit of luck, it would even win him approval from his own CID team.

It was left to Alf Houldsworth, the one-eyed reporter from the local *Evening Dispatch*, to ask the question Tucker had expected would come earlier. "Superintendent, is it your opinion that this crime is another in the series committed by the man who has come to be called 'the Lancashire Leopard'?"

A little buzz of excitement ran through the room, followed by sighs of dismay as Tucker said, "I'm afraid it's too early for us to say. We are keeping an open mind on the matter."

Houldsworth did not sit down after his question as the convention demanded. Instead, he smiled a crooked smile and persisted, "Even from my visually disadvantaged position, that looks like an evasion, Mr Tucker. It is now thirty-six hours since this murder. Time, surely, for you to have considered the *modus operandi* of the killer. You must have formed an opinion on this matter."

Houldsworth, a popular man among his peers because of his long experience and his formidable capacity for alcohol, got a titter of amusement on his joke about his eye and a mutter of agreement for his conclusion. Tucker, who hadn't studied the evidence and did not easily form an opinion, decided he must give a little more. "It is possible that Hannah Woodgate is not this man's first victim – I think I can say that we are confident that our killer is a man, in this case. We have an open mind on whether he has killed before."

A young reporter from one of the nationals said with what was almost a sneer, "Then surely the matter should be passed from Brunton CID to the Serious Crime Squad, without further delay."

Tucker smiled. How foolish of this callow youth to play into his hands on a matter of police procedure. "I'm afraid you are quite wrong there. We shall remain in charge of this case whether it proves to be an isolated murder or one of a series. The Serious Crime Squad will offer us help as and when it is needed. I am in charge of this case and will remain so."

He hesitated, then decided that a mention of the egregious Peach was inevitable if he was to convey his own masterful overview of the case. "I have already asked Detective Inspector Peach to take charge of the day-to-day conduct of the case for me. Should it prove necessary, he will be supplemented by resources and personnel from the Serious Crime Squad. What I can tell you is that we are already exchanging information on this and previous crimes with the Serious Crime Squad."

Intoxicated with the exuberance of his own verbosity, thought Alf Houldsworth. Gladstone, that was; well, the Grand Old Man had nothing on this twat, except a few brains and a lot of integrity. As the audience filed out at the end of the media conference, it was Houldsworth who interpreted the rhetoric for the benefit of those less familiar with Thomas Bulstrode Tucker. "If old Droopy-Drawers is talking to the Serious Crime Squad, that's it," he said. "We can start planning headlines about the

Lancashire Leopard pouncing on another innocent victim."

Alf Houldsworth was right, of course.

At the beginning of November, a twenty-six-year-old married primary-school teacher in Preston had been strangled at around midnight when walking home from visiting her sick mother on the edge of the town. On the twelfth of December, a woman of forty-one had been killed by the same method on the outskirts of Clitheroe, as she walked home from her local public house. There was no sign of sexual assault in either case.

Both women had been wearing trousers at the times of their deaths and there was no disturbance of their clothing. Neither woman had had sexual intercourse in the hours before her death. The pattern and the method of killing was the same as in the death of Hannah Woodgate, and the killings had so far proved equally motiveless.

Peach got his Brunton CID team together and gave his instructions. "This is almost certainly the third in a series of killings. That doesn't mean we ignore our normal procedures for a death like this. We treat this initially just as if it were a one-off. That means we turn over the local dung-heap and see what we can find. She was at the dance at King George's Hall on Saturday night. The first thing to find out is whether anyone followed her home from there. That's a job for DCs Murphy and Pickard."

He caught Tony Pickard casting his eyes heavenwards after a look at Brendan Murphy. "It may be bloody boring, Tony, but you lads are paid to be bloody bored. There were four hundred people at that dance: say two hundred men. Most of them you should be able to eliminate. There'll be the ones who went home with their girlfriends and the ones who walked home in groups. Then there are the groups who shared taxis. I know that people can go out again after they've got home, or double back after they've left a group. But time is helpful to us here; one of the useful

31

things we have is an exact time of death, so let's use it. From what Hannah Woodgate's friends have told us about the time they left her, it seems pretty certain that she was dead by twelve twenty a.m. – she would have reached her house otherwise.

"Unless it's possible for a man to have been on his own and in the area where she was found by twelve fifteen, you can eliminate him. You and Brendan are both local men, so you know the ground: that's why you've been chosen for this job. Be as bored as you like, but be bloody thorough – no Yorkshire Ripper-type cock-ups, or you'll have me to answer to. You can have four uniformed coppers from different beats to help you get through this quickly. I want a list of possibles within twenty-four hours. Then we'll follow them up."

Peach nodded then to the man beside him, who introduced himself. "DI Parkinson, Serious Crime Squad. You may be wondering why we are so ready to assume that there is only one man involved. Everything about both this killing and the previous two indicates that this is so. There were people still awake in houses within fifty yards of where Hannah Woodgate died, but no one heard anything. There was no suggestion of a gang-bang, nor of any other sexual shenanigans. And if, as we think, this is a third killing by the same man, then you should know that we are sure that the murders in November and December involved only one man."

Peach grinned mirthlessly. "That's one of the few bloody things we *are* sure of. There isn't much to pass on to you from the other two murders. That's why I'm saying we observe our usual procedures, just as if this was a one-off. House to house is giving us a few names to follow up in the area, and we'll have a go at the usual suspects while you lads and lasses are getting some lists together for us."

A woman detective constable at the back of the room said, "Have we any indication at all of the man's age?"

Peach shook his head grimly. "None whatsoever. You'll

have to keep your eye on all of us, love." There was a ripple of laughter round the room at the weak joke, nervous rather than amused. No one liked a killer, and least of all one who struck like this.

DI Parkinson said, "If we assume for a moment that this is the Leopard, there are certain things of which we should all be aware. The first death was on the third of November. The second was on the twelfth of December. This one was on the fifth of January. It looks as if the frequency is accelerating as he gets more confident. And all the signs are that he is getting confident: the first two killings were in isolated areas, whereas this one was in a heavily populated part of a town, with lights still on in some of the nearby houses. We're all guessing here, and he's enjoying that. But my guess is that if we don't find him quickly, he'll kill again. He's sitting on his own somewhere and laughing at us. Unless we get closer to him, he's going to show us again before too long just how clever he thinks he is."

On this early January evening, darkness dropped in quickly over the narrow streets of the old cotton town. It threw a cloak over the frenzied activities of the augmented team of sixty officers who were working on the death of Hannah Woodgate.

Much of the work was conducted around the Murder Room which had been set up in the Brunton CID section, where by the early evening officers who had worked alone or in pairs all day were exchanging information and making sense of their efforts within the larger context of the investigation. There was a steady chatter of computer keyboards as information and lists were fed in and cross-referenced.

Brendan Murphy watched his list of men who might have followed Hannah home from the dance lengthening as information was fed back to him. Tony Pickard was still out in the town with the uniformed officers, checking the stories of those who claimed to have gone home with girlfriends or in groups. Much of the checking had of necessity to be done in the evening. People arriving home from work found themselves involved, however peripherally, in a murder investigation.

Even Superintendent Thomas Bulstrode Tucker stayed an hour longer than usual at his desk. He had hoped that Peach would come in, to be regaled with the success of his chief's media conference. It would have been satisfying to emphasise the importance of good public relations in modern police work to that stocky figure with the toothbrush moustache and shining bald pate, who reminded him so much of a more compact and muscular Oliver Hardy. He rang Barbara and asked her to record the interview with Sally Etherington when it appeared on the evening news. Her reply was not as complimentary as he would have wished. But he knew that nevertheless she would record it; it would be ammunition for the games she played at her coffee mornings.

As the man in charge of the investigation, he went down to the Murder Room, found that Peach was not there, and gave an impromptu pep talk. It began, "I am glad to see how thoroughly my orders are being implemented by DI Peach. It is important that you give him every possible support . . ."

The male and female officers listened dutifully to his words. Most of them held Peach's opinion of the man who commanded them in CID, but they were making their careers in the police service, and rank was rank. Peach had made himself into a local legend by his carefully measured contempt for the man he called Tommy Bloody Tucker, but he had no wish for further promotion. As Tucker had become less efficient, more atrophied in his bureaucratic isolation, he had paradoxically become more dependent upon the man he would have loved to send on his way.

For Percy Peach produced results. He might pretend to a scepticism about the system, and in particular about the man who represented it to him, but he waged a war on crime which was forceful and unremitting, nailing villains with an energy which was his own brand of integrity. Tucker rode upon his back, and both of them knew it. Tucker had realised years ago that as long as Peach was making arrests for major crimes on their patch he had to tolerate his insolence. He had examined the alternatives often enough, and come each time to the conclusion that even the insufferable Peach was the lesser of two evils.

At half past six, Tucker left the station and drove home to his comfortable house on the outskirts of Brunton. It is one of the ironies of the case, and indeed of life itself, that this most ineffective head of the investigation into the death of Hannah Woodgate passed within a few yards of her murderer on his way home.

Five

I t was now after nine o'clock at night. In the front room of the small terraced house, the only light came from a seventy-five-watt bulb, its dim illumination further diminished by a dusty shade.

But Peach had set his man on a chair directly beneath that dismal light, and he was watching for the first signs of fear in his face. It was a mean face, thin and lined, weasel-like with low cunning. But the mind behind the face was no match for Percy Peach, and both these old antagonists knew it.

The man had switched on both bars of the electric fire when they came into the front room of the grimy little turn-of-the-century house – the parlour, as it was still called by the old lady they had left in the living kitchen on the other side of the wall. There was a smell of burning dust from the rarely used elements of the fire. The room, musty when they had begun this, was now hot and airless.

Peach's eyes, coal-black and unblinking, never left his adversary. "You might as well admit it, Billy. You were out last Saturday night. Putting yourself about a bit. Getting well out of your miserable depth. Panicking, eventually."

"I never left the 'ouse, Mr Peach. I told you."

"You were seen, Billy. Outside the Wagon and Horses. Up to no good, as usual."

"That was earlier. I was 'ere from ten o'clock onwards. Tucked up in me bed by eleven." He repeated the words in a whine, as if it was a formula which might become true if he repeated it often enough.

"And who says so?"

The watery blue eyes narrowed as a small smile of cunning flashed momentarily into the narrow features. "Me mother does. You can speak to her now, if you like."

An old lady, suffering from the first stages of Alzheimer's, who still saw her son as a mischievous boy who got into occasional scrapes; she would bring herself to believe her own lies by the time they had prepared a case. Whom Peach knew he could never put into the witness box for cross-examination, in any case. Billy and he both knew the score here.

It had been a long day and Peach was suddenly weary. His brain told him that this was a pointless exercise, but he knew that it must be completed: you didn't leave any stones unturned when murder was the crime. Or, as he was now almost certain in this case, triple murder. He used his irritation that this pathetic creature should be holding out against him to drive him on.

Billy Bedford was a wretched figure. His pink shirt was grubby at the neck and frayed at the cuffs; his thinning, greasy grey hair was dishevelled from the number of times he had run his hand through it since he had sat down opposite Peach. But his long experience of petty crime, of hours of questioning in the interview rooms of police stations, now stood him in good stead. He made his watery grey eyes carefully blank and folded his arms across his thin chest, challenging Peach to break his story. "Ain't done nothing," he reiterated stubbornly.

Peach knew that Bedford was only here because of his grubby past, and that that held no more than a string of convictions for minor, slightly comic, crimes, the kind even the police laughed about behind Bedford's back. And here was that same Billy Bedford, outsmarting and outlasting that scourge of villains, DI Peach.

"You're a flasher, Billy. Tried and convicted. And God knows what else you are!"

"Nothing else, Mr Peach! And I've given all that up. I've told you."

He had, several times already in the last forty minutes. And he would go on doing so, unless Peach could frighten him.

"Flashers often go on to bigger things. You know that, Billy, and so do we." That wasn't strictly true. It was something of a rarity, and the ones who did were younger than fifty-four-year-old Billy Bedford. And they usually moved through the dark world of indecent assault and rape before they killed anyone. But it wasn't unknown; it was possible – and so it had to be explored.

And Bedford didn't know the statistics which Peach carried in his head. For the first time, he looked scared. "I 'aven't done nothing. I told you."

But he couldn't keep his arms folded. His hands clasped in his lap, massaging each other in slow motion, the filthy fingernails appearing and disappearing in the dim light. Peach saw the first real apprehension and went for it, like a welterweight seeing his chance for a punch. "I told you, Billy, you're out of your depth this time. This one is big. And very, very nasty. The girl was killed. Strangled, as she looked into the eyes of her killer, we think. Pressed down into the snow, with thumbs crushing her windpipe and a knee—"

"It's not what I'd do, Mr Peach. Not my sort of crime, 'onest it isn't!" Bedford was desperate to stop the flow of detail, to fracture the picture of violence that was being built up before his widening eyes. "I've – I've been a nuisance to women, God knows, but I've never hit them."

"Not strictly true that, Billy, and we both know it. Four convictions for flashing, and the last time you assaulted the woman."

"I wasn't charged with that. Only with the flashing. I only put my hand over her mouth to try to stop her when she started screaming."

They glared at each other, their faces four feet apart as they sat forward on the edges of their chairs. Peach caught the stench of Bedford's breath, gusting at him in waves in the overheated room. He could smell the fear as well as see it now, and he went in for the kill. "And when the man had finished with this pretty young girl, when he saw the life die in her eyes, he threw her in the back of a derelict van and slipped away. Just to stop her talking, he did that. Or to stop her screaming, like you did with that other woman. Or to give himself more pleasure than he could get from just a flash. You tell me which, Billy Bedford!"

Bedford wasn't used to this direct attack. Policemen usually kept the details of crime from him when they pulled him in to question him, hoping to make him uneasy by keeping him in ignorance about what he was accused of, looking to collect the bits of information which he might reveal if he jumped to the wrong conclusion. And he wasn't used to being questioned by inspectors – even Peach had only been a detective sergeant when they had last crossed swords. This blunt confrontation by top brass in his own home threw him off balance. "You can't set me up for the Hannah Woodgate killing. I've known her since she was a kid!"

"And now she's a young woman, Billy. Or was. A pretty one. Innocent. Just the kind to get a man like you excited."

"But I knew her, Mr Peach, and I've never—"

"So she knew you, Billy. And recognised you. So you had to shut her up."

"But I didn't!" Bedford's voice changed from a whine to a scream. They heard the sound of movement on the other side of the thin wall.

"Maybe you panicked. Just felt you had to stop her screaming. That would be your best defence, Billy, now you're in the frame for this. Go for manslaughter – say you didn't really mean to kill her."

"But I didn't kill her at all! I wasn't even—"

"You were seen earlier in the evening, within a quarter of a mile of where she died. Not a lot earlier, either. We have a witness to that." He watched the thin fingers twining and untwining in Bedford's lap.

The man's gaze followed Peach's and rested on his hands. But he made no effort to still their movement; he watched them as though the fingers belonged to someone else. "I didn't do it! I wouldn't do anything like that! You're not going to pin this on me!"

But he could hear the panic singing in his own voice. In the world in which Billy Bedford moved, the creed was that the pigs could pin most things on you, if they had a mind to. And the squat ball of muscle opposite him certainly looked as if he had a mind to fix him for this.

Peach heard the panic, and read the signs. Guilty or innocent, this man would just go on with his denials now, shouting his innocence like a child pinned into a corner. Peach wracked his tired brain for a new tack, then felt into the pocket of his jacket. "Want a fag, Billy?"

The mobile hands moved forward a couple of inches, then stopped abruptly. "No. Keep your snout!" The prison word was out before the mobile lips could arrest it.

Peach gave him a sour smile, signifying that the intensity of the interrogation was to be relaxed a little. "Just as well, that. I gave up smoking five years ago. Might find you a stick of chewing gum, if you talk sense. You see, I'd like to help you, Billy. To help you to help yourself, perhaps. If you didn't do this, where were you at midnight last Saturday?"

"I was here. At home. My mum'll tell you."

"I'm sure she will. But I don't think I'll even bother to ask her. I like to leave old ladies with clear consciences. Besides, I saw the Amitriptyline tablets on the table in there. Fifty milligrams. After one of those, she wouldn't know whether her son was in Brunton or Bombay."

They had lowered their voices now. And at this moment there was a knock at the door and a frail voice quavered, "Are you all right in there?"

"Right as rain, Mrs Bedford," said Peach, opening the door and smiling reassurance at her. "And we've just about finished our business in here now." He went into the shabby but clean living kitchen. As the eighty-year-old resumed her scat by the fire, he felt a surge of painful sympathy for this woman who had never broken a law in her life but who had found her final years so disrupted by the seedy crimes of her son.

She stared into the crimson glow of the fire. "He didn't do it, you know. Not this one. He wouldn't do that, wouldn't Billy. Not kill a girl."

So she'd been listening at the door, as he thought. No sign of Alzheimer's tonight in the old girl. Peach reached into his suitcase, glancing towards the parlour door. His exhausted adversary had not followed him into the room. He produced a can of stout, pulled aside the curtain to the scullery, and found a single glass, into which he carefully poured the dark liquid, trying not to react to the sharp beads of eyes which followed his every movement.

He set the glass down on the hearth beside the old lady's rocking chair and spoke softly into her ear. "Between you and me, Mrs Bedford, I think you're right. But we have to be certain, you see, before we can leave him alone."

His voice had scarcely been raised above a whisper, but Bedford must have heard enough to know he was speaking. He came through the door from the parlour and stared suspiciously at the conspiratorial pair by the fire. Peach straightened and considered him without affection. "We were just saying, Billy: if you really did have nothing to do with this and you want to convince us of that, the best thing you can do is to give us a lead on who did do it."

"I ain't no grass, Mr Peach!" The old lag's instinctive reaction. The petty criminal's fear of reprisals from bigger fish in his murky pool.

Peach went over to him, resisting the impulse to grip the shabby cardigan, to stare into the narrow features from close range. There was no call to upset the old lady whose only link with the modern world was this miserable son. "This is murder, Billy! Not shoplifting. Not opening your raincoat to show how little you've got to people who've seen much better. Murder. Understood?"

"Yes, Mr Peach." Bedford spoke in a choked voice, as if Peach was actually holding him by his collar.

"So if you hear the slightest whisper of who might have done it, you get on the blower to Brunton CID right away, see. There'll be someone there ready to listen, harder than they've ever listened before to Billy Bedford. And we'll protect you. No one will ever know where it's come from. Understood?"

The watery eyes stared for a moment into his, then dropped. Slyness mingled with fear in the mean face. "Information about this might be worth a bit if I could come across it, mightn't it, Mr Peach?"

Peach had to resist the impulse to shake the skinny frame until it rattled. He said between clenched teeth, "Don't push it, Bedford. Just keep your grubby ear to the ground and let us know immediately if it picks up anything. Until we know something different, we'll keep you in the frame."

He smiled briefly at the frail figure by the fire. "I'll say good-night then, Mrs Bedford. Look after yourself now." She did not look at him, but raised the glass of stout a couple of inches towards him as she gazed into the fire.

Peach wondered as he climbed wearily into his car what those two would be saying to each other now in that shabby old living kitchen. This job took you into some strange places.

The man who had actually killed Hannah Woodgate was altogether more at ease than pathetic Billy Bedford.

In his comfortable, centrally heated room he sat back in an armchair and watched the television news. He enjoyed the performance of Superintendent Tucker in the "News from the North-west" section. He watched it with the detached air of a connoisseur of such items. He would have asked different questions himself: this girl was letting the old windbag off the hook far too easily.

Why didn't she pin him down more? Why didn't she confront him with the fact that the police team of sixty had been up and down the town all day without uncovering anything of value to them? Why didn't she ask him if he expected to make an arrest in a day? A week? A month? A year?

He laughed out loud at his thoughts. If he were a betting man, he'd be willing to wager that they'd be no nearer to him in a month than they were now. But he wasn't a betting man: he only dealt in certainties. And he wouldn't become overconfident, just because he knew the police machine was failing. He hadn't taken anything for granted so far, and he wasn't going to start now. Plan carefully. Never act in a hurry. Keep the bastards guessing! Enjoy it all with a straight face as they got more and more frustrated.

They were bringing in extra resources from the Serious Crime Squad, the paper had said. That was just to reassure the public, who thought these sods were much more efficient than they were. Let's see what Joe Public thinks in a week or two, when the team of sixty they keep boasting about has got no nearer to the truth. They won't think so highly of the boys in blue then, will they? Sixty of them against one clever man, and they can't catch him. Superintendents, inspectors, all the cream of the CID, and they can't catch one man! The thick sods!

He poured himself a generous whisky, filled the glass up with water, sat back to watch a comedy programme with his feet up. It was good to think that with all this frenzied activity being mounted against him, he needed to do absolutely nothing in response. He hadn't left anything of himself behind at the scene of the murder; there had been nothing of that "exchange" at the scene of a crime which these clever buggers talked so glibly about. Apparently the killer was supposed to leave something of himself which the experts could pick up. Well, bollocks to that! If you knew about these things and were careful, you didn't leave anything. No fibres, no hairs, nothing from which they could get DNA. And the gloves he'd used for these first three were at the bottom of the canal with stones in them. Up yours, forensic!

If you were cleverer than these overpaid cretins who were supposed to catch you, you would always come out on top. Cleverer included lying low, for a while, anyway. It was satisfying in any case to have a rest and watch these silly sods chasing around like blue-arsed flies.

There would come a time, of course, to remind them again how dumb they were. But for the moment you could enjoy your triumph. Pity it had to be so secret, but there it was. Other people who had killed had written to the police and taunted them, but he was far too clever to take such pointless risks. They knew well enough that they were failing, and in time the public would be telling them so and calling for blood. Good phrase, that!

In a little while, it would be time to frighten the public some more. He dwelt for a while on that thought in bed before he went to sleep.

Six

"Ｉt's time you settled down, our Lucy! I've said it before—"

"And you'll no doubt say it again! Change the record, Mum. I keep telling you, I *am* settled."

Detective Sergeant Lucy Blake was undergoing the kind of grilling that can only be given by a mother to a daughter. It was worse now that her father wasn't around to say, "Give the girl a chance, Mother!" And the maternal examination of her life and its goals was more concentrated, now that she had her own place and didn't live at home. She had her own neat little modern flat, three miles from the centre of Brunton, where town met country, and she loved it. But she still spoke of this rural cottage where her mother lived as "home", still enjoyed being greeted so cheerily by the villagers who had known her since she was a girl.

Her mother regarded Lucy's flat as a strange and temporary departure. Agnes Blake had always known that her daughter would have to leave her house and probably the village eventually, but she did not regard this new flat as representing that final break. No one stayed for long in flats anyway, did they? Flats hadn't existed round here, when Agnes Blake was young, and there was something essentially transient about them. Lucy had been born when her mother was forty and her beloved dead father was fifty; Agnes Blake clung unconsciously to the notions of a generation which was almost gone.

She returned to her theme. "When I say 'settled', I mean

45

properly settled." Her brow furrowed. She didn't want to put her pictures into words. She knew quite well that they were old-fashioned, and knew even more clearly that her daughter would laugh at them. Good-naturedly, even lovingly, but that wouldn't help. Agnes set her lips in a prim line, refusing to respond to the smile which danced about the girl's mouth as she looked at her. "You know what I mean, our Lucy, perfectly well."

"You mean find myself a nice man. Settle down. Have babies. Dress them up pretty, for Granny to parade around the village."

Agnes smiled in spite of herself. It was an appealing picture, and she couldn't deny that her ideal for Lucy was something of that sort. "Is that so bad a thing to hope for?"

"Maybe not. But I've got to shape my own life, Mum. You know that. You've told me before that you want just that."

Agnes supposed she had. You found yourself mouthing these modern notions, not wanting to seem a reactionary parent. But she'd picked up another idea from *Woman's Hour* the other day, and she produced it now, as nonchalantly as she could. "You're twenty-six, my girl. Nearly twenty-seven. And your biological clock is ticking, you know. You can't leave these things for ever."

Lucy grinned at her across the comfortable room. It was a thought she had had for herself, one which she had thrust away at the back of her mental filing cabinet. But she couldn't admit that to her mother. "You'll be reading the *Guardian* next, Mum, and campaigning for gay rights. I'm not ancient, you know, not yet! There's plenty of time. Women are having their babies much later – it's the modern trend, with joint mortgages and bigger incomes for women."

Agnes shook her head and said stubbornly, "You'll be thirty before you know where you are."

And you'll be seventy, thought Lucy, and still not a grandmother. She felt suddenly guilty, in a way she would never have anticipated. This was another of the trials of being an only child. Trying to move away from the thought, she said, "Anyway, you have to have the right man to be the father of your children, don't you? 'Marry in haste and repent at leisure,' your generation used to say. Well, I've seen plenty of that, and so have you."

"I wasn't suggesting you married in a hurry. You're putting words into my mouth. But I won't deny that I'd be happy if you had a nice man to look after you. There must be plenty interested, with your looks."

Lucy smiled. "I don't need anyone to look after me. I'm a detective sergeant in the police now, for God's sake." She wondered what her mother would say if she knew that she'd found a nice man. That she'd spent four days at New Year in his house, that she'd only gone back to her own flat because she wanted to retain her independence, and to guard against things moving too fast.

She wanted to tell her mother about Percy Peach. Indeed, she had been determined to tell her on this visit home. But it wasn't easy to tell the mother who had such dreams for her that she was attracted to a stocky bald man who was ten years older than her – and divorced.

There was no denying that it was an unlikely pairing, until you knew Percy Peach as well as she did now. Tommy Bloody Tucker had assigned her to be Peach's DS as a punishment to him, and Peach had started off in the best male chauvinist tradition – she smiled now as she thought of their earliest exchanges. They had enjoyed a few laughs together over the New Year about those early days. But there was no getting round the fact that Percy was an acquired taste. He'd be nice to her mother, she was pretty sure, to please Lucy. But she had never seen Percy Peach straining to be nice: it might well be a disaster.

Agnes Blake saw the faraway look swim into her daughter's ultramarine eyes, and divined far more from it about the state of the girl's affections than Lucy knew. There was a man, then. She hoped he was suitable, that if he was he would be

47

long-term. There must be something wrong about him, or he would have been revealed by now. She said suddenly, before she was aware of the thought herself, "You need someone to look after you, with this man they call the Lancashire Leopard prowling about in Brunton."

"I'm in no danger from him, Mum. But it's interesting to see how we go about catching a man like this, a serial killer – I've never been involved in a case like this before."

Agnes glanced at her quickly. "You're involved, then?"

"Yes. The whole of the CID is, really. So you see, I'm in no danger, Mum, as I said."

"You're no nearer to catching him, then."

It was a statement, not a fact. Lucy was startled, as children are wont to be by a parent's shrewdness. "Not really. But we shall get him. It's early days yet." That sounded as defensive as Tommy Bloody Tucker, she thought. "There's a very big machine in operation, now. We've been given extra resources."

"His first two murders were on each side of here, you know. One on the outskirts of Preston, one in Clitheroe. Each of them within eight miles of here. They questioned all the men in the village. And now there's a third one, right on the doorstep of this new place you've bought for yourself."

"Hardly that, Mum. A good two miles from my flat."

"You might be safe while you're at work, with all those hefty policemen around you, but you still have to go home on your own. Working all kinds of odd hours, getting home in the dark. You just promise me you'll be careful, my girl."

"I'll be all right, Mum, really. You're not to worry about me. Anyway, what about you? You must come home here in the dark in January, with no street lighting to help you." She wished as soon as she had said it that she had bitten back the words; it sounded as if she had been trying to frighten her mother. The truth was that she had almost told her about Peach, to reassure her, and then had shied away again from the revelation.

She climbed into the bulbous blue Vauxhall Corsa. "I have to go and help interview someone about the case now," she said importantly. She knew that the news that Agnes Blake's girl was involved in the hunt for the Lancashire Leopard would be round the village by the time her mother had finished her part-time stint in the supermarket, that her prominence would be exaggerated in the evening exchanges in the Hare and Hounds.

She smiled at the thought as she waved to her mother and drove away. In her wildest imaginings, she could never have conceived quite how important her part would become in this local melodrama.

Neither the autopsy on Hannah Woodgate nor the work of the Scenes of Crime team were able to provide the police team with much that was useful.

The PM confirmed what the pin-point haemorrhages in the eyes had suggested in the back of the abandoned van – that the victim had died from strangulation. Analysis of the stomach contents and the internal organs showed that the last meal had been eaten some six hours before death and that a very small quantity of alcohol had been consumed at some time during the evening – certainly not more than a pint of cider. There was no evidence of any illegal drug intake, either in the stomach contents or elsewhere on the body.

A bruising on the right shoulder indicated that the girl had probably been seized from behind and spun round while fleeing from her assailant. She had died facing him. her killer had forced both of his thumbs hard into her neck, constricting the carotid arteries until she died. The slightly greater pressure on the left side of the throat suggested that he was probably but not certainly right-handed. He had worn thick leather gloves, possibly cycling or motorcycle gauntlets, but just as possibly thick leather gardening gloves, of the kind on sale at Boots, Woolworths and a host of other retail outlets. Not only were the broad thumb-prints upon the neck consistent with such gloves, but one of the strips of

Sellotape placed on the victim's neck at the place where the corpse had been found revealed tiny traces of such leather when examined under a microscope.

All the evidence was that the victim had died mercifully quickly. She had unfortunately been wearing fine leather kid gloves during her last brief struggle for life, so that there had been no chance of finding hair or skin beneath her nails which might help to identify her killer. There was no evidence of any sexual assault, nor of any kind of interference with the clothing. There were no marks on the body to indicate any form of torture before death.

From the point of view of detection, all this was negative, apart from the minor piece of information about the gloves. Torture, like sexual assault, would almost certainly have left them with some traces of the assailant, some clue which could be followed up, which might in due course clinch an arrest.

SOCO were equally bleak about the area where Hannah Woodgate had died. The snow, which they had hoped might be useful to them, had in the end only helped to confuse matters. It meant that almost everyone who had trodden the area had worn boots or wellingtons, so that there was little chance of identifying the killer by any distinctively soled footwear.

There had been considerable contamination of the site around the van before the SOCO team had arrived to rope it off. A CID officer, DC Pickard, had conducted a detailed examination of the broader surrounding area soon after the body was discovered, but this also was covered with the footprints of local residents who had been drawn to the scene by the discovery of the body. It had not been possible to identify the precise spot where the victim had died. Of the sole-marks from numerous wellingtons and boots, none could be identified as worn by the killer of Hannah Woodgate.

At the end of his PM report, the pathologist made one more suggestion. Everything about this killing – the swift, ruthless dispatch of the victim, the absence of any injury apart from the neck and throat, the apparent lack of any indecent assault – replicated the deaths in November in Preston and that in December in Clitheroe. Even a copy-cat killer would be unlikely to have shown the same restraint, or to have replicated the killing so exactly. This killing was almost certainly the work of the same man. The police should think in terms of a serial killer.

They were looking officially for the man everyone was now calling the Lancashire Leopard.

Peach decided he would interview the former boyfriend of Hannah Woodgate at Brunton nick. To those unfamiliar with them, police stations could still be frightening as well as dismal places. And Peach was a great one for putting on the frighteners. He sent DC Pickard to bring Jason in.

He turned out to be a good-looking boy, tall, with fair hair and an attractive, rather shy smile. Peach wetted his lips and prepared to remove the smile. "You're here of your own free will, Mr Wright. Helping the police with their enquiries into a most serious crime. The most serious of all, in fact. Murder. But you should understand that you are not under arrest. Not yet." He gave the lad the most businesslike in his huge range of smiles, implying that it was probably only a matter of time before the boy was thrown into a cell.

Jason looked round the windowless interview room, trying to convey the impression that he was perfectly calm, that he felt under no threat. The survey did not take him long. The room was no more than ten foot square, with a small, square, heavy table in the middle of it, on which stood a heavy cassette recorder. The walls were not plastered; the bricks were covered with light green emulsion paint, badly scratched at the bottom by chairs and feet. His own chair was the only one on his side of the table; there were two on the other side, occupied by this aggressive inspector and the pretty girl with the beautiful reddish hair, who had introduced herself before they came into this room as Detective Sergeant Blake. He felt as though the single harsh light in the centre of the ceiling was shining directly into his face.

Jason thought he could show how calm he was by volunteering information, without waiting to be asked. He said, "I wasn't Hannah's boyfriend when she died, you know. She'd picked up someone new at university, I understand, some chap who lives down in Surrey." It didn't emerge as nonchalantly as he had planned, mainly because he could not keep his voice steady as he spoke. The quaver was because Hannah lay dead, not because he was nervous, but he could hardly start to explain that to this unsympathetic man with the dark eyes and the even darker moustache, who studied him so unnervingly.

Peach said, "You understand right, lad. Chap by the name of Tony Palmer. He's very cut up about what happened to Hannah. He'd have to pretend to be, of course, if he'd killed her. But we've had him checked out by the local fuzz; he's in the clear. He was in Guildford on the night in question, with five of his mates. Not here in Brunton, like you."

Lucy Blake sensed that this was a young man who was still stricken by the death of a girl he had idolised. That didn't mean he hadn't killed her whilst in the grip of some fierce fit of resentment, of course, as Peach would swiftly have reminded her. She said gently, "We need to eliminate you from our enquiries, Jason, in the same way as we have eliminated this other lad in Surrey."

"If we can, of course," said Peach curtly.

Jason wondered if this was the tough cop/friendly cop routine he had heard about as one of the methods the police used to prise one open. The truth, had he known it, was that it hadn't been worked out like that as a tactic: Peach and Blake each used their own strengths, did what came naturally to them, and found that they complemented each other as an interviewing pair. There was nothing planned about it, but it meant that Peach was prepared to give his sergeant her head nowadays, even when she sometimes appeared to be undermining the effects he created by his more robust approach.

Jason looked from Blake's soft smile to Peach's bristling aggression and said uncertainly, "I saw Hannah that night, yes. But I didn't kill her."

"Where did you see her?" Peach knew the answer to his question perfectly well from the researches of Tony Pickard and Brendan Murphy, but one of his maxims was "Always give 'em the chance to lie". That way you could expose them from the start, go in for the kill, and press them into telling the truth in more important areas. Peach had been a dancing, quick-footed batsman in the Lancashire League until a couple of years ago, and he had always found that an early boundary persuaded the bowler to bowl less searchingly for the rest of your stay. No one dispatched a loose lie over the ropes more effectively than Percy Peach.

"I spoke to Hannah in King George's Hall, on the night she was killed. I was at the dance on that Saturday night." Jason chose his words carefully, convinced that if he strayed accidentally into any error this man would pounce upon it like a dog upon a bone.

"Pity, that. Shame you couldn't have been in Manchester, or Liverpool, or Timbuktu. You'd have been in the clear then."

"I'm in the clear now. I didn't kill her."

"Correction, lad. You may not have killed her, but you're not in the clear until you can convince us of that." Peach smiled, as if he considered that a highly satisfactory state of affairs.

Lucy Blake said, "When did you last see Hannah, Jason? At what time in the evening, I mean, as accurately as you can remember."

"I danced with her. Some time between ten thirty and eleven, that would be."

"Did she seem in any way distressed at the time?"
"No."

"She didn't say that anyone had been bothering her during the evening?"

For an instant, Jason was tempted to invent some distress in Hannah, to point the finger towards some mysterious danger and away from himself. Then he saw Peach's baleful, unblinking scrutiny and said, "No, she didn't. You can't hear a lot on the dance floor, of course. Not while the music's playing. It's too loud to allow you much conversation."

He allowed himself an apologetic smile, and found it returned by a brief and savage one from Peach, like a tennis shot being volleyed fiercely back across the net before you could get into position. "You didn't have much of an exchange with Hannah, then?"

"Not while we were dancing. I took her back to where she was sitting with her friends at the end of the music and – well, I asked her if I could take her home at the end of the evening."

"And she told you to piss off and you were infuriated by that refusal, and followed her anyway."

"No!" Jason was horrified by the way in which his candour had been received. He had expected to be congratulated upon his honesty, but this little sod seemed determined to put the worst possible interpretation on everything he said. "She was quite polite, even sympathetic. She just said she didn't think it would be a very good idea."

"Hard to take, sympathy, isn't it? When you've been close to someone I mean, and you see them feeling not attraction but pity. Enough to make you lose your rag completely. Do things you later regret. Things which horrify you, in the full light of day."

"No!" Jason hated this smiling torturer, would have done almost anything to remove the smile which beamed upon him from beneath that shining bald pate. Peach hurt him more because he was so near to the truth of what he had felt on that fateful night. He had felt first humiliation, then frustration and anger, as Hannah's kindness came through to him as pity. "I didn't do anything! I would never have done anything, not to Hannah! I never saw her again, after that dance."

"Good lad! Now, if you'll just tell us how you got home and at what time, and then give us the name of someone who can confirm this, we can all stop wasting our time." Peach flashed his teeth in a tigerish smile.

Jason noticed for the first time that the inspector's upper canine teeth were missing in an otherwise perfect and very white set; although what should have been the fangs were missing, he was reminded vividly of Count Dracula. "I . . . I did look round for Hannah, at the end, but I didn't see her. She must have left quite quickly with her friend, Anne, I think. I walked home on my own. I must have arrived at about twelve thirty or twelve forty, I think. I . . . I'm afraid I can't think of anyone who can confirm that. Everyone at home was in bed."

Peach raised his eyebrows more than Jason Wright would have thought was humanly possible. Lucy Blake said quietly, "The time when you arrived home is not so vital, Jason." There was a pause, in which Wright realised that she meant that he could have arrived home at twelve forty having murdered Hannah. He gulped for oxygen in the airless room as Lucy said, "What we'd like is someone who could confirm where you were at about quarter past midnight."

"That's when she died, isn't it?" His voice rose on the question. For a moment, it looked as if he would burst into tears. Then he controlled himself, looked down at the table between them, and said in little more than a whisper, "I was two miles away from where she died, walking up Preston New Road on my own; seeing how beautiful the new snow looked on the hedges; wishing I had Hannah beside me to enjoy it with me."

There was another pause, whilst they considered this picture. Then Peach said quietly, "You can go now, Mr Wright."

Jason looked up at the man who had seemed so determined to trap him, and this time there were tears in his eyes as he said dazedly, "But I haven't anyone to vouch for what I'm saying."

"No. That isn't necessarily damning, though. The guilty can usually give a convincing account of themselves, with witnesses to prove it. And lots of perfectly innocent people don't have alibis."

Peach glanced at DS Blake, then gave the boy his least threatening smile. "We don't believe you killed Hannah Woodgate, Mr Wright. If we should have second thoughts, we've got your address."

Jason realised that his ordeal was at an end, as abruptly as it had begun. He said, "Yes. I shan't be going away. I'm on a business studies course at Brunton College of Technology."

Peach's smile was again curiously without any threat. "Yes, we know that. And you're a local lad. Keep your ear to the ground, see if you can pick anything up. See if you hear of anyone behaving strangely. You probably realise that this bloke has killed three times now. And I think he's a local. If you hear of any odd bods that you think might even possibly be our man, let us know. Don't worry about wasting our time: we'll be checking out a vast range of people in the next few weeks, including names given to us by all kind of crackpots. And don't think anyone you name will ever know where the information came from."

Earnest requests for help from amateurs now, thought Peach as he went back to his office. A sure sign of desperation, that. He'd be asking Tommy Bloody Tucker for his ideas if things got any worse.

DS Blake guided Jason Wright through the labyrinth of the CID section and back to the reception area. She smiled into the exhausted young face as she prepared to leave him. "You have to be pretty good, to convince DI Peach, without witnesses. Try to get on with your life without Hannah Woodgate now. Look to the future, not to the past. And rest assured: however long it takes, we're going to get whoever killed Hannah."

Seven

"You're telling me you still haven't got anyone in the frame, a full two days after the body of this Woodgate girl was discovered?" Superintendent Tucker believed he saw an opportunity to put what seemed a rather muted DI Peach in his place.

"No, sir. Not unless you make it a pretty big frame."

Tucker looked puzzled for a moment, then resumed even more truculently. "It's no use playing with words. Have you or have you not got someone for this murder?"

"No, sir."

"I wonder how you spend your days sometimes, I really do. You have a team of sixty and you produce nothing. Or very nearly nothing. And I told the Chief Constable the other day what a quick and incisive detective you were."

Peach shut one eye and regarded his chief narrowly through the other one. "Most unwise, sir."

"I might have known you wouldn't even appreciate it when I tried to help you. What do you mean, anyway, when you say that you might have people in the frame if it was a very big frame?"

"Pretty big, sir, I think I said. I've had DCs Pickard and Murphy compiling a list of all the men who were at the dance in King George's Hall on Saturday night and can't account for their movements afterwards. There appear to be between thirty and forty of them."

"Yes, I see. That seems a sensible place to start."

It was a bloody obvious place to start, you gormless

57

old windbag, thought Peach. The place where any young constable with six months service behind him would have started. "Thank you, sir. I'll pass on your encouragement. It's tedious work, as you can imagine, but necessary, I thought."

"And what has this tedious but necessary exercise produced? Have you lined up two or three suspects from whom our man must come?"

"Not two or three, sir, no. Twenty or thirty would be nearer the mark, at present. But we're whittling down the list all the time. If you'd like to apply your expert eye to it, and use your vast experience to—"

"Don't bother me with the detail, Peach. I've told you before, it's my job to keep an overview of the situation, to make sure the team is working, to keep the CC and the public informed of our efforts."

"Yes, sir. I remember that, now. I'm always reminding the lads and lasses who are working twelve-hour days of the overview that you have of the situation. I tell them just how valuable that is. In detail. I shall—"

"Twelve-hour days? You're not going overboard on the overtime budget, I hope. I gave strict orders that—"

"Sorry if I've got this around my neck again, sir. I thought you told the nation on television that 'no stone will be left unturned' and 'no resource will be left untapped' in the hunt for the Lancashire Leopard. I'm sorry if I misunderstood you, sir, but I thought—"

"You thought nothing, Peach! Because you know perfectly well that one has to say such things to reassure the public. That these statements have very little to do with the practical running of the station, where we have to husband resources, to be prudent in the use of public funds, to—"

"Yes, sir. I appreciate what you mean, now. Shall I leak it discreetly that the hunt for the Lancashire Leopard has been stepped down, then? Alf Houldsworth of the *Evening Dispatch* tried to buttonhole me as I left last night, but I said I hadn't any news to give him. I'm sure he'd appreciate a little titbit like this, especially if he got it before the rest. Might make quite a little spread of it, I should think, and it's only fair that the old bugger should get first crack at—"

"PEACH! You will not speak to the press!" Tucker delivered the monosyllables clearly, loudly and very slowly. "Is that crystal clear?"

"Very clear indeed, sir. Sorry I misunderstood. It's just that I know how you pride yourself on your relationships with the media, and—"

"You will leave any bulletins to the press officer, and any major announcements to me or the Chief Constable."

"Yes, sir. Of course, sir. Sorry, sir. It just seemed a major change of policy for us to de-escalate the search for the Lancashire Leopard, and if poor old one-eyed Alf was going to miss out on—"

"Leave poor old one-eyed Alf to look after himself!" said Tucker grimly, as the headlines swam before his mind's apprehensive eye. Bluster didn't seem to have cowed this awful lieutenant of his; he decided to try sarcasm. "And of course we're not de-escalating the search. I just thought that after two whole days with the extensive team I have secured for you, you might have produced some results. Or is that asking too much of you?"

"Depends what you mean by results, sir, doesn't it? I'd say we're narrowing the field, myself. We've narrowed it quite a lot, in the two whole days you mentioned. Rather more than the Serious Crime Squad had been able to narrow it in two whole months, in fact. We're comparing notes with them and using their help too, of course."

Tucker stored away the thought of two days of his investigation against two whole months spent fruitlessly on the previous two murders: it might be useful, that, if the CC or the media got on his back. He said dismally, "I suppose there's no doubt now that Hannah Woodgate died at the hand of the same man who killed the previous two women?"

"None whatsoever, sir, I'd say. MO exactly the same, and

59

none of the women sexually assaulted. But you'll have read all that in my report, sir." He nodded at the unopened file marked "Confidential" on the superintendent's desk.

"Of course." Tucker, who had started guiltily, tried again to assert himself. "But all of this is very general stuff, isn't it? Compiling lists, narrowing the field. It might be good enough for the general public, but it doesn't deceive old hands like me. We're old sweats together, Peach, in CID work." He leaned forward, allowing Peach to assimilate the nightmare vision of Tommy Bloody Tucker as a colleague at the crime-face. "I want names, Peach. Accounts of villains you have put in the frame and gone after."

Peach studied his chief for a moment, his dark eyes unblinking. Then he abruptly spat the words, "Billy Bedford."

Tucker recoiled a foot – almost as if he had been slapped on the cheek with a wet cod, thought Peach pleasurably. The superintendent said stupidly, "Billy Bedford?"

Peach realised with delight that Tucker didn't know the man, whereas he could guarantee that every other member of Brunton CID would have recognised the name immediately. "Flasher, sir. Mucky magazine type. Several previous convictions. Did time for the last one. Fifty-four. Lives alone with his mother."

Tucker's eyes lit up. "Can he account for his whereabouts at the time of the murders?"

"Not satisfactorily, sir, no."

"Then why isn't he in a cell?" Tucker stuck out his chin in his most decisive manner.

Peach took a metaphorical swing at it. "Because he didn't do it, sir. Not in my opinion. Of course, if you'd like to have a go at him yourself, I can arrange—"

"No!" Tucker's eyes widened with apprehension at the thought of real police work, as Peach had known they would. "I trust my staff, as you should know by now. If you say he didn't do it, that's good enough for me."

And if I was wrong, you'd hang me from the nearest lamp

post without a moment's hesitation, thought Peach. Aloud, he said, "Your loyalty to your team has always been one of your most valued virtues, sir. Binds us together in the pursuit of crime, I often think, that does. The knowledge that you would never ever let us down."

Tucker peered suspiciously at the round countenance with its smile of contentment, but found the eyes now fixed upon a point a foot above his head. "Yes, well. Who else have you been to see?"

"We've had the ex-boyfriend in here, sir. Gave him a bit of a grilling in an interview room."

"And?" Tucker reflected upon the fact that this supremely irritating man, whose flow of words could not be arrested when he was on the wrong tack, seemed to stop and require prompting on the rare occasions when you actually wanted him to speak.

"Well, he admits he was at the dance on Saturday night. And he admits that he was still smitten by the dead girl, that he asked if he could take her home, that she refused the request."

Tucker sought for a penetrating question. He could not keep the excitement out of his voice as he came up with, "And can he account for his movements at the time when the girl was being killed?"

"Not satisfactorily, sir. He says he walked home. Alone. There doesn't appear to be anyone who can corroborate his story."

Tucker struck his most authoritative pose; his chin was almost as high as his nose. "Then why isn't he in a cell? And why wasn't I told this earlier?"

Peach was suddenly weary of the man. He snapped, "Because we've no evidence to put him there. Because there's nothing at all to connect him with the previous deaths. Because he didn't do it. In my opinion and that of DS Blake, who interviewed him with me. Sir."

He rose and left, without taking his eyes off his superior officer, without waiting to be dismissed.

61

J. M. Gregson

Friday, January 11ᵗʰ

Clyde Northcott was inspecting his pay packet and looking forward to the weekend.

The money was never as much as you expected, even when you'd done the overtime. Six hours at time and a half he'd put in this week, and he had well over two hundred pounds to come, but the figure was still less than he'd expected. Big lump of tax off it. Fucking Government! he echoed the ritual phrase of all the other lads on his shift; it was nothing to do with politics – you said it whichever of the parties was in power. That didn't seem to make any difference to you, nowadays. The single blokes were paying for all these brats, supporting all these sponging girls who had kids by God knew who and then called themselves single mothers.

It wasn't fair on the single workers like him, who sweated all week to pay the rent for their own places and didn't live off the state. He went with the rest of the lads to the pub near the gates of the electrical works, but he only drank in halves. When you had what he had to excite you, you didn't need to drink.

They talked about the Rovers and the next day's match, and whether the board would shell out any more money for strikers when so much had been misused. Clyde kept his end up in the football conversations, even wrapped a blue-and-white scarf round his neck in freezing weather, but in truth he wasn't all that interested in soccer. Bikes were more his thing. When you had a three-fifty engine between your thighs and a grip you could twist to accelerate man and machine faster than any car, you were the Captain of your Soul. Clyde liked that phrase. It had stuck in his mind from a poem they had read at school, long after all the other words from it had gone. He liked doing things which made you feel the Captain of your Soul.

He talked a little about the Yamaha, as he always did when

the opportunity arose. A seventeen-year-old with acne who worked on the next bench in the works said, "He'll bloody kill himself, will Clyde!"

Clyde turned his head, gave the boy a slow grin. "Fancy a ride on the back, Dermot?"

"I wouldn't bloody ride behind you if you paid me the fucking Lottery!" said the boy. "Wall of bastard death, that is." He looked round at his companions for supporting laughter.

There was a little, because you were usually safe enough when the subject was motorbikes. But no one took too many liberties when they were joking with Clyde Northcott. He was six feet three, lean, fit and very black. He had a two-inch patch of carefully trimmed beard on his chin, which combined with the flashing whites of his eyes to make him look more menacing than the white and Asian youths who worked with him. He was a bit of a loner, Clyde. He didn't seem to have any close friends. And he could handle himself: he had grown up in council homes, where you learned to do that or suffer.

And he was a crazy bastard to boot. That was the most important thing of all to remember. Clyde was vaguely aware that his companions were a little afraid of him. He wasn't quite sure why that was so, but he knew that he enjoyed the feeling that it gave him.

The young men stood in a little group outside the pub for a few minutes, talking about women, joking, getting ready for the night and the weekend. The rest of them looked after Northcott for a few moments as he went back to get his bike from the works car park, where he had left it for safety.

"He's a mad bugger, is yon," said one of them, and they all laughed their agreement and relief.

In the Murder Room at Brunton CID, DCs Pickard and Murphy were comparing notes. They had reduced the men who had been at the previous Saturday's dance and who remained suspects to six now, from an original list of thirty-seven.

The thirty-one they had eliminated had either been able to come up with a checkable account of themselves or had had some sort of alibi for one of the previous murders. In that respect, having the Lancashire Leopard as a quarry was a help: once you accepted that the same man was responsible for all three deaths, you could discount people who could prove that they could not have done any particular one of them.

Of their remaining six men, three were students who were out of the town and would need to be checked in the next day or two. In all probability, the three would be able to show that they were also away from the area in early November, when the first woman had been killed. If any of them had been at home when all three of the women had been murdered, that would be highly significant. A lucky break for the police, the press would say, ignoring the fact that it had been turned up by the patient and laborious sifting of thirty-seven possibilities.

Of the other three, one was a twenty-five-year-old man with two children who had attended the dance without his wife's knowledge, left home on the following Sunday morning, and as yet not been located. His wife was "fairly sure" he had been in the house when the first two women had met their deaths, but he would need to be found and checked. The wife thought that their marriage was at an end and said she would refuse to have him back in the house, but marriage was a strange institution: even the spouses of wife-beaters were sometimes willing to protect the men who had abused them.

The other two men were commercial travellers in their late twenties, who were on the road during the week. One was divorced and lived alone, the other was in a childless and apparently unhappy marriage with a wife who was on the way to becoming an alcoholic.

Commercial travellers, like long-distance lorry drivers, always excite the interest of policemen searching for serial killers. They have the transport and often the opportunity, for few people, even wives, can be certain of their whereabouts from hour to hour, and particularly overnight. These occupations seem also to carry more than the normal quota of loners, men who find it difficult to get on well with large groups of people or to form deep and lasting relationships.

At twenty past six, Tony Pickard said, "We've done enough of this for one day. Fancy a drink before we go home?"

"You're on!" said Brendan Murphy immediately. "But it's only because I haven't got a pretty little woman waiting at home, mind."

A few minutes later, Brendan sat in front of a pint of Guinness with a fine white head, into which he drew eyes and a nose and a mouth by the delicate use of his little finger. People expected him to drink Guinness because of his Irish name – you couldn't always get Murphy's – and he had no great objection to the stereotyping: he had acquired a taste for stout by now. "Expect Percy will want to interview the commercial travellers himself," he said.

"Probably. One thing's for certain: our respected detective superintendent, Tommy Bloody Tucker, won't go near them!" said Tony Pickard with feeling. "He'll tell the television and radio people how capably he's directing the hunt, how hard his boys are working, but he won't have a clue what we're about at any particular moment." At the end of a hard week, a little ritual denigration of the hierarchy was an automatic, cathartic relief. He took a small, exploratory sip of his bitter and sighed with satisfaction.

"Percy Peach won't let him get away with too much," said Brendan. "He's a right stroppy little sod, Percy, and he's the only copper I've ever met who doesn't give a bugger about rank."

Tony Pickard smiled. "On balance, we're lucky having Percy. He drives us hard, but he drives himself even harder. He's a cantankerous little bugger, as you say, but in the end he's on our side. I sometimes think he says all the things we'd like to say, but he manages to say them better."

65

J. M. Gregson

Tony took a longer pull at his bitter this time, waiting for his companion's reaction. They were both relatively new recruits to the CID section at Brunton, so it was good to know how other people felt about things.

Brendan grinned. "He's a character all right, is Percy Peach. The kind of bloke you're always talking about, even when he's not with you. Like now. I reckon he treats Tucker the way he does because he knows the old windbag can't do without him."

Tony Pickard nodded. "Do you reckon Tucker knows about Percy and Lucy Blake?"

Brendan sipped his Guinness with care: the trick was to drink it almost to the bottom of the glass and still leave the face you had etched staring at you from the froth. "Probably not. I bet Percy still gives the stupid bugger the impression that DS Blake is one of the crosses he has to bear."

Tony Pickard laughed. "I wouldn't mind bearing DS Blake myself occasionally. She's got more curves than any sergeant I've ever met. Mind you, most of the others have been males, with moustaches and B.O.!"

They exchanged a few meaningless male fantasies about the nubile Detective Sergeant Blake and the possibilities of bedroom exercise available to the fortunate Detective Inspector Peach. It was harmless enough – just part of the winding-down process at the end of a busy week for two single men who were beginning to make their way as CID constables.

Clyde Northcott, studying himself in the mirror, decided to trim an eighth of an inch off the little patch of closely cropped beard on his chin. He had already showered; now he put away the scissors and applied a touch of aftershave, enjoying the brief icing of his skin, watching his face in the mirror to check that it did not wince, smiling a little at himself and his foibles.

He had left it as late as possible to smoke the crack. The small cocaine rock disappeared swiftly. He put the pipe

66

carefully away in the drawer, feeling already that sense of omnipotence which always surged through his veins after the crack. You took it as late as you could, for the effects didn't last for more than a few hours. But in those hours, you felt that you could do anything.

He put on the new shirt he had bought at Next and made himself ready for the disco. He was a good dancer, they said, but that wasn't of great importance to him. He enjoyed the strobe lights flashing, picking out and glamorising shapes which disappeared as swiftly as they had arrived; the near-darkness as the music surged in a crescendo; the movement of women's bodies, close to but not touching his own.

He couldn't analyse quite why he enjoyed it so much, but he knew that it excited him. Yet he didn't want to carry it through as some of his companions did. He didn't want to end up in a clinch with some girl at the side of the floor; he was disgusted when he found couples at it like dogs in the darkness outside. Not that there would be much of that tonight: that was for the summer darkness, rather than the winter.

Winter suited Clyde best. He pulled on his leathers as though they were armour, savouring how closely they fitted round his lean and muscular frame. Then he took a last look at himself in the mirror, pulled on the thick gauntlets, and went out into the night.

Eight

S uperintendent Tucker was in his office on a Saturday morning.

No one could recall when this had last happened. Percy Peach, receiving a summons from on high, left the busy Murder Room and wondered as he climbed the stairs whether there would be a plague of frogs by nightfall.

Tucker pulled an armchair from the edge of his office to replace the upright chair which was normally placed in front of his desk. "Do sit down, Percy," he said. He had forced a wide smile on to his long face. Peach could see more of his teeth than he could recall ever seeing before. They reminded him of the yellowing keys of a neglected piano.

"It's all hands to the pumps, in a case like this, Percy," Tucker began weakly. "It's good to be in charge of a team who are pulling together so well."

"Yes, sir." Peach's fertile mind had already suggested a range of possibilities for his chief's unprecedented presence here on a Saturday: a sense of duty did not figure among them.

"I thought we should have a talk together at this stage – exchange a few confidences, perhaps. We're old hands, you and I, Percy. Two old sweats together, as you might say."

You might, I wouldn't, thought Peach. Any more than I would dream of exchanging confidences with a flatulent old fraud like you. And you've called me "Percy" three times in under a minute: that's a danger signal if ever I heard one, but I can't figure out what the danger is, yet. He donned the blandest of his own formidable range of smiles and said cautiously, "Confidences. I see, sir."

Tucker wondered why this man who was normally so difficult to shut up would now hardly speak at all, when he needed a response to help him on. He said desperately, "I don't suppose I should be talking to you at all about this, really. Not if I went strictly by the rules."

"I see, sir. Before you go any further, I think I should tell you that I'm not interested in joining the Masons. I'm flattered to be asked, of course, and I'm sure it's nothing like as corrupt an organisation as people say, but—"

"I wasn't inviting you to join the Masons, Peach!" A vision of that round countenance with its vacant smile beneath the bald head sitting beside him at the lodge swam before Tucker's horrified imagination, and he had to shake his head violently to dissolve this horrid fantasy. He made an immense effort to be affable. "Percy, we've worked together now for several years and—"

"Seven, sir."

"Seven. Is it really? Well, we've seen things come and go. And a few people as well. We've had our successes and our failures and I think it's now time to—"

"Before you go any further, sir, I don't want one."

"Don't want what?"

"A transfer, sir. I'm happy at Brunton. Happy with the team I have to work with here. If you're thinking—"

"No, no, Peach . . . Percy. I wasn't thinking of that at all! I wouldn't dream of fracturing a relationship which has been so successful. We have been good for the service, you and I. We have given them successes which I venture to say in all modesty they would never have achieved without us."

"In all modesty. I see, sir."

"What? Yes, that's right. Well, this is what I wanted to talk about, though as I say, it's a matter of some delicacy."

"Delicacy, sir?"

"Yes. I'm speaking to you in the greatest confidence, of course, and perhaps I shouldn't even be doing that."

"Do be careful, sir. I wouldn't like you to compromise your integrity."

"My integrity?" This was obviously not a concept with which Thomas Bulstrode Tucker was familiar.

"One of the proudest things in Brunton police circles, your integrity is. I often tell the lads and lasses that."

"I see. Well, I prefer to think in terms of efficiency."

"Yes, sir. Well, that's all right then. I often tell the team exactly how much I think of your efficiency, also."

Tucker peered suspiciously at the round countenance with the cheerful smile and the eyes beamed at a spot two inches above his head. "What I'm saying is that we make an effective unit, the two of us. And efficiency deserves its rewards, does it not?"

Bloody hell, he's going to tell me they're about to promote him, thought Peach. If this garrulous old fart is to move even further up the ladder, I should win the bleeding Lottery. And I never buy a ticket. Despite himself, his smile became a grimace. "Rewards, sir?"

"Yes, Percy, rewards. Merit does not go unrecognised in the modern police service, you know. Look at me."

"Yes, sir. I do. And I tell the rest of the lads to do that, almost every day."

Tucker leaned forward, brought his face to within two feet of the black toothbrush moustache on the other side of the desk, narrowed his eyes to indicate a moment of intimacy. "Well, then. And may I tell you that it is possible that I haven't finished yet."

Oh God in heaven, look down and release me from this torment, thought Peach. The bugger's saying he's going to be promoted. The office and its furniture swam briefly before his eyes. When his vision cleared, he found Tucker with his head slightly on one side, tapping the side of his handsome nose and leering. "And it may well be that you too will move up the hierarchy, Percy. At the same time as me. If you . . . I mean if we . . . play our cards right." He tapped his nose again and threw a cunning smile at Peach.

In this mood, he makes Mephistopheles look like Shirley Temple, thought Peach. He said weakly, "I'm happy where I am, sir."

Tucker smiled his elder-statesman smile, slid his left hand under the lapel of his jacket in the Napoleonic gesture he reserved for his moments of advice. Peach resisted the temptation to ask him if he felt a right tit – this man would never understand, anyway. The superintendent said magisterially, "There is no reason why you should not remain contentedly under my direction, doing essentially the same job, while attaining a higher rank. You must trust me in these things, Percy."

Peach thought that on the whole he would rather trust Captain Hook, but it did seem that the man on this occasion had a point. He said cautiously, "Promotion, while remaining contentedly under your direction. That sounds almost too good to be true, sir."

Tucker was unaware of any irony. He beamed and repeated, "Trust me, Percy, trust me. It may surprise you to know that the CC has a very high opinion of your abilities."

I bet it surprised you, thought Peach. But you'd go along with it, as long as it meant praise for you and your department: you're not quite as stupid as I like to make out. And not stupid at all where your own interests are concerned. He tried not to let his distaste show in his face as he said, "That is gratifying, sir, but I don't quite see how—"

"Come, Percy, you and I are men of the world. We know how these things work. I have had some good results in my CID section in the last few years, and that is bound to be recognised sooner or later. And if I can lift my most valued member of staff up the ladder a rung or two behind me, I am happy to do so."

For the first time in seven years, Peach was speechless in the presence of his chief. In the face of this effrontery, even his nimble brain and agile tongue were atrophied. His jaw

71

dropped a little, in the face of this hypocrisy from a man they both knew would like to give him a single ticket to hell.

Tucker was delighted by this unaccustomed silence. He held his hand up with the palm towards his DI. "Don't bother to thank me, Percy. And don't breathe a word of this to anyone. And remember, promotion, if it comes, will come as the product of our results. We must find the Lancashire Leopard. I feel confident that almost as soon as we arrest him, DI Peach will become Detective Chief Inspector Peach."

And Tommy Bloody Tucker will become Chief Superintendent, thought Peach. It's a mad, mad world, my masters.

Wednesday, January 16ᵗʰ

It was a grey, bleak day, but the visibility was better than you would have expected. The council house was one of a row at the top of a gentle rise, and you could just see the dark shapes of the distinctive skyline of Liverpool in the distance.

The woman who opened the door was in her mid-thirties. Her prettiness was still evident, but fading fast. She looked apprehensive as Lucy Blake showed her warrant card. "Mrs Plant? I'm Detective Sergeant Blake and this is Detective Constable Pickard. We'd like a few words, please."

"What about? I've done nothing. I've nothing to talk about . . . not to pigs." She checked herself on that word: it was one of his, when she thought she had rid herself of him for ever.

"No one's suggesting you've done anything wrong, Mrs Plant. And if you're worried about being seen with the police, we'd be better inside the house, wouldn't we?"

She stared at them for a moment, in which they could see the fear in her eyes. Then she turned abruptly and led them into a living room which seemed clean and fresh, which was shabbily furnished but very tidy. She shut the open window and turned back to them. "It's Debbie Edgar now, not Plant. I've gone back to my own name. This is about Terry, isn't it?"

It was probably just fancy, but Lucy thought that she could smell the fear on the woman. She said, "It is, yes. But no one knows we've come here. And no one will."

Debbie Edgar wasn't reassured. She'd heard promises like that before. They might mean it as they said it, but no one could guarantee such things. She said, "You found me, didn't you? What's to stop him?"

"We have our methods. The ones we used to find you are not available to Terry Plant. If you can tell us a little about Terry, we'll go away and leave you in peace."

She glanced at the clock on the mantelpiece. It was one of the few items in the room which had not come from the Salvation Army or the Church Furniture Centre; her mother had given her the clock. It showed her now that the children would be home in half an hour. She wanted these people out of here before then: they were a link with the past which Debbie wanted all of them to forget. She said wearily, "What's he done now?"

Tony Pickard said, "Nothing, that we're aware of, Ms Edgar. Nothing that we can charge him with. He's been looking for you. We encouraged him to give up the idea."

Her eyes flashed white with fear. "He'll take no notice of that. He'll find me, if you have."

Lucy said firmly, "He won't, Debbie. The source of our information isn't available to him." She didn't say that the woman who had told them that Terry Plant's wife might be somewhere around Liverpool was now in Styal Prison for six months, where Terry Plant would certainly not get to her.

Debbie could not let it go; she was desperate for reassurance. "He'll use the same methods as you did."

Lucy shook her head, smiled gently. "He won't, Debbie. He might guess you've gone back to your maiden name, but there's no way he can connect you with this area. And he won't be able to arrange for computer searches of employees, as we could."

Debbie Edgar breathed a little more easily. "He might even have forgotten that I trained as a nursery school teacher . . . I never worked when I was with him. I've got myself a job at the local nursery school. Just mornings, but it gives us some money. And I was eligible for this place, once I had a job locally." She was trying to be matter-of-fact, but her pride in the way she was picking up her life crept into her tone in spite of herself. She looked from the green, intelligent eyes of Lucy Blake to the grave, rather handsome face of the tall young man beside her. "I don't see how I can be of any help to you two, though."

Lucy said, "It may be painful, but we'd like to ask you a little about your life with Terry Plant. Believe me, it's important, or we wouldn't have taken the trouble to find you and we wouldn't be bothering you now."

"What kind of things?"

"Was he violent?"

For a moment, Debbie thought she would refuse to answer, would fling them out of this new home she had worked so hard to create. Then she heard herself saying simply, "Yes. Yes, he was."

"To you? To the children?"

Debbie glanced briefly at Tony Pickard, then stood and moved to the door, nodding at Lucy Blake to follow her. In the small kitchen where the pots drained on the sink, she pulled up her sweater and shirt and showed the livid scar between the top of her breast and her shoulder. "That was a broken bottle. A memento to remember him by, when I'm going to bed at nights."

They went back into the living room; Lucy gave a tiny nod to Tony Pickard. She said, "It wasn't an isolated instance, Debbie, was it?"

"No. It began after we had our first child. He was always very sorry afterwards, in those early days. I suppose that's why I stayed: I thought he might stop doing it. But it got worse."

Tony Pickard said, "What age are your children?"

74

"Rosie's thirteen now. She can look after the others for an hour, if I need it."

She looked suddenly guilty, as if she remembered that this was the law she was talking to. "I don't though, unless there's some sort of emergency. Keith's ten and Mandy's eight."

"Did he hit the children?"

"He did, yes. He started to hit Rosie. That's why I left."

Tony Pickard nodded, made a note. Did he ever hit the boy?"

"No, he didn't. Keith was only seven when Terry went inside, mind, but somehow I don't think he'd ever have hit him."

There was a tiny pause before Lucy Blake said, "I know this is difficult, but can you tell us anything about the kind of violence he offered to you and Rosie? Was there any pattern to it?"

Debbie Edgar looked for a moment as if she would refuse to answer. Then she said slowly, "It wasn't drink, the way it is with a lot of them. Sometimes he'd had a drink, but most times he hadn't. And it wasn't connected with sex – I didn't refuse him, and at the end he wasn't that interested. I don't know whether he had other women or not, and eventually I didn't care."

"So it would be after some kind of argument?"

"Yes. But he wasn't predictable. Sometimes I could talk to him without even a threat. Not often in the last year or two, though. He thinks I shopped him, but I didn't. He swore he'd kill me, when he got out."

Lucy said gently, "Well, he's been out since last September, now, and he hasn't got near you."

"Yes. I reckoned he'd be out by then, with remission for good conduct. That's a joke, after the way he treated me!"

"Do you think it was a power thing, when he hit you? Was it because he saw you as a threat to his dominance?"

Debbie smiled bitterly at the younger woman. "I tried applying all the psychiatric nonsense myself, to see if I

75

could cope with him. Perhaps it was the need to dominate which drove him. Sometimes I thought he just hated all women – he used to shout his mouth off about all of us." She looked from one to the other of her questioners, sensing their heightened interest. "Why do you want to know all this? Has Terry attacked someone else?"

"Not as far as we know, Debbie. But he's a violent man, as you say, and we like to keep an eye on such—"

"You suspect him of being this Lancashire Leopard, don't you? The man who's killed three women near where we used to live . . ." Her voice tailed away as her eyes widened with the horror of the thought. She had lived with this man, shared her bed with him for ten years and more, felt his hands upon her, in tenderness as well as in violence.

Lucy said as briskly as she could, "We're checking out all men with a history of violence, that's all. The fact that—"

"The dates tally, don't they? He came out of Strangeways in September, and the first murder was after that."

"On the night of the third of November, yes. And the second killing was on the twelfth of December. But we haven't any evidence against your former husband. It's just that we're checking out anyone—"

"But it could have been Terry, couldn't it? If he's on his own, and roaming about the area."

Tony Pickard said quietly, "It could have been a lot of men, Debbie. That's our problem. Do *you* think it could have been him?"

She shook her head in bewilderment, contemplating this ultimate horror of the relationship she was trying to bury. Her voice was scarcely audible as she said, "I don't know."

Pickard had watched her intently as she unravelled the life she had shut away from her. He now said quietly, "You say Terry's violence to you was never connected with sex. Did he ever put his hands round your neck – threaten to strangle you?"

Debbie Edgar looked at him for several seconds, her eyes widening with the terror of her recollection. Then she stared at the empty fireplace and said, "He did, yes, sometimes. Especially in the last years. He put his hands round my neck and pressed until I couldn't breathe. Then he'd laugh and tell me what a slender thread my life hung by, how easily he could kill me. But he always let me go after a second or two." She looked up again, fastening her eyes upon Lucy Blake's alert face beneath the red-brown hair, as if she could only trust a woman to be honest about this. "That *is* the power thing, isn't it?"

"I suppose it is, Debbie. But it would need someone better qualified than any of the three of us in this room to know how significant it was."

They left her standing on the step, a lonely, anxious figure, staring down the road for the first glimpse of her children returning home.

Saturday, January 19th

The murderer sat in front of his television set, watching a late-night showing of *The Silence of the Lambs*. It was a strange film to use to wind oneself down, but he felt the tension easing out of his limbs by the end of the first hour of it. He treated the film as pure escapism, and saw no relation to his own life. This Hannibal Lector was clearly a monster and clearly mad.

He listened to the late night news on Radio Lancashire. There was no mention of the Lancashire Leopard. But then he had known that there wouldn't be. He only watched and listened to the news bulletins to reinforce his sense of security. The police team engaged in the hunt numbered more than sixty now. And they weren't even getting near.

At 1.30 a.m. he opened a window to the cool night air and sat for a few minutes in a chair with a mug of tea, exulting in the absolute silence of the world around him. Out there, he knew, there would be police officers searching for him, vigilant, nervous, wondering as they moved through the cool night air if the Leopard might be abroad.

He felt better now. Calmer. Earlier in the evening, when he had been out, he had felt a restlessness, a desire to show them again how futile their efforts were. But he had conquered it. You didn't take hasty, impulsive actions when the stakes were high. You moved in your own time, took action only when you knew it was safe, when it suited you. Your enemy might be baffled, but you didn't underestimate him. Not if you wanted to go on giving yourself kicks like the ones he had enjoyed so much.

While he remained master of the situation, there could be no danger. He was confident now that he knew everything about the hunt which was being raised against him. He certainly knew enough about what was going on to know when to strike. And where. He had found another possible victim, but he would be as meticulous as ever in his preparations. That was the secret of his success.

Soon the Leopard would be ready to kill again.

Nine

C lyde Northcott stood with his long legs on the ground on each side of the Yamaha. He revved the 350 c.c. engine, listened to the smoothly accelerating roar with deep appreciation, savoured how slight was the vibration between his thighs even when he opened the throttle almost to the full. A great machine, the Yamaha, well worth the sacrifices he had made to get it. Much better as a companion than these expensive girls. And much more reliable. He eased the bike gently on to the road.

Clyde didn't speed in the built-up area, despite the power of the bike and his mastery of it. When you were young and black, you attracted police attention like a hornet at a tea-party. And when you had a throaty motorbike to make them jealous, you had to be extra careful. He'd had his usual small rock just before he set out, and he felt like racing up through the gears, but he controlled himself. That was the advantage of good coke rocks, he thought: they put you on a high, but they made you extra smart as well. Your brain seemed to work that little bit quicker, your mind seemed to rid itself of every consideration save the matter in hand.

Restraining himself made his pleasure all the greater when he passed out of the town and on to the open road. He kept a close watch for any pig cars or motorbikes as he moved on to the dual carriageway of the A59. Then he watched the needle on the speedo move swiftly through the numbers, as he roared smoothly up to the ton and sped past Clitheroe. He held it between a hundred and a hundred and ten for four miles of almost deserted tarmac, passing a solitary car as if it were standing still, catching a fleeting glimpse of the woman driver's white, surprised face as he overtook with a brief wave of his gauntleted hand.

The party was out beyond Gisburn, somewhere, just off the main road. He found the house easily enough: a big, rectangular box of a place, with all the lights on and music already blaring out. He had come quite late, for he did not like to be one of the first at any function. He hated standing around attracting attention and trying to make the small talk which would never come easily to him.

He scarcely knew the girl who was giving the party – taking advantage of her parents' cruise in the West Indies to use their house for her own purposes. She worked with him at the electrical components factory, but she was office staff, and they rarely deigned to communicate with the shop-floor workers. He had only been invited because she knew one of his companions, a fellow-biker, who had taken the opportunity to win a little cheap popularity with his fellows by stretching his own invitation to include four.

Clyde parked the Yamaha carefully in the shadows at the side of the three-car garage. You didn't want any casual damage from party revellers when you were only insured for third party, fire and theft. Unlike many of the people here, he had to be careful with his possessions. He put his bottle of wine on the big table which had been set up as a bar in the wide hall of the house, then went and peeled off his leathers in a room his hostess called the family room. This Tracey didn't even know his surname, he thought. Well, that wasn't her fault; left to her own preferences, she would never have invited him.

Had he but known it, Clyde Northcott was quite wrong about that. Tracey Wallace, the girl who lived here, was well aware of all his names. She had spotted the tall, handsome youth across the works canteen and made a point of making the cursory acquaintance which was all she had needed to invite him here. It was not surprising that she should do

The Lancashire Leopard

so. Clyde was a striking figure, with a carriage which proclaimed that he owed allegiance to no one. He did not seem to have a girlfriend, and to an impressionable girl of twenty who had come to work straight from Cheltenham Ladies' College, even the vague air of menace he carried upon his lean black frame seemed to add to his attractions.

Tracey came in with a glass in her hand while he was peeling off his leggings. "Glad you could make it, Clyde. I was beginning to think you weren't coming," she said.

She had a small, pretty face. Her curly blonde hair hung about her ears in what was no doubt a highly expensive style, though it looked to Clyde rather like damp rats' tails. He said, "I was always going to come. Thank you for asking me," and immediately felt as conspicuous as he had years ago when invited to children's parties, the lone black boy in a sea of white faces.

He poured a can of lager into a glass with elaborate care, tilting the glass and pouring slowly to make sure the foam did not spill on to the carpet, postponing the moment when he would have to look again into the face of Tracey Wallace. She said, "You're an expert at that, I can see," and gave him a wide smile while he tried to shrug away his embarrassment. He could see through the open door that drinks were already being spilled, could imagine what the reactions of his own parents would have been if he had dared to hold a party without their permission in their little terraced house in Bolton.

He wondered why he so constantly remembered that; he had been in homes from thirteen, when his father had gone away and his mother had what was always referred to as her breakdown. His increasingly distant memories of the family home couldn't have any reference to this girl, or this place. He shrugged the distant image away and gave Tracey a smile. The cocaine coursing through his veins made him feel happy and in control; he wondered why the power did not extend to his tongue, so that he might put aside this bubbling girl without offending her.

81

But he was reprieved. A crowd of slightly tipsy girls came in from the lounge, where the music was playing so loudly, and took her attention, demanding drinks, teasing her about her posh house, enjoying the delicious idea of using the place without her parents' consent. Clyde took his lager and moved silently and swiftly into the dim room where the music blared.

He stood at the side of the big square room for a moment, then was drawn into the dancing in the centre of the floor. It was not one of the brasher tunes. Some stringed instrument – a sitar, perhaps – twanged plangently at the outset, and then a solo violin took up the melody for a time, before the backing group came in on the chorus. Clyde let his supple body writhe sensuously to the music, his limbs seeking out the soft rhythm which underlay the tune, his eyes almost shut, his hands caressing the air in a gentle arabesque.

He found some of his friends from work. They stood together at the side of the room, watching the girls, drinking slowly, tapping their feet in line with the beat as the evening became more frenzied. Tracey Wallace came and pulled Clyde on to the floor and he danced for ten minutes with her, his slow smile lighting up the ebony features, his eyes watching her mobile, pretty face and her bare arms that gyrated wildly to the music. At the end of the track, she reached up to him, running her fingers through his tightly frizzed hair, pulling his face down towards hers, fixing her lips upon his in a long, slow kiss.

After a second of surprise, Clyde lifted his arms and stroked the top of her back, feeling the delicate shoulder blades beneath the smooth silk of her blouse. He felt the tip of her tongue against his teeth, damp and exploratory. She smelt nice. He drew his head back slowly after a moment, enjoying the soft caress of her hair against his mouth and cheek as she sank her face against his chest. He held her at arm's length for a moment before he released her, his face breaking into a slow smile as he looked down into blue eyes clouded with desire.

When eventually she slid her hand through his fingers and left him, he went and got himself another lager, trying not to analyse for the moment what he felt about this unexpected encounter. He had never had a prolonged relationship with any girl. And he had certainly never had the running made to him by a posh girl. He tried to imagine for a moment what the absent parents he had never seen, never would see, would make of him, what they would say about any relationship between him and this fair-haired girl with the carefully rounded vowels and the expensive clothes.

His musings were abruptly terminated by a sharp dig in the middle of his back. He turned to meet a broad-shouldered youth with an open-necked shirt, fair hair, and a flushed, panting face. Clyde was twenty-three; this man was probably a little younger than him. About the same weight, but three inches shorter. The man said, "Friendly warning, pal. Lay off Tracey. She's spoken for!"

The accent was different from what you normally heard around Brunton. Public school, Clyde thought: he had become something of an expert in these matters over the last two years at the electrical factory. The combination of this manner of speech with the blunt, working-class phrases lent a curious overtone to the words. In Clyde's drug-heightened assessment, the effect was that of a boy trying to be a man. He smiled down into the breathless face, imitated the accent a little as he said, "That's not at all politically correct, is it? We aren't supposed to treat women as property any longer. Or hadn't you heard?"

"Don't try to be clever with me, you black bastard! I was giving you a friendly warning, that's all. The next one won't be so gentle!"

He glanced over his shoulder on the last words, and Clyde knew in that moment that this aggressive prat wasn't alone, that he felt he could rely on the assistance of a group to support his threats, if it should come to it. Clyde thrust down the temper he felt rising, forced a half-smile on to his lips. "Cool it, mister! I'm not looking for a fight. You can keep your girl, if she's silly enough to want you. I'm more into motorbikes. And for your information, it was Tracey who was making the running, not me."

He turned and walked away, his senses alert for any movement behind him. But the pink-faced young man did not follow him. When Clyde turned, he saw him standing on the other side of the room, glaring malevolently after his adversary but making no attempt to follow. Clyde raised his right arm and waved the fingers of his hand in a slow, dismissive gesture.

He found the other three who had been invited here with him as a group and stayed with them for the next hour. The trio were all a little drunk and confused, not capable of properly articulated conversation. But there was a certain safety in numbers, so Clyde stayed with them when he was not dancing.

There were a couple of Asian youths, but he seemed to be the only black face in the house. Was he the token black invite, the role he had played too often before in liberal gatherings? He didn't think so, now. Tracey Wallace had wanted him here for his own sake, to judge by her actions on the dance floor. He smiled a little, half at that thought and half at the dismay he had brought to the public school swain.

The party was getting noisier and more disorderly. Tracey had made the mistake of leaving the central heating on high, and all the windows in the place were open, as the temperature soared with the numbers and their activity. Half an hour after midnight, someone stumbled drunkenly into a coffee table which was covered with glasses and it overturned with a noisy crash. An ironic cheer came from the adjoining room at the noise, then spread through the house as it was taken up by the revellers. Clyde wondered where Tracey Wallace was, whether she comprehended the damage that was being done to the family home as her party lurched towards chaos.

As if responding to a cue, she appeared at his elbow. He

began to speak to her, but a crash of electronic guitars from the big speakers drowned his words, and she seized his arm and pulled him on to the middle of the carpet to dance. He felt a splinter of broken glass beneath his heel as she pulled him towards her. It was time to be out of here.

But she had both his hands in hers. As the beat of the music slowed, she said, "Smoochy one, this!" and pulled him close against her, grinding her pelvis hard against his thigh as they gyrated together around the floor. He looked over her head for any sign of his earlier adversary, but there was too much smoke and too little lighting now for him to see much beyond the couples who were locked together and moving slowly in time to the music.

Clyde tried to tell her how he had been warned off, wanting to let her know for her sake as well as his, but she did not want to hear. She pressed her face against his chest. He could feel the tongue which had caressed his gums earlier finding its way between the buttons on his shirt, licking the sweat at the top of his chest. It was exciting, but it was also disquieting; he pressed her firmly against him to stop it, feeling her little giggle of pleasure and amusement as he did so.

When the music ended at last and she looked up into his face, he could smell alcohol upon her breath, though she was perfectly steady upon her feet. "Nice!" was all she said, very softly. She let his hands go reluctantly and he stood back a pace, giving her a smile which was meant to be friendly but not intimate. You never knew who was watching: he was confident he could handle lover boy, but you didn't want a punch-up, especially with things sounding so raucous all round you and most people pissed. Not if you were black.

He said, "I'll have to be off soon," and made it a leave-taking from her, turning swiftly and moving away into the hall without looking back. There were couples on the stairs; other pairs were climbing clumsily over them to disappear into the bedrooms. The music blared out from the speakers as loudly as ever, but there were fewer people dancing now.

Clyde Northcott went into the family room, found his leathers amidst a pile of coats, and began to pull them on. He did not allow himself the sensual pleasure he usually derived from the slow donning of this tightly fitting armour, but simply slipped into it and zipped it up as quickly as he could. Without knowing the reason why, he found himself wishing he had left an hour earlier. There was no sign of Tracey when he went back into the hall. That was a relief. He went swiftly out into the welcome coolness of the night air.

The Yamaha was untouched. He wheeled it out with a small sigh of relief from the shadow of the huge garage where he had left it, and prepared to mount it and depart. He was reaching into the holder for his helmet when a voice said harshly, "Time of reckoning, nigger!"

It was not the fair-haired youth who had confronted him earlier. That man stood beside the speaker, who was a good two inches taller than him. This man had a shaven head and a baseball cap with a National Front logo above the Union Jack. He wore a short-sleeved shirt and loose-fitting combat trousers above his boots; his forearms gleamed bare in the residual light from the house.

Clyde Northcott stood with his helmet in both hands in front of him. Three of them, at least. The cocky sod who'd just spoken had his earlier challenger on one side and another, slighter figure on the other. The third man stood two feet behind National Front, too deep in the shadows for him to see more than an outline. Twenty yards behind the trio, on the steps of the house, he saw Sam Cook, who worked on the next bench at the factory, who had got him the invitation to come here. Sam paused on the steps, then turned back into the house. Cowardly bastard!

Clyde called over the heads of his enemies, "Get the others, Sam! Bring them out here!" Then, as calmly as he could, he said to the man in front of him, "Let's just leave it, shall we? It's been a decent rave, this. No call to end the night with a punch-up, is there?"

The man who had challenged him earlier in the evening had looked over his shoulder when Clyde called for help. Now he whirled back and said viciously, "I warned you to lay off Tracey, Sambo! You chose to ignore it, so now you're going to get what's coming to you!"

The face which had been pink in the overheated house was white with fury now. The public-school accent sat oddly on the crude threats of violence. For a second, Clyde found himself threatened by an unexpected desire to laugh at the incongruity of it. He watched the oblong of light which was the open front door. No one appeared in it. He heard a tiny tremor in his voice as he said, "I told you, I never made the running with Tracey. I'm telling you now, I don't intend to take it any further with her. Let's leave it at that, shall we?"

National Front spoke again, grinding his fist into his palm, mocking Clyde's words in a high, effeminate tone. "'Let's just leave it at that, shall we?'" He moved forward a pace, and the other two followed as if drawn on strings. "No! We won't leave it at that, you black bastard! You're going to pay for putting your dirty paws on Mark's girl."

It looked as if Sam Cook wasn't coming back. Either he hadn't gone looking for the others, hadn't found them, or they had decided collectively to keep out of this. Clyde said, "Look, I don't want a rumble. Someone could get hurt. If you let me ride away quietly, you won't see me again."

National Front smiled. "Someone *is* going to get hurt, Sambo. But it isn't any of us."

The music was louder than ever through the open windows of the house. Someone was singing raucously along with it. There were shouts from within. Laughter. Another crash of glass. But no one came out. No one was suddenly silhouetted against the orange oblong of light.

Clyde Northcott said decisively, "I've had enough of this! I'm going."

"Not yet you're not, nigger!" shouted National Front, and launched himself upon the lone figure by the big motorbike.

He was a heavy man, and Clyde, side-stepping his bull-like rush even as he hurled his helmet at the man called Mark, avoided him easily and landed a glancing blow on the shaven head as he passed. The man who had challenged him earlier in the evening, however, caught the helmet and flung it aside, then followed his companion in with surprising force and speed. His knee caught Clyde, who had been watching his fists, in the side, partially winding him. Not Queensberry Rules at all from the public schoolboy.

The third man seemed to have disappeared, but National Front was back on his feet in an instant, an enraged bull now. He came at Clyde with a massive grunt, reaching for him with both hands, looking to hug him to his great chest, transformed in an instant from ox into angry gorilla. His idea was to hold the black man whilst his companion put in the blows which would down him, but Clyde realised this. His leathers were a help: fitting tight against his body, they gave the opposition nothing to get hold of as their hands flailed the air.

Their contest shut out all other sights and sounds, every other consideration but inflicting pain upon each other. None of them even heard the wail of the sirens in the distance. But the third of Clyde's adversaries had heard it, and melted away into the darkness.

Clyde managed to land a heavy blow into mouthy Mark's face: he felt bone crunch under his knuckles an instant before the yell of pain hit his ears. More fortuitously, he managed to get a knee into the groin of National Front as he whirled to confront him. His enemies weren't done yet, but there were two of them, not three, and both of them were hurt. "Come on then, you buggers!" he yelled, furious now, crouching with his fists in front of him. "Who's next for the nigger to chop?"

It was at that moment that he caught the glint of steel in the gloom, saw the long arms of National Front down by his knees, as he crouched and moved stealthily forward through the darkness. "Don't be a bloody fool!" Clyde yelled, but the big man only grunted and moved closer to him, too concentrated now even to hurl his insults. Mark was still doubled up with his face in his hands, trying to feel what damage had been done to him as the blood ran between his fingers.

There was only one to worry about now, but he had a blade.

Clyde feinted to go at his adversary's left side, then grabbed the arm holding the knife with both hands as the man thought he saw an opportunity to stab at his chest. Clyde's eyes were glued to the steel as it flashed above him, his every effort directed to protecting himself from that deadly blade. He could see it clearly now, not more than six inches from his face, held in the bare arms of a gorilla who was suddenly very strong.

There was an instant when the two of them were poised crazily against the night sky, each grunting with the effort of their contest of strength. Then Clyde slid a smooth leather-clad calf behind the balancing leg of his opponent and threw him heavily to the ground, with a shout of triumph. In an instant, his knee was on the arm of National Front; he threw his full weight like a hammer upon the bicep, yelling in triumph as he saw the helpless fingers release the knife, exultant as his ears caught the scream of pain from his defeated enemy.

Clyde snatched up the knife triumphantly, realising only in the moment of his victory just how frightened he had been. "What next, then, nigger-baiter?" he yelled into the gorilla's face, holding the blade against the throat of his terrified adversary.

"The next thing is an arrest," said a cool voice from the darkness behind him. "Drop the knife and turn round. Very slowly, please."

Clyde Northcott felt the knife slip through fingers that were suddenly nerveless. He turned and saw four uniformed policemen with truncheons at the ready. The bright blue lights of two patrol cars blinked blindingly from the darkness behind them.

They put Clyde in the back of one car, National Front in the other. He heard a policeman radioing for an ambulance for Mark and his broken nose.

The last thing Clyde heard as they shut the door upon him was National Front saying, "We was going home quietly when the nigger pulled a blade on us."

Ten

P ercy Peach had never quite believed in the worthiness of lace. To be fair, he had never given it a lot of thought. Now he was convinced in an instant of its value.

He did not often change his mind so quickly on important issues. But these circumstances were quite exceptional. The lace around the periphery of Lucy Blake's new green bra and pants was probably of a very high quality. He could not be certain about that. What Percy was certain of was that lace had never had such a setting to display its virtues.

He allowed himself a soft moan of pure pleasure, found he liked the release it afforded him, and repeated it at greater length.

"Please don't endanger your elderly frame by such painful excesses of desire," warned Lucy Blake, without turning round. She was standing in front of the full-length mirror of her wardrobe, brushing her lustrous auburn hair methodically with long, unhurried strokes and humming softly. Very Edwardian, thought Percy. He didn't mind that; they liked their women to be curvaceous rather than skinny, the Edwardians, and Percy was right with them there.

He lay beneath the duvet on the double bed and watched the delicate movements of the lace around the bottom that he felt had now been made more desirable than ever. With difficulty, he recovered the power of speech. "H-h-hand made, is it, that lace?" he said tremulously.

"Lace? Oh, that. I hadn't really noticed the lace. Yes, I expect it is."

91

"They'd have been extra-careful, if they'd known where it was going," said Percy. He liked an intellectual conversation.

Lucy laughed; transferred the brush to her left hand; resumed a more vigorous and slightly less co-ordinated brushing. Percy allowed himself another moan, then a gasp of pure lust as she dropped the brush and had to retrieve it. "Bloody 'ell, Norah!" he panted. It was an expression he had used a lot lately.

"I'm beginning to be quite jealous of this Norah," said Lucy. But she went on humming as she moved about the familiar bedroom. It felt different with Percy in it. Less private, but she didn't object to that. She finished brushing her hair, turned towards the bed and kicked off her slippers. This time Percy's moan had a clear note of anticipation.

"You're making me self-conscious," she said. "I can't concentrate on an orderly retirement with you huffing and puffing, you fool!" She reached out and switched off the bedside light.

It was a mistake. Percy had her wrist in an expert grip in an instant, and she was beneath the duvet and within his arms in one continuous movement. It was the way he had taken many a slip catch. The secret when you swooped was not to snatch, but to let the ball settle into your eager fingers, rather than clutching at it. Percy took this particular catch one-handed, letting the mound beneath the green pants settle firmly into the fingers rather than the palm of his right hand, closing the fingers with perfect timing when he knew the catch was secure.

"Ooooh! What a happy accident!" he muttered into an ear he found near his mouth.

"That was no accident, that was my lace gusset!" a muffled voice said from somewhere beneath his chin.

The lace proved as rewarding to the touch as it had been to the eye, and with considerable interest he traced its lines around the perimeter of these garments which stretched thin as gossamer between him and paradise. "Built-in foreplay, this is," he said happily to the ear; he hoped it was still approximately where it had been.

And then, with a little assistance, the gossamer was gone. It was a moment or two later that he said, "You now have it in your hands to make an old man very happy, my dear!"

So she did. And he was.

It was twenty minutes later that she said, "Were you serious about Tucker wanting to promote you?"

He started out of his warm, honeyed drowsiness. "Bloody 'ell, Norah! If you're going to bring him into bed, you could at least give me warning!"

"If you persuade Tommy Bloody Tucker to promote you, after the way you treat him, it will be a greater feat than getting me into bed with you."

"But infinitely less pleasurable. Let's talk about your bottom. I need a cerebral exchange." His active right hand sought an introduction to the debate.

"Let's talk about Tommy Bloody Tucker. That should cool your ardour and keep your ancient pulse in check."

"It'll certainly do that, girl. All right. And I didn't say Tucker wanted to promote me. I've not gone that daft. And neither has he."

She sighed, stretching her toes luxuriously towards the foot of the bed, while imprisoning that wandering right hand firmly in both of hers. "So tell me exactly what he said."

"I couldn't do that. I've got better things to do. But the gist of it was that he was hoping to make Chief Super for himself."

"That's bloody ridiculous! Everyone knows how you carry his section on your back! How can anyone ever think of promoting someone like Tucker?"

Percy enjoyed her righteous indignation on his behalf almost as much as the more overt demonstration of her affections she had just given him. She quivered with indignation against his thigh as she spoke, and he wished he could prolong that sensation indefinitely. Instead, he said, "It's the way the world works, love. His CID section has had a certain success, so they look to promote the man at the helm."

"Except that he's not. Not really. He's no idea what's going on, most of the time. Anyway, from what you said, he's at least had the decency to insist that your contribution should be recognised."

"Oh, how little you understand of the wicked ways of the world, my pretty! I'm willing to teach you a little more though, if you'll just—"

"No. Keep your hands still and your mind on the tale you're telling!" She pressed her nails firmly into his wrist to emphasise her point.

"Oooh, I do love you when you're masterful, lass! I never saw much in this bondage before, but if that's what you're into, I'm quite willing to—"

"Tucker! Or I'll throw you out of this bed!"

"Oh, all right. My reading of the situation is that someone has realised quite well who does the work and perhaps even what a prat Thomas Bulstrode Tucker is. Perhaps it's even the Chief Constable – Tucker claimed he'd commended me to the CC, which in Tucker-speak means that the CC has spoken favourably of me to him and he has claimed the credit for his department. He's trying to engineer a promotion for himself, but he realises he can't do it without recommending me for Chief Inspector."

"So you think that if Tucker wants to become Detective Chief Super, he'll have to see you made a DCI?"

"Precisely. So it's not on."

"What's not on?"

"Promotion for me. Not if it means that that jumped-up git is going to strut about as a Chief Super. I'll give him a message about where the monkeys put their nuts. With precise instructions."

She thought for a moment. He was full of surprises, this lover of hers, even now. "You can't do that. You deserve to be promoted. Everyone knows where the successes of Brunton CID have come from."

"Maybe. But I'm happy where I am. I never wanted to go further than Inspector. And certainly not if it means that twerp clambering further up the ladder."

She was silent for a moment. "It won't work, Percy. You're the one who's always telling me I'm not cynical enough about the system. Well, try this for size: the system is bound to recognise the success of a small CID section like Brunton's with a promotion for its chief. You said yourself, that's the way the world works. So Tucker will get promoted anyway, and someone will become Chief Inspector as a result. Someone more obsequious and less deserving than Percy Peach. He wants you because he depends upon you for his results, but he'll take someone more comfortable if you let him."

He considered what she had said. She was correct, of course. Sometimes you were too close to a situation to see it objectively. He said reluctantly, "You could be right, I suppose."

She snuggled a little nearer. "I am. You know I am. Thank you for telling me about it."

"It was very boring. I feel I deserve some reward for it. Sort of tit for tat, as you might say!" And with a swift and accurate movement, he secured an ample breast in his left hand. Very ambidextrous, was Percy. Noted for it, in his cricketing days.

It was Lucy's turn to feign surprise. "Oooh, DI Peach, you're full of surprises! If I'm not careful, you'll be asking for second helpings!"

So she wasn't. And he did.

Monday, January 28*th*

Terry Plant had proved an elusive quarry. The hunt for him had been stepped up after DS Blake and DC Pickard had interviewed his ex-wife Debbie, but no one had been able to find him.

He had left the house where residence was provided

95

for newly released prisoners after no more than ten days, removing his meagre possessions from his room without any notice to the manager who ran the place on behalf of the charitable trust. It was by no means unusual that he should disappear like this without leaving a forwarding address. Indeed, it followed a depressing pattern for men of his background, who disappeared swiftly rather than pay the maintenance that was required of them for an estranged wife and children.

No one deployed many resources to find him until the hunt was stepped up for the man now known as the Lancashire Leopard. Plant was by no means a leading suspect: there was nothing to connect him directly with any of the three killings. But then there was nothing to connect any individual directly with them yet: the Leopard had left too little of himself behind at any of the murder sites.

But Plant needed to be investigated. He had a history of violence, which according to his wife was not sexually related, and the killings had all taken place in the four months since he had been released from Strangeways. And enquiries now showed that Plant had been in the East Lancashire area at the time. He had been back to the street of his former married residence a week before the first of the killings, trying unsuccessfully to find out where his wife had gone. And he had been sighted in Brunton three days before the death of Hannah Woodgate.

But the police machine failed to locate him. The dubious people who were his known associates before his three years in prison either hadn't seen him, or weren't admitting to it. It began to look as if he had now left the area. Then, in a situation that bordered on farce, he made a present of himself to his hunters.

The building society raid he and his fellows tried to commit failed because it was badly researched, badly planned, and badly staffed. An impressive trio of deficiencies in any crime.

At 08.20 on a grey and blustery Monday morning, Terry

96

Plant and his companion appeared behind the woman who had come to open the door of the Burnley Building Society branch in the centre of Preston and hustled her within the premises. With threats of what would happen if she made a sound, they shut the door behind them and prepared to rob the place at leisure.

So far so good. The plan at least had the virtue of simplicity. But things went wrong from this point on. For a start, the woman they had ambushed was almost hysterical with fear at the sight of the baseball bat Plant produced to threaten her and the toy gun brandished by his companion.

She was meant to lead them to the strongroom and provide them with the keys. Initially unable to speak with fear, she was eventually able to convey two vital facts: first, that there was very little cash in the strongroom anyway at the start of a week, and second that she did not have access to the keys and did not know where they were kept. Their increasing threats were counter-productive. She fell prostrate at their feet and wept for mercy from her captors.

Moreover, their plan depended on the fact that they had entered the place unnoticed save for the woman now proving so unhelpful. They did not know it, but this too had been bungled. A man rearranging the engagement rings behind the grilled window of the jeweller's across the street had noticed the two men with a suitcase, lingering suspiciously long outside the window of the bakery higher up the street, and watched as they bundled poor Mrs Shorrock through the door of the Burnley Building Society. When he saw the door shut behind the trio, he crept back into his shop and dialled 999.

The farce was completed by the third man in the con-spiracy, the driver who was to whisk them swiftly away from the scene of the crime with their booty. He had stolen the vehicle from a pub car park after midnight. There was little risk of it being reported yet: punters who had a drop too many and left their cars rarely returned to collect them before nine o'clock on the next day. So far so good.

But the crime depended on a slick timing which proved beyond the skills of the trio involved. The driver was supposed to cruise down the street of the building society branch, pick up his colleagues as they emerged from the door with their takings, and drive swiftly away to Fulwood, where the stolen car would be abandoned and they would transfer to their Mondeo and be away down the M6. A doddle. In planning.

But not in execution. When the driver arrived on the dot of the prearranged time of 08.27, there was no sign of his companions. It must be taking them longer to get into the strongroom and fill the suitcase than they had anticipated. Plan B: drive round the block, wait briefly, return exactly five minutes later. 08.32. He was there, bang on time, again. But as he cruised cautiously down the street, he saw the two police cars, one on each side of his rendezvous point.

He kept his head, stared resolutely straight ahead, moved slowly past the fuzz, accelerated cautiously away to Fulwood and to freedom. He was the only one of the trio to escape with his liberty.

Terry Plant and his companion came like battery chickens to their doom. Having achieved nothing within the building, they stuck their heads cautiously out to look for their driver and means of escape. They were promptly arrested. The man with the toy Armalite rifle dropped it as he was bidden, but Terry Plant made an ill-advised attempt to use his baseball bat on the armed police who were shouting the words of arrest into his face. Assault on a police officer and resisting arrest would be added to his other charges.

And he would now be investigated thoroughly as a possible Lancashire Leopard.

Eleven

I t was a situation tailored for the skills of Percy Peach. Two blokes brawling, with a knife involved. One, possibly two, on drugs. So much drink and noise at the party that the police had been called to restore order, twenty minutes after midnight. One in hospital, two arrested.

And now, in the cold light of this late January morning, it had got even better. Two youngish single men caught red-handed in violence; who lived alone in the area; who had provided blood samples; who must be outside suspects for the Lancashire Leopard case which was bringing increasingly hostile headlines to the police; who must thus be thoroughly examined while they were under lock and key.

And it seemed to Peach that it could only get better still. Two men softened by a night's stay in the cells and a police-station breakfast. Two men feeling forlorn and foolish after a night spent in solitary confinement, reviewing their situation. Two men who had been foolish enough to refuse legal representation for their interviews. Two men who were now in separate interview rooms, each wondering what the other was saying to the police.

And passing between them, increasing the flood of panic like a frenzied Sorcerer's Apprentice, Detective Inspector Percy Peach.

Peach decided to see the black boy first. He arrived in the room with a sorrowful "Oh dear, oh dear, oh dear!", set the tape recorder running, named himself and DC Brendan

99

Murphy to the microphone, all without taking his eyes off the stony black face of Clyde Northcott.

He studied his quarry for a moment and said, "In a lot of trouble, aren't you, Mr Northcott? Standing over a defenceless man with a knife at his throat. Lucky our lads got there when they did, I'd say, or you could have been facing a murder rap this morning." He looked as if he was disappointed that this was not the case.

"I didn't start it," said Clyde carefully. You had to watch your step with this lot. Perhaps he should have taken the brief when it was offered, but it had seemed at the time as though that would be an admission of guilt.

"Really? Well, it's up to you what you say of course. We'll come to that later. You've got a lot of fences to jump before you get there. Drugs, for instance. Using and supplying. Blood sample full of crack." Peach looked at the notes on the blood test in front of him, whistled silently, then shook his head sadly.

"I wasn't—"

"Cocaine rocks, was it? Mix it with the baking powder yourself, do you, or is it supplied to you wholesale?"

"I don't mix my own. I had one rock at the beginning of the evening, that's all."

"That's all, he says, DC Murphy. Dangerous attitude that."

"Yes, sir. Riding for a fall, I'd say. Probably astride a powerful motorcycle under the influence of drugs, in fact, at the beginning of the evening. Very lucky he wasn't stopped."

This tall DC with the curly brown hair and the soft brown eyes seemed as bad as the inspector, thought Clyde desperately. He'd been prepared for the tough cop/friendly cop routine. No sign of that here. It looked as if both of these sods were going to be tough. He said, "The only coke rocks I had were for my own use. I take one occasionally at the beginning of an evening. I don't supply."

Peach turned sideways to look at Brendan Murphy and

gave his DC a broad grin. "This lad thinks we fell off a Christmas tree." The idea seemed to give him great amusement as he turned back to the anxious black face. "What about the rock you had in the pocket of your motorcycle leathers? The only one you hadn't managed to dispose of during the evening, was it?"

Clyde's heart sank away towards his feet and he felt his palms damp with a cold sweat. He'd forgotten altogether about that single rock he kept in the leathers as a spare against emergencies. It had seemed a sensible precaution at the time; now he could not understand why he had ever risked anything so dangerous. "I . . . I know it looks bad but—"

"Bad? It looks bloody awful, lad. Makes me almost sorry for you. But not quite. How much crack did you sell during the evening? Quite a lot, I should think, in a gathering like that."

"I didn't sell any!" Clyde heard his voice rising, tried to control his breathing but couldn't. "I told you, I'm a user, not a supplier. That was just a spare I keep there for my own use. I'm a fool, but not a seller!" His words came in quick, uncontrolled bursts as his breath gusted out unevenly. As a result of this delivery, the phrases sounded unconvincing, even to himself.

"'A fool, but not a seller'. Well, the first part of that's certainly right." Peach leaned forward, fastening the dark-brown eyes with his own black pupils from no more than three feet. "I'll tell you what I'm going to do, Mr Northcott. I'm going to go away and talk to another naughty boy now. Give you time to think about your position. To think about what you're going to tell us. Mug of police tea, if you're a good lad. Two mugs, if you're a bad one."

He left with a laugh which sounded to Clyde Northcott much more like a snarl.

Paul Dutton, the man Northcott knew only as National Front, had felt his confidence seeping away in the ten hours he had spent waiting to be questioned. He told himself that the police had the same sympathies as he had; that they saw enough of what the blacks and the Pakis were doing to the country to sympathise; that they would accept his version of events and have a quiet laugh about it afterwards as they put the nigger away.

In the small hours, with the drink inside him still helping, he had been confident of it. Shivering in his cell in the bleak grey light of morning, it had seemed less certain. He wished now that he'd got the legal bloke who attended their NF meetings to come and speak for him – but the bloke wasn't fully qualified yet, anyway, so they might not have allowed him. He remembered his advice anyway. Take a line and stick to it. Let them try to disprove your story, if they want to.

In these circumstances, they surely wouldn't want to. Lucky for him the bloke had been a Sambo, really.

Peach viewed the massive figure with a distaste he did not trouble to conceal as he set the recorder going and announced that the interview with Paul Dutton would be conducted by DI Peach and DC Pickard. He paused for a moment, letting his eyes run over the heavy forearms and the florid, truculent face. Then he said, "Well, Mr Dutton. Landed yourself in a lot of trouble, haven't you? Let's hear what you have to say for yourself."

"I shouldn't be here at all. The nigger pulled a knife on me!"

"Going for wrongful arrest, are you? Well, that should be interesting. Pity you didn't ask for a brief, though – doubt if he'd have advised that."

Dutton looked from one to the other. Tony Pickard's white face looked as blank and unrevealing beneath its neat black hair as Peach's was happily mobile. Paul leaned forward, spoke as confidentially as he was able. "Look, you know what they're like as well as I do. The nigger should never have been there. He was trouble all night, was Sambo."

Peach looked at Pickard. "Be able to add racial abuse

to causing an affray, by the looks of things. And we've hardly started yet. Good thing we've got plenty of charge sheets." He turned back to Dutton. "Perhaps that's where you'd better begin your story, sunshine. Much further back in the evening."

Perhaps they were just going through the motions. Perhaps they thought just the same about the nignogs as he did. Perhaps when he gave them the details Sambo would be for the high jump. He'd better make it convincing – that would be a help to them as well as to him. "I told you the nigger was causing trouble all night. He was dancing with Mark's girl, Tracey. Had his tongue down her throat and her knickers half off, apparently."

"Apparently? You didn't see this yourself, then?"

"Well, no."

"Pity about that. Be better if you'd at least been there, if you want to argue with what other people said."

"Listen, if you're going to take any notice of what the nigger says—"

"If you mean Mr Northcott, we haven't even asked him for his version of this yet. But do carry on with your story, Mr Dutton." Peach looked quite eager, as if he had a lively taste in fiction.

"Well, Mark warned him to stay away, but he didn't."

"So you attacked him. Tried to beat him up. Bit off rather more than you could chew, though, as it turned out."

"No! It wasn't like that at all!"

"Really? Tell us how you think it was, then."

Paul summoned all his meagre resources to try to make it convincing. "We were getting ready to leave when—"

"We? Just who does that mean, Mr Dutton?"

"Me and Mark Foster and Jack Cox."

"Three to one. I see."

"No! The nigger had others with him," Dutton said desperately. "They set on us. And the nigger pulled a blade!"

"I see. But he didn't try to use it. Curious, that."

"Eh? What d'you mean, he didn't use it?"

J. M. Gregson

Peach slid a sheet out from the sheaf in front of him. "Mark Foster has a broken nose and a tooth less than he had yesterday. The doctor who examined you last night has recorded bruising to your upper thigh and left side and a shallow graze on your upper left cheek . . . from which, incidentally, we took a blood sample. No sign of knife wounds."

"So? The nigger was putting himself about a bit. He's probably used to it, the trouble he causes."

Tony Pickard said, "More used to it than you, Paul? You're the one with the previous record, after all. Won't help you much, when it comes to sentence, a previous caution for assault."

Dutton said in a voice suddenly bereft of all conviction, "There won't be any sentence. Not for me, 'cause I'm not guilty, see? I told you, Sambo came at us with a knife. Assault with intent to cause serious—"

"But he didn't, did he, Mr Dutton?" Peach's patience was running dangerously thin. "I've just read out the list of injuries to you. None of them caused by a knife. None of them could conceivably have been caused by a knife."

"I tell you, he pulled a knife. Whatever else happened, he pulled a knife. The nigger. Your blokes found him with it in his hand. He was threatening me when they arrived."

Peach studied him for a few seconds, in which the sound of Dutton's uneven breathing seemed unnaturally loud in the claustrophobic room. Then he said, "Maybe. It's how you all arrived at that situation that interests me. Mr Dutton, I'm going to give you a few minutes to review your position. Perhaps when I return you will be prepared to tell me a more realistic story. DC Pickard will see that you get a mug of police tea, to encourage inner cleanliness."

He rose and was gone before the big man could find a word to say.

"Decided to tell us all about these drugs, have you, Mr Northcott? Much the best thing, if you do. Supplying crack

104

is a serious charge, and we can't do deals, but if you are prepared to give us information about those higher up in the chain I'm sure it would stand you in good stead when your case came—"

"I didn't supply drugs! I never have. I've been a fool, but not that much of a fool. I've never dealt. Not even when I was asked to. Not even pot." Clyde hadn't meant to say all this at once, had meant it to come out gradually, as he was sympathetically questioned. But now he was just desperate to stop this bald-headed tormentor from talking.

"You're sticking to this?"

"It's the truth. That's why."

Peach, having made the dramatic re-entry he wanted, now slowed the pace of the exchange to allow his quarry serious thought. "Mr Northcott, we have quite enough evidence to obtain a search warrant, to enable us to examine your residence in detail. I have to tell you that we shall probably do so, later today. Now, what would we find there in the way of drugs?"

Clyde thought swiftly. He didn't think the squat little man was bluffing. "Two, maybe three rocks of cocaine. The same size as the one you found in my leathers. In the bottom drawer of the kitchen unit. Underneath a pot towel."

"All right. Now, you've been arrested in the middle of a fight, with a knife in your hand and cocaine in your bloodstream. More crack was found on your person. You say you do not supply drugs to others, that any charge in this area should be confined to the lesser one of possession. I think that in these circumstances you need to convince us of that. The best way, I can assure you, is by full co-operation. Are you willing to offer us that?"

Clyde wondered whether he should trust him. Everyone said you should never trust the pigs. But he couldn't see that he had much option. "All right. But I don't know much. What is it you want?"

"Only where, when and how you got your rocks." A flash

of the normal Peach aggression and contempt in the blunt answer. But his voice had remained quiet.

Clyde Northcott took a deep breath. He'd decided while they were out that he wasn't doing drugs any more, anyway. But it was a big thing to tell this lot everything they wanted, all the same. "I don't know the bloke's name."

"All right. Was it always the same one?"

"Yes. I think so. Man in a big anorak, with the hood turned up. Not white, but not as black as me. Behind the Ugly Heifer. In the car park. Tuesdays. Ten o'clock." He felt as he had when he was a child, taking nasty medicine all in one gulp.

Peach glanced at Brendan Murphy, received the tiniest of nods. It was probably correct: the Heifer had a reputation for drugs. The supplier would be a small-time, but he could lead to bigger fish. The Drugs Squad would appreciate the information. "All right. If you've told us the truth, you needn't worry about them finding out where the information came from. The man in the anorak will be supplying a lot of people as well as you."

It was Brendan Murphy who said quietly, "There's still the other matter to clear up, Clyde. Last night's tasty little fracas."

Clyde looked at the wide brown eyes, the long Irish upper lip. Was he going to get a more sympathetic hearing from this man than he had earlier from Peach? He said, "There was a woman at the bottom of it."

Brendan smiled. "There often is."

"Yes. Not that it was her fault, really. There needn't have been any trouble."

Peach said more aggressively, "Suppose you give us your version of the whole evening. From where you joined the orgy to where you were found with a knife at someone's throat when our lads arrived."

"I arrived later than most people. Parked my bike in the shadow of the garage – I didn't want it to be in any danger of damage."

106

"The Yamaha 350. Nice bike." Northcott looked his surprise. "Used to ride one myself, sunshine. Older model, of course. When you were a . . . when you were in infant school and falling off your fairy-cycle, I expect."

"Well, I went inside and took off my leathers, in what they called the family room. Went and had a drink. Then Tracey Wallace, the girl whose party it was, asked me to dance."

"And that's when the trouble started. Tasty piece, Tracey. Tongue down her throat, hands round her bum. And she objected."

"No! It wasn't like that! Not much more than friendly. She . . . she did kiss me at the end of the dance. But it was her who was making the running, not me."

"If you say so. But lover boy didn't see it like that?"

"That bloke Mark? No, he didn't. He came and warned me off. Said Tracey was his girl. Public-school twat!"

"Called him that, did you?"

"No. But I did tell him I hadn't made the running. Told him his girl wasn't just a piece of property, could make her own decisions."

"Conciliatory, that. Just the thing to stop a shindig."

"Well, he annoyed me. He—"

"He went to a public school, I know. Unfortunately, there's no law against it. Even DC Murphy here went to Queen Elizabeth's Grammar School, and I try not to hold it against him."

"It wasn't that. It was that he seemed to think he only had to warn me off to send me packing."

"I see. Well he didn't succeed, obviously. Or we wouldn't be having this illuminating conversation now. Let's have the next thrilling instalment."

"I kept away from her. Not because I thought that there was any reason why I should, but because I didn't want trouble. And it wasn't as if I was that keen on the girl, anyway. She'd made all the running."

"But you had another go at her before the evening was out, nevertheless."

107

Clyde was disturbed by how much they seemed to know about this. They must have talked to National Front about the events leading up to their arrest. He shuddered to think what story he would have told them. He'd better try to make his own version as convincing as he possibly could. Even if it made him seem less than gallant. "It was Tracey who had another go at me, if you must know. The lights were pretty low by then and I was hoping it wouldn't be noticed, but it obviously was. We danced close together for about ten minutes." He remembered her tongue between the buttons of his shirt, tickling away the sweat from the smooth skin at the top of his chest. Not a detail they needed to know, that. "We separated at the end of the dance and I decided it was time to go."

"Very sharp of you, that." .

"I put on my leathers as quickly as I could and went to get my bike. I had a fear they might have been out there damaging it, but—"

"They?"

"Mark and his pals. I didn't know who they were at that time, but I was pretty sure he wouldn't be on his own."

"And what about you? Were you alone?"

"I turned out to be. I'd hoped the lads who'd been invited to the party with me would be around if I needed them, but they weren't, as it turned out. They were pretty drunk by then, anyway."

"So what you're claiming is that you were on your own and not looking for trouble. That Paul Dutton and Mark Foster sought you out."

"Yes, if those are their names. There was a third man as well, but he didn't take any part in the attack. I think he must have heard the police sirens, when the rest of us didn't."

"So you're standing on the gravel by the garage, facing three blokes who want to give you a kicking in the darkness. Have I got the picture right?"

"Yes."

"And that's when you pulled the knife. When you saw what the odds were."

"No! I didn't have a knife! I've never carried a knife!" This squat little opponent on the other side of the table had let him tell his tale fairly quietly for a while. Now, at the crisis of it, he was throwing in this again. Clyde wondered how he was ever going to make him believe the truth of this.

Peach watched him for a moment. Then he said quietly, "When you were arrested by police officers you were standing over a man with a knife at his throat, Clyde. You had better tell us how you got there."

Clyde licked dry lips, tried to take his time, to put conviction into the words he would use. "There were three of them, as I said. I told them I was on my way and they'd not see me again, but they wouldn't have that. They came at me together – just Mark and National Front, that is – the third one disappeared once the fighting started. I managed some sort of blow on the face of this Mark, the one who said Tracey was his girlfriend."

"Quite an effective sort of blow, actually. He's still in hospital."

Clyde wondered whether to say he was sorry, then decided it was better to stick to the truth. "He seemed to be out of it. That was when that National Front gorilla pulled the knife." He waited for Peach to deny it, but this time the man said nothing. "I told him not to be stupid, or something like that, but he took no notice. We grappled a bit, and I managed to get my leg behind him and throw him down. That's when he dropped the knife. That's when I grabbed it and stood over him."

"And that's where the lads in blue came in. Good thing for everyone, that. No knowing what might have happened next, with cocaine and adrenaline coursing round your veins in equal measure."

Peach stood up. "Don't go away, Mr Northcott. I'll be back soon. Talk to DC Murphy if you want a bit of counselling."

*   *   *

Paul Dutton's condition had not improved in the twenty minutes without Peach. That was because he had been considering his situation. It appeared that the people he had thought would be kindred spirits regarded him as a racist thug. These soft-as-shit liberals were running everything now, even the police.

As if to reinforce these thoughts, that nasty little sod of an inspector came into the room like a thunderclap. He was speaking even as he came through the doorway. "Lot of talking still to do, sunshine. Suggest you start telling the truth, pronto." He switched on the tape recorder. "Interview resumed at 10.17."

Paul didn't know what to do. He'd refused a brief scornfully at the beginning of the morning, on the ground that he wouldn't be needed. Should he ask for one now? Could he ask for one now? He watched the cassette turning slowly, waiting for his next batch of lies. It seemed to have an almost hypnotic effect. He tore his eyes away. "I've told you the truth of what happened. I don't need to alter anything. The nigger put Mark in hospital. He pulled a knife on us." He came back to that like a chorus in a bawdy song.

Peach regarded him with a happy smile. "Sticking to that, are you? Well, it's your own look-out, sunshine. Not what we've heard from others, though."

"You've been listening to the nigger? You're not going to take his word against—"

"Against what, Dutton? Against your word? The word of a man who has a record as a brawler and a bully? Who can hardly open his mouth without breaking the law of the land? For your information, Mr Northcott has lived in Lancashire as long as you. Longer, in fact, because he's a year older. And yes, we've listened to what he has to say, just the same as we've listened to you."

"But you're still going to take the . . . take his word against mine. And you call that bloody fair, do you?"

Peach looked at Dutton as if he was something he had

trodden in on a dark night. Without taking his eyes from the broad, meaty face he said, "Tell him, DC Pickard, please."

Tony Pickard chose his words carefully, but delivered them with a certain relish. "We have statements, Mr Dutton. From independent witnesses, who saw everything which happened in front of that garage. Typed and signed, as a true record."

Paul's heart leapt to his throat and for a second his head swam. There couldn't have been anyone who saw what had happened. They'd been on their own, hadn't they? Well, they had when they started shouting at each other – he couldn't be sure if anyone had come out of the house after that. He heard the uncertainty in his own voice as he tried to bluster. "If you're going to take the words of the . . . of that bastard's friends—"

"The people who have spoken to us were not friends of Mr Northcott." Tony Pickard was quite enjoying this. "We shall not reveal who they are at this point, though copies of statements will of course be made available to your lawyers if and when the matter comes to court. But you might wish to know that your friend Mark Foster talked to us in hospital. I understand, incidentally, that he is being discharged about now. His statement is being prepared for his signature. It is interesting to note that it differs from your version of events at almost every important point."

Paul thought desperately as the last threads of his confidence were torn from him. "He must be concussed. That black bastard hit him so hard he can't remember things clearly. You should never have—"

"His isn't the only statement we have, Mr Dutton." Peach's voice pierced his rantings like a sliver of ice. "We shall be asking for a statement from you, in due course. Asking for you to sign a written record of it. Allow me to remind you of the official opening of such statements: *This statement is true to the best of my knowledge and belief and I make it knowing that if it is tendered in evidence I shall be liable to prosecution if I have wilfully stated in it anything which I know to be false or do not believe to be true.'"*

Peach sat back on his chair, not troubling to conceal his evident distaste for the man in front of him. "You would be well advised to consider those words, Mr Dutton. I do not believe that you are as stupid or as unintelligent as the picture you have so far presented of yourself. In compiling your own statement, you should think about whether you really want to get yourself even deeper into trouble than you are at this moment."

He turned back at the door, just as the huge frame was slumping into despair. "By the way, I shall be back presently. Want to talk to you about another matter altogether. I'd like to administer a truth drug, but all I'm allowed is Brunton police-station coffee. Let's hope it has the same effect."

"Well. Mr Northcott. We may not need to retain you much longer, if you continue to co-operate with us."

Clyde didn't trust the smile beneath that jet-black moustache, but he noted the last phrase with hope. Perhaps it meant that they believed him. He said, "What I've told you is the truth."

"And nothing but the truth. I know – they all say that." Peach beamed delightedly. "We don't intend to charge you with carrying an offensive weapon or malicious wounding. As far as we can gather from independent witnesses, you were the victim rather than the aggressor. What would have happened to our National Front representative if our lads hadn't intervened is mere speculation." He beamed conspiratorially at Clyde, then assumed a straight face as if he were donning a mask. "We shall need to have a look round your place of residence: we shall have no difficulty in obtaining a search warrant to do that. If a search of your abode reveals that you have told us the truth about those cocaine rocks, you will not be charged with the supply of drugs. You will almost certainly be charged with possession.

I cannot of course say what the outcome of any such charge will be."

He was silent for a moment, wondering if Northcott knew what he was hinting at: that he would probably get away with no more than a caution. There was no trace of what was going on in the brain behind that black face, smooth and handsome as if it were a polished ebony effigy.

Clyde fingered the little rectangular patch of tightly clipped hair on his chin and came to a decision. "You don't need a search warrant. You can come and look round as soon as I can open the place up for you."

That probably meant that there were no more drugs than the amount he had admitted to. Good. But Northcott didn't know what other things they might be seeking. Also good. Peach said, "Right, lad. Always happy to cut down on the red tape. Now, while you're here, we want to ask you a few routine questions about another matter entirely. All right?"

"All right."

There was no hint of fear in those smooth features. Peach told himself he wouldn't have expected it, even if this was their man. "Can you tell us where you were on the night of Saturday the fifth of January, Mr Northcott?"

Clyde furrowed his brow. "That's three weeks ago."

"Yes. Just over that. It was the night it snowed. About two inches, by the end of the night."

Northcott's face cleared. "I remember now. I was at home. I was going to go out to Whalley with a few other biker lads. But I called it off when it snowed. Motorbikes are lethal on snowy or icy roads."

Peach smiled grimly. "I remember. Is there anyone who can confirm your presence in your home that night?"

"No, I don't think there is. Why, is it important?" Then they saw realisation flood into the hitherto unrevealing features. "That's the night when that girl was killed, isn't it? You're thinking I might have killed her!"

Brendan Murphy said hastily, "We're not thinking any such thing, Mr Northcott. Inspector Peach said 'routine

113

enquiries' and these are just that. The more people we can eliminate from suspicion, the more attention we can concentrate on the few who might have done it."

"Well, you can't eliminate me. There were other people in the house. I live in a bed-sit. But no one will be able to confirm that I was there, because I didn't speak to any of them that night."

How could he be sure of that so quickly, with the night in question twenty-three days in the past? Because he knew he wasn't in the house at all, perhaps? Peach said evenly, "That's a pity. Still, it's understandable, when someone lives alone. Would you be able to tell us where you were on the night of November the third? That was also a Saturday."

"No. Not at this distance."

"Or December the twelfth? That was a Wednesday."

"No. We have bikers' meetings, but they're usually on Fridays."

"Pity. Well, I'd like you to make a note of those two dates. If you can remember where you were and what you were doing on either of them, it would be a great help to us. Especially if you could suggest someone who might confirm it."

There seemed to be a threat in the last phrase. Unless Clyde was imagining more than there was. He said, "I'll try. I can't promise anything."

"No. Perhaps if you talk to your friends it might stir a memory. For the earlier dates I mean. Do you have a steady girlfriend, Mr Northcott?"

"No." Clyde wished at that moment that he had some regular girl, that he wasn't such a loner.

Peach and Murphy were reflecting that in all probability the Lancashire Leopard didn't have a girlfriend, either.

"DC Pickard will be taking your statement in a few minutes, Mr Dutton. I hope you'll see fit to revise what you told us earlier, but that's up to you. Now, will you tell us

114

please where you were on the night of Saturday, the fifth of January?"

He glared at them. He knew what they were after, immediately. Knew that they had switched to the Leopard inquiry. Did that suggest anything? Had Dutton been prepared for this, from the moment he was pulled in for something else entirely? It was interesting that he should seem to be expecting this. But you had to allow for the fact that the kind of men he associated with were probably fascinated by violence; that they had probably discussed the Leopard and his identity at length.

Dutton said, "That was the night it snowed. The night that girl was killed."

"Hannah Woodgate, yes. Where were you?"

"At the dance. The one she attended. At King George's Hall. But you can't fit me up for this, Peach. I'm not stupid."

"It appears not, despite all the evidence to the contrary over the last twelve hours. Six quite good GCSEs, I see from your record. At the same school as Hannah Woodgate. How did you get home that night?"

"By car. Four of us together. The driver was quite sober. We take turns, you see."

"How very sensible of you. What time did you get in?"

"Twelve thirty. We sat talking in the car for twenty minutes or so, before he dropped me off. I was the last one, see."

It had all been volunteered too promptly by this previously uncooperative man. He had it ready, complete with the reason why he had been so late into his house. With only a single one of his friends needed to confirm the alibi, they noticed.

It was Tony Pickard who two weeks earlier had taken Dutton off the list of men they had checked out from the dance, on the grounds that he had gone home in a group. The DC now said grimly, "We'd better have the driver's name. You know why."

Dutton gave it to them with a sour, contemptuous smile. They knew he could probably get to the man before they could, if that should be necessary. Pickard said, "Can you tell us where you were on the night of the third of November? That was also a Saturday."

"Three months ago? No chance."

"Think about it. When you come up with an answer, let us have it. Be in your own interest, that." Pickard stared into Dutton's belligerent face until the big man dropped his eyes. Peach thought that this newish DC was training up nicely.

It was Peach who said, "Can you recall where you might have been on the night of Wednesday, the twelfth of December, or has a convenient amnesia also obliterated that date?"

Dutton tried to relax, to force contempt into his voice. "I'll let you know, if I remember."

"Splendid! I don't suppose you have a regular girlfriend, do you, Paul?"

"Why the bloody hell should you think I don't?"

"Certain qualities I have seen in our short acquaintance. Are you saying I'm wrong?"

"I don't have a girl. Not at present, I don't. Not that it's any business of yours, pig!"

"Oh, it might be, Paul, in due course. Unless you can come up with some convincing evidence as to where you were on at least one of those dates. Be in your interests, as we've said, that would. But it's up to you, of course." He glanced down at the sheet in front of him. "You'll be charged with causing an affray. With carrying an offensive weapon with intent to use it. With actual bodily harm. In view of the fact that we know you brought a knife to last night's gathering, we shall need to search your flat. We shall need you with us. Someone will accompany you from here, when you've been charged and released."

They expected him to argue, but after a few seconds he nodded dumbly.

*   *   *

Peach had a Holland's meat and potato pie for his lunch. A very present help in times of trouble, Holland's pies.

But today even that failed to restore his normal cheerful optimism. It wasn't a bad morning's work. Terry Plant in the nick in Preston, and two other suspects for the Leopard whose premises they were going to inspect later. Blood samples and stray hairs from both of them, for DNA sampling.

But there was nothing to compare them with, as yet. The Leopard left so little of himself behind at the scenes of his crimes that he was still anonymous. They might collect DNA samples from all over the place, but they would still have to wait for something to compare them with.

They were sitting here waiting for the next murder, hoping that this time the Leopard might leave a little more of himself behind.

Twelve

S uperintendent Tucker was not looking forward to this. Peach was sure to be reactionary and unhelpful: he rejected all the modern ideas. And for some reason he didn't seem to like notions which came from his chief; that would surely make it even more difficult for him to take it on board. The bolshy little bugger clearly didn't take kindly to direction.

The fact that Peach was working ten or twelve hours a day on this Leopard case had only made him more difficult. He seemed to think it allowed him to be more tetchy with his superintendent as well as those working beneath him. Peach needed to be kept in his place, there was no doubt about that. But Tucker had to be careful; the last thing he wanted was for the man to throw up his hands and demand that the superintendent responsible for directing the biggest criminal hunt in Brunton history actually did his job.

Well, Thomas Bulstrode Tucker told himself, this was part of management. Your staff must know who was boss, when it came to it. He ran a finger round the inside of his immaculately pressed collar, licked his lips, and buzzed for DI Peach to come up from the Murder Room.

Coffee, Peach noted. On a tray, with cups and saucers. Ginger nuts. He was being treated like a visitor from outside. Danger. Tommy Bloody Tucker was looking to pull a stroke of some kind. Better let him make the running then; Tucker wasn't good at that.

"How's the case going?" said Tucker nervously. He didn't

118

need to identify which case: smaller criminal investigations went on, as they had to, but the Leopard was now dominating the station's thinking as completely as the public's.

"We're continuing to eliminate people. There's not a lot else we can do. The man left nothing of himself behind at any of the crimes. Motive doesn't seem to be much help: we've already eliminated the immediate circle of family and close acquaintances for all three of the women involved. We're having to work on opportunity, and that leaves too wide a field." This was all in the written summary which lay unopened on Tucker's desk, but Peach didn't trouble to taunt him with that; he was too busy watching for whatever fast one the man was trying to pull.

"Yes. Yes, I see. Well, it may be that I can offer you some help there."

That would be a first, thought Peach. Time to baffle the bugger with science, if he was about to speak. "We've got these two hard men who were involved in a knife fight on Sunday night. One of them on drugs, the other a known hard man with a record of violence. Both live alone; both of them have not as yet been able to alibi themselves for any of the three killings. But nothing specific to tie either of them up with the Leopard."

"Yes, I see. Well, it may be—"

"Even managed to justify a search of their residences in each case, but it hasn't produced anything you can call a clincher. We turned up a few drugs at the black boy's place, a few dirty mags and a knuckle-duster in the National Front lad's flat. Interesting, but you can hardly say either is a direct tie-up with the—"

"No. Well, perhaps—"

"And we've found this bugger Terry Plant we've been looking for, for a fortnight. You remember, the bloke who used to beat his wife up, who went inside for GBH in a warehouse robbery."

"Well, it might just have slipped—"

119

"Silly sod virtually gave himself up. Most inept building-society job you could imagine, in Preston. He's a thick bugger with a history of violence, man who went looking for his wife as soon as he came out of Strangeways, but whether he's the Leopard is another matter entirely."

"Yes, I see the difficulties. And that's why—"

"The murders began five weeks after he came out of stir, of course, and again he hasn't an alibi for any of them, so—"

"PEACH! For God's sake shut up for a minute and let me get a word in! I have a suggestion to make."

Peach looked as hurt as a child who has tried to please and met brutal rejection. His face quivered towards tears for a moment. Then surprise stole slowly over his revealing features and he said in tones of incredulity, "A suggestion, sir?"

As if the most astonishing thing of all to him was that his superintendent should have an idea of his own, thought Tucker angrily. Well, this idea might strictly speaking have come from the Chief Constable, but there was no way this wretched man Peach was going to know that. The superintendent said pompously, "Yes. Now that you have finally deigned to listen, I have a suggestion to put before you. A suggestion which any objective person would find helpful, I believe."

Defensive, that. Peach put on his objective person's face. It had an open mouth, raised eyebrows and eyes that were so eager that they seemed in danger of boring, gimlet-like, into the features of his informant. "Yes, sir?"

Tucker gulped at his rapidly cooling coffee, then shut his eyes. He couldn't concentrate when that moonlike countenance gave him its full attention. "I think it's time we had a psychologist in. Oh, I know you'll pour scorn on the idea, but we must move with the times. It's a forensic psychologist I'm talking about. They've proved that they can be useful in other cases of this kind and I'm now going to insist that we use one."

120

He had expected to be interrupted by an outburst of indignation long before this. He opened his eyes warily. And found that Peach's eyes were no longer on his face. They were fixed on that point a foot above his head which the inspector seemed to find perennially attractive; Peach's mouth munched appreciatively on a ginger nut, then fell into a gratified smile. "Delighted you agree, sir."

"Agree?"

"Yes, sir. As one of the old school, I thought you might not be in favour. But the Chief Constable rang across to me last night after you'd gone home, to see how the investigation was going, and I cleared it with him. He seemed quite enthusiastic about the idea."

Tucker's chair seemed suddenly slippery beneath him. With some difficulty, he pushed himself into an upright position and said, "I see. Well, you seem for once to be ahead of me. I'm glad to hear it. Well done, in fact." He forced a bleak smile. "Well, if you'll just get back to work now, I'll see what I can do about arranging—"

"All arranged, sir."

"What?"

"Ten o'clock Thursday morning. Dr Wishart from Manchester University. Good man, I believe. Helped the Greater Manchester Police in similar situations. They speak very highly of him."

"Do they, indeed? Well . . . er . . . it's good to know we think upon the same lines, Peach, isn't it? Sign of a healthy team."

"Yes, sir. You'll be attending the meeting, I expect. I'm sure Dr Wishart will be glad of your contribution. He said he'd need to be put in the picture about where we've got to, so your overview and insights will be almost essential."

"I'm not sure I'll be able to make it, Pea— . . . er . . . Percy. I have a press briefing tomorrow afternoon. Normally I'd leave it to the Press Officer, but in a case of this magnitude it hardly seems fair to leave him on his own. And then I shall be meeting with the Serious Crime Squad superintendent on Thursday, to see what extra help I can get for you. But I shall be most interested to hear what this trick-cyclist fellow has to offer us. If anything, of course."

So the forensic psychologist had become just an intrusive nuisance, once it wasn't Tommy Bloody Tucker's idea. Pity this Dr Wishart wasn't a psychiatrist, with the power to section superintendents, thought Peach, as he went contentedly back down the stairs.

When you were working as hard as he was, you needed a little cheap amusement to keep you sane.

Wednesday, January 30th

When they brought him up from the cells at Preston prison for this latest interview, Terry Plant wore a resigned, defeated air. He had been remanded in custody at the brief court hearing. Now it seemed the police wanted more information from him, when they already had a watertight case.

Lucy Blake was struck, as she had been on previous occasions, that a violent man should appear so ordinary. This was a man who had beaten his wife; who had started to hit his daughter; who had coshed a warehouse night-watchman hard enough to put him in hospital for weeks; who had threatened a junior woman employee in the Burnley Building Society with a baseball bat and tried to use the weapon upon a police officer when he was arrested. A dangerous man – and danger should surely parade itself in more obvious terms than this.

Terry Plant was slight and narrow-shouldered, with slicked-back black hair that imitated the style of an earlier era. His brown eyes looked empty of emotion. He was small-featured, with a nose that was smallest of all. Not ugly, but nondescript. You would have passed him by without a second glance in the street or in most other places. Perhaps men who hit women and children should have some kind of badge on their forehead, thought Lucy. At least that National

Front thug that Peach had interviewed had been happy to proclaim himself for what he was.

She watched the man with interest as she said, "I am Detective Sergeant Blake and this is Detective Constable Pickard."

"I've said all I've got to say. You're not getting the driver's name because I don't know it."

Don't grass. The only bit of the criminal code that this bungler understood. He would probably be in and out of prison for the rest of his life now, thought Lucy. He would make shallow resolutions to reform, disappoint a series of well-meaning people who would try to help him, age prematurely, die miserable. But you might be quite wrong, Lucy Blake, she told herself firmly.

She said, "That's as may be, Mr Plant. DC Pickard and I are here to talk to you about another matter altogether."

A flicker of interest crossed the professionally vacant face. Then he said, "Whatever it is, I won't be able to help you. I ain't a grass."

Tony Pickard smiled. "You won't be incriminating anyone else, Terry, whatever you say to us about this. This only concerns you."

"If it's that bitch who used to be my wife, I don't want to know. We're finished."

"But you went looking for her, when you came out of Strangeways. One of the first things you did."

"Yes. I didn't want this divorce she's pushed through. But I've given up on her now. Sod her, wherever she is. Anyway, how'd you come to know I was looking for Debbie?"

"Only because we thought we'd like to know where you were, Terence Plant. A touching concern on our part, you might think." Pickard's tone switched from mocking to menacing. "You went missing, a week after you'd come out of Strangeways. Not what you were supposed to do, that, Terry. Where did you go?"

The brown eyes narrowed, feeling the threat in his tone. There was no point in trying to deceive them, because they'd get the truth eventually, from the man who was inside with him for the building-society job. "With a mate. In Manchester. It's not easy, when you come out of the big house, you know." The last sentence had the automatic whine of the long-term offender.

"A mate you'd been friendly with in Strangeways, no doubt." Pickard paused, then took the silence for assent. "You were planning the raid you attempted in Preston, weren't you?"

Plant looked as if he was going to deny it, then said with what little spirit he could muster, "Well, what if we were? You've got us banged to rights for that."

Pickard grinned at him. It was true; their little exchange was strictly speaking irrelevant. But it was part of the necessary softening up process for what was to follow. Show a man the hopelessness of his position in one area, and he might be less able to resist you in another, more vital one.

It was Lucy Blake who said, "Are you telling us you were living in Manchester from the date at the beginning of October when you disappeared from Brunton? Right through to last Monday morning, when you were arrested in Preston?"

Plant immediately looked more shifty. "Basically, yes. Except that we stayed the odd night around Preston when we were setting up Monday's job. We looked at a few building-society and bank branches before we chose that one." There was the glimmer of a ludicrous professional pride.

Lucy ignored it, said coldly, "You were seen in Brunton on January the second."

"So what? I said we were 'around Preston', didn't I? What's Brunton . . . ten miles away?"

He was scared again, anxious to take them away from Brunton as a place where he might have been spending time. That might mean no more than that their getaway driver had come from the town, that Plant didn't want to reveal that. She made a note to pass on that thought to the DI investigating the building-society job. But Plant's anxiety might also stem from something quite different. "Where were you on the night of Saturday, January the fifth, Mr Plant?"

"I don't know. How the hell should I? It's nearly a month ago."

"Twenty-five days, yes. It snowed that night, in Brunton. Does that ring any bells?"

"Remember it snowing. I can't remember where I was or what I was doing. I wasn't in Brunton."

"And could you give us the name of anyone we could contact to confirm that?" She was patient, matter-of-fact, implying that no great issues hung upon his answer – almost as if she was bored with this.

"No, I couldn't. What's it to you, anyway?"

"To us? It's a matter of some importance, actually. I can tell you that it would certainly be of help to you, if you could account for yourself on that night."

"Well, I can't. I was in Manchester somewhere, that's all I can tell you."

Lucy Blake made a note of that, reminding herself also to check whether it had actually snowed that night in Manchester as well as Brunton, since Plant claimed to remember the snow too.

Then she nodded to Tony Pickard and he said, "Let's see if your memory is any better for some other dates, Terry. November the third of last year, for a start. Another Saturday. Clear night with a crescent moon, in case that jogs the memory of a nocturnal animal like you."

"No. It's too bloody long ago. If you're trying to fit me up for other jobs, it won't work. There weren't any others, until Monday."

"Of course there weren't, Terry! And that was such a fiasco you're giving up crime forever, sticking to the straight and narrow from now on, I know. We've heard it all before. Save it for the judge. Just tell me where you were on the night of Saturday, November the third, there's a good boy."

125

"I can't. But there's no bloody reason why I should. I know my rights!"

"Rights, is it, now, Terry?" Tony Pickard folded his arms and smiled, then unfolded them and leant forward. "Listen to me, Plant. You're a bloody thug and everyone knows it! We don't have to prove that; you've proved it admirably yourself, and you're going down for a five stretch at least for the latest episode. I don't give a damn what happens to scum like you, but I'll tell you this much: it's in your own interests to batter that thick head of yours into some action. Tell us where you were on these dates. In fact, find some means of *convincing* us where you were on these dates, or we'll become very interested in you!"

Plant recoiled as if he feared physical violence; like many men who hand out casual beatings to the defenceless, he was quickly afraid when anyone threatened to assault him. And Pickard had sounded ready to hit him; even Lucy Blake glanced quickly sideways at her companion, ready to intervene if he showed any sign of letting his anger take over.

But Tony Pickard had not lost control. His white, unlined face was glaring at Plant, but his voice was perfectly level as he said harshly, "Let's try another date, Terry. The twelfth of December. A Wednesday. See if you can remember where you were on that night."

Plant shook his head dumbly, his eyes widening. Lucy was sure that he knew where this was leading now. If his horror was simulated, he did it well. But then you would have expected no less from the killer who took such pains to leave nothing of himself behind at the scenes of his crimes.

Once he had realised what this was about, they left him alone, knowing that eventually he must speak, that he would not allow the silence which was so threatening to him to stretch for ever. After a good thirty seconds, Terry Plant said hoarsely, "The Lancashire Leopard. Those are his dates, aren't they? You're trying to fit me up with that. It's . . . it's bloody laughable!"

126

Tony Pickard had relaxed with the mention of the Leopard. He said, "But you're not laughing, Terry. And on this side of the table we don't find the notion funny at all."

"I didn't kill those women. I've never—"

"We had a look round your place, Terry, a colleague and I. Well, the place your dubious friend who'll go down with you enabled you to share. Found a few interesting things. One of them was a pair of gardening gloves. Unused for horticulture. Unused at all, apparently, as yet. The kind of gloves the Leopard wears, when he's throttling women. They're bagged and in our Murder Room now. Anything to say, Terry? Any explanation of why those gloves should be found in an apartment in Hulme which has no garden?"

Plant was panicking now. He said desperately, "I don't know about no gloves. I never saw any gloves. I never bought them. They . . . they must be Keith's, if they were there at all."

"Oh, they were there, Terry. Hidden away, of course, ready for the occasion when they would be used. Under the mattress you slept on, as a matter of fact. And curiously enough, your friend Keith denies any knowledge of them."

"They weren't mine. I didn't buy them. They . . . they must have been there before I ever used the place."

"Unlikely, that, Terry. Be difficult for you to convince a jury of it, when the time comes, I should think."

Lucy Blake decided that this had gone as far as it could usefully go. She said, "Think about it Terry. When you're in your cell tonight, think hard about it. If you've no explanation for the gloves, you'd better come up with an account of where you were on at least one of those dates, and provide someone convincing to support your story. Otherwise we shall be back."

The warder locked the door upon a thoroughly frightened man, who had suddenly become a focus of much more interest in the prison.

Superintendent Tucker got the news of Blake and Pickard's

visit to interview Terry Plant at lunch-time as he prepared for his press conference. It seemed to him at the time like manna from heaven. In retrospect, it proved nothing of the sort.

At the conference, Tucker was ruffled by some hostile questioning. It seemed, said the man from the *Express*, that the police were getting precisely nowhere, despite the extra personnel allotted to the case, despite the passage of almost four weeks since the death of the Leopard's third victim Hannah Woodgate, despite the nightly fears of hundreds of women in the north-west of England.

Tucker said that it was a particularly difficult case, because the Leopard left nothing of himself at the scenes of his crimes. He was unusual in that there were no traces of sexual assault on his victims. That made things more than usually difficult for the police and the forensic services.

So the message was that it would be more helpful all round if the killer raped his next victim before he killed her, said the woman crime reporter from the *Mirror*.

That was a ridiculous suggestion, and in the worst of taste, said Tucker; as usual he was more easily nettled by a woman journalist than he would have been by a man. He insisted that the police should be congratulated on their industry: they had painstakingly eliminated hundreds of possible candidates for these murders.

So the man in charge of the case had nothing to tell them, suggested the local man, Alf Houldsworth. They were no nearer to an arrest than they had been a month ago. The only message the papers could give to their readers were the old clichés: the Leopard is too clever; the police are baffled.

There were signs of merriment at Tucker's expense and he produced the card he had meant to keep hidden until much later. He told his critical audience that a man was even at this moment in custody, that he was helping the police with their enquiries.

He had their attention immediately. Even for Thomas Bulstrode Tucker, the adrenaline could pulse through his veins, and it had the same effect as upon other people. It made him a little more excited, prompted him to say a little more than he would have done in a calmer moment. He told his listeners that while nothing was settled yet, certain evidence which might be helpful had been unearthed. No, he could not give them a name. Yes, he was very optimistic about an announcement. When? Within the next forty-eight hours, he hoped.

It got him off the hook. His audience dispersed with some excitement. The radio and television bulletins that night carried the news that a man was being questioned in connection with serious crimes in East Lancashire; that the man in charge of the case thought that he probably had the Lancashire Leopard under lock and key.

The murderer watched the television reports of these latest developments with acute interest. At ten o'clock on that Wednesday evening, he poured himself a small whisky, added a precise three times the amount of water to it, and began to think about what he should do next.

That Superintendent Tucker had shown himself up for the wally he was. The public didn't realise that yet, but they soon would. The police were chasing their own tails, were nowhere near him.

It was time to show people just how futile were the efforts of that self-inflated balloon Tucker and his underlings. He had already researched the area of his next strike. Success came from careful planning and cool execution. The first he had already put in place, the second was just a matter of following the straightforward methods of the previous three.

Tomorrow, or the next night, he would make his move. He was so excited that it took him hours to get to sleep.

Thirteen

Thursday, January 31ˢᵗ

In the end, Superintendent Tucker decided to attend the session with the forensic psychologist. If the initiative was successful, he would wish at some time in the future to claim credit for it. Even he would hardly be able to do that if he had conspicuously ignored the man at the time.

Dr Hamish Wishart was a small man with a trimmed ginger beard, a mop of rather untidy matching hair, and intense blue eyes. He brought a flat black briefcase into the room, which was crowded with CID officers whose expectations ranged from the optimistic to the openly sceptical. Tucker got the meeting off to a good start by getting their visitor's name wrong in his introduction. Wishart corrected him humorously and Tucker, whether from caution or a fit of the sulks, hardly spoke for the rest of the meeting.

Peach gave a summary of what was known so far. It was succinct, partly because there was really so little to report. No clothing fibres; no blood to test against samples acquired from suspects; no semen; no possibility so far of any DNA profile. Tucker winced as Peach ended with, "Bugger-all to show from the efforts over many weeks of a team that has grown from thirty to sixty."

Wishart smiled. "Not quite nothing, Inspector. We can deduce certain things about the criminal from his behaviour. Not definitive, but worth bearing in mind. Such as that your man is a planner. As you say, he has left very little of himself behind. That does not happen by accident. He

130

has taken care that it should be so. Perhaps elaborate care. Would you agree?"

Peach nodded. "Yes. He's also mobile. My guess is that he parks some distance from where he actually kills, because there was mud around at the scene of the December killing and snow at the time of the third death in January. But we didn't find any tyre tracks near either body. Nevertheless, we can presume that he's a driver, I think, because of the sites of the killings. They are quite widely spread within East Lancashire, and he must have had some method of getting there and getting away swiftly afterwards. The first two bodies were found quite quickly, but no suspicious characters were reported in the area."

Brendan Murphy said, "It could be either a car or a motorbike, of course." Only those involved knew that he was thinking at that moment of the smooth black features of Clyde Northcott, who had still not been able to come up with an alibi for the three nights of the murders. "We've checked stolen vehicles on the night in question, and are satisfied that none of them were used in connection with any of the murders. So the probability is that our killer is a motorcycle or car owner, probably using the same vehicle on each occasion. Door-to-door enquiries have given us a few vehicle sightings, but none which tally on two of the occasions, never mind all three."

Wishart nodded. "More evidence of how careful your man is. What we have to try to do is to construct a net with smaller holes. Too often a man like this gets through the net, simply because the holes are too big. We need to narrow those holes. So far we know that he's a driver, probably but not certainly with his own vehicle, and a careful planner. Let me suggest something else which might save fruitless work; which might narrow the holes in our net a little. That is that you should eliminate flashers and people with convictions for minor sexual crimes. This man has scrupulously resisted any form of sexual assault. It is almost certain that flashers, gropers, even rapists and

131

deviants like necrophiliacs, would not have been able to resist sexual assault of some sort."

Tony Pickard said, "There may have been verbal assault on the victims before they died, of course. We don't know what awful things this man might have said before he killed."

"True enough. But sexual criminals talk to excite themselves as well as to torment their victims. It is very rare that obscene suggestions or threats are not followed up by some form of physical sexual attack."

Peach said, "All the killings have been late at night. It may be the time of maximum opportunity for our man, but the chance to isolate women and kill them is by no means confined to the time around midnight when he seems to operate. Can we draw anything from that time?"

Wishart shook his head. "Nothing conclusive. But it probably means he has a job. Probably works what most of us would regard as a regular day. I think otherwise it's likely that by now you would have had an assault during the day on an isolated housewife. There are plenty of them around, now that so many women go out to work, and we know this man is a planner."

Lucy Blake nodded. "A man with a regular job looks likeliest. We checked out people like barmen, who work in the evenings and could have killed immediately afterwards. But the geographical spread of the killings works against them. Dr Wishart, you said we should probably not be looking for someone with a history of sexual crimes. What about people with a history of violence?" She glanced across at Tony Pickard, who gave her a smile of recognition, so that she knew they were both thinking about Terry Plant.

"That's much more likely. Especially if the violence is towards women, and especially if it's not related to sex. That would be quite an unusual combination, I have to add."

DS Blake smiled. "We do have one such candidate. He's safely under lock and key at present, because he's on remand for another offence." There was a little stir of interest in the crowded room, and Lucy added hastily, "He doesn't strike us as highly intelligent, though, as we said earlier the Leopard might be."

"I think I said a planner. He need not be highly intelligent in the conventional sense of the word. The proverb says that genius is an infinite capacity for taking pains; I do not care for that definition myself, but on that basis your man might be a genius. I prefer to think of him as a very careful criminal. A planner, who very probably enjoys the minutiae of planning."

Brendan Murphy said, "Would drink or drugs be likely to be a prelude to these crimes?"

Wishart smiled. "Good question. The short answer is that we don't know. But it's hardly likely that the man was high on either drink or drugs at the time of the killings, or he wouldn't have executed them with such cold efficiency and made no mistakes. I'd say you'd be wasting your time sifting through candidates who have serious drink or drug problems. Your man almost certainly won't be an alcoholic or an addict."

"But he might use drugs as a stimulant, to make him feel in control?"

"Yes. Just as he might use a small quantity of alcohol. Cocaine can give people a feeling of mastery, just as alcohol can. The effects vary with individuals, as you know."

Peach noted Brendan Murphy's satisfaction and knew that he was picturing the ebony face of Clyde Northcott standing over Hannah Woodgate. He said with a touch of acid, "Before all of you begin to put forward your individual preferences for the Leopard, perhaps we should draw this together. I think we've given you what we have in the way of information, Dr Wishart. It's pitifully little. Would you like to summarise your thoughts for us?"

Wishart nodded and looked down at the notes he had made during the meeting, stroking his small beard thoughtfully, for all the world as if he were concluding an academic seminar in the University of Manchester. "What we're trying to arrive at in our discussion is what the Americans call an 'offender profile'. They draw a distinction between organised and disorganised murderers – a simple enough idea, but one they have found useful. The Leopard is an organised killer. He is not a confused loser, but a man who plans his killings carefully and probably enjoys that planning. You have had three carefully organised crime scenes; one might just be luck, but three can only be produced by an organised criminal. He will have a job, very possibly one in which organisation of his time is paramount, whether that is within his own control or enforced by others. He may well be delighted to be frustrating a large police hunt: that is probably one of his satisfactions. He may or may not be married or have a partner; even if he lives with someone else, he will be something of a loner. He will not have a history of sexual crimes, but he may well have indulged in violence towards women which was not directly related to sex."

He put down his ball-pen and smiled at his audience. "None of this is gospel, and I don't want it to prevent you from opening any doors you think need to be opened. It is merely a summary of my thoughts at the moment, based on the existing evidence."

A typical academic disclaimer, thought Peach. He muttered to Hamish Wishart as the meeting broke up that the only way he was going to get more evidence was if the Leopard acted again.

This brought an unexpected response. Wishart said, "I agree. And I didn't want to raise it in the meeting, because it wasn't going to help anyone. But if you look at the three killings, the intervals may be significant. Thirty-nine days between the first and the second; twenty-four days between the second and the third. It is now twenty-six days since the death of Hannah Woodgate. I think it likely that the Leopard will be planning to kill again, quite soon."

*   *   *

Michael Devaney was an innocent-looking figure. He had a round, unlined face and features which looked not yet fully formed, as malleable and changeable as a child's. Percy Peach had looked at his picture and said that, while each individual feature was regular enough, no one had taught them the value of team work.

Yet Devaney was twenty-nine and had a responsible post. He also seemed to have most of the characteristics of the Leopard profile which had been outlined by Hamish Wishart in the morning's meeting.

His official title was Care in the Community Officer. It was quite a new post, designed to foster the sort of mutual awareness and assistance in the community which everyone recalled nostalgically from the days of narrow terraced houses and outside lavatories. There had been a lot of those in Brunton, and the worst had been cleared years ago and replaced by modern blocks, and new and more acute social problems.

Devaney's job had been created by a well-meaning council to try to alleviate some of these. It was too little and too late. Michael had no one place of occupation and few powers. He popped into the youth club and tried to seem in touch with its members; he liaised with parents' associations and gave them guidance on the latest state of the illegal drugs industry; he sat on the Asian/British Mutual Understanding Committee; he helped transport pensioners to the Red Cross Centre for their weekly day out on a Wednesday; he tried to find those, mainly but by no means exclusively the old, who were dangerously isolated on the new estate, and alert others to their plight.

It was a job which needed the services of a superman. And Michael Devaney was no superman. On the face of it, he seemed the kind of well-meaning but largely ineffectual man you might have forecast for the kind of money the Council had decided was appropriate for the post.

But in the world of fear which gripped Brunton as the

135

town waited for the Lancashire Leopard to pounce again, Devaney was in a vulnerable position. He had been reported to the CID section by three separate women as behaving suspiciously. But they had been able to produce little more than the facts that he was a man who lived alone; who had no girlfriend; who seemed to have little social life outside his work; who probably could not account for himself on the nights of the murders.

The female CID sergeant who took the calls made polite noises and a note of the man's name and address. You could not ask the public to help you and then ignore their suggestions. Michael Devaney had to be checked out, though her private feelings were that it would be fruitless work.

So far, so lukewarm. It was surprising how many people there were in Brunton and its neighbouring towns, in the villages and hamlets of the Ribble Valley, who fitted this description. Perhaps that was some kind of comment on English society in the new century. DS Blake noted that Devaney fitted most of the criteria suggested by Hamish Wishart at the end of the morning meeting.

And then something quite surprising turned up.

Michael Devaney had a record. For violence. For violence against a woman. And for violence seemingly unconnected with sex. When he was nineteen, he had hit a woman of twenty-two so hard that she had needed eight stitches over her left eye. She had not wanted to press charges and it had never come to court. Devaney had got away with a police caution, but that meant that the incident had been recorded and was easily resurrected now by the computer.

There had been no recurrence. Or, as Tony Pickard remarked to DS Blake on their way to interview Michael Devaney, no recorded recurrence.

They met him in his tiny, crowded office in the Community Centre. He sat behind a desk covered with letters and memoranda awaiting his attention. There was barely room for the two upright chairs they carried into the room to sit on for their exchange: they felt uncomfortably close to their man. He apologised that he couldn't open the window: "We have to keep them locked against intruders, you see, and I'm afraid I've mislaid the key. I'm scarcely ever in here, so it doesn't matter that much to me."

In all truth, it wasn't warm in the room; the only window was on a north wall, so that there was no heat through the glass from the pale January sun outside. But perhaps Michael Devaney was already feeling the heat of his situation. Lucy Blake said, "I'll come straight to the point. There's no way of wrapping this up nicely, even if I wanted to. We're part of the investigation into the three murders committed by this man the media have dubbed the Lancashire Leopard, and we're here in connection with that."

No noticeable surprise, apart from a moistening of the lips that was entirely understandable. He said, "Has someone reported me to you? Did someone suggest that you should come here to see me?"

Did he have a persecution complex? Perhaps it wasn't just a complex: he looked like a man who would easily be persecuted. And he was right: no fewer than three women had said that he merited this visit, though Lucy could not tell him that. She said with a smile, "You should not be unduly alarmed. You are one of several hundred men who have been questioned about these events. We should be happy to cross you off that list; if we can eliminate you from our enquiries, we shall be one tiny step further along what is proving a very long road."

He did not respond to her smile. Instead, he said, "Needless to say, I didn't kill these women. Proving it may be a different thing. But I don't have to prove it, do I?"

Tony Pickard said, "Indeed you don't. Though if we can't be satisfied that you have no connection, we shan't of course be able to cross you off our list. Where were you on the night of January the fifth?"

The bluntness of the question, the suddenness with which it had been posed, from no more than three feet from his

137

face, made Devaney recoil as if in fear of being struck. "I can't recall. Not just like that. I—"

"You must have thought about it, surely? Any single man, living on his own, would certainly have thought about where he was that night. I did myself."

"No. No, I didn't. We're not all the same, you know."

"No. Otherwise three women who have been brutally murdered might be alive today, eh? Well, think then, Mr Devaney. Where were you on the night of Saturday the fifth of January?"

"In bed. In my flat. If you think it's any business of yours."

"Oh, we do, Mr Devaney. And was there anyone tucked up cosily in bed with you? Anyone who might remember a night of passion clearly enough to support your story?"

"I was on my own. I had a stiff whisky and went to bed at about eight with three aspirins, because I had a shocking cold. I thought at the time it was going to develop into 'flu."

"Really. So you had to have time off work, then. That at least we will be able to check on." Pickard smiled as if he knew the answer to that one already.

"No. It was only a cold. It lasted for the best part of a week, but I didn't have any time off." He looked then at Lucy Blake, as if he hoped for a little more sympathy from a woman. "I'm a bit of a one-man band in my job of community liaison officer, you see. Everything just ceases to happen if I'm not around . . . there's no one to take over."

She said dryly, "Your devotion to duty is no doubt highly commendable, Mr Devaney. From our point of view, and yours as well, it would be useful if there was someone or something to support your story that you were not out in the town on that Saturday night."

"Well, I'm sorry, Sergeant, but there isn't. I didn't know the wretched girl was going to be killed, did I?"

They raised their eyebrows a fraction at the adjective, letting him know that he had made a mistake in this bizarre game. Lucy said quietly, "I know it's a long time ago, but we are finding that most men who live alone have given some thought to the point. Can you tell us where you were on the nights of November the third and December the twelfth?"

"No. It's too long ago." The answer had come too promptly, as if he had been waiting for the question with his blank denial. Perhaps he realised that, for after a few seconds he added, "I'm usually pretty well exhausted after a day's work with the elderly – I help at the Red Cross centre whenever I can. I was probably listening to music in my flat – I don't watch television much."

He had thought about it enough to realise that the second of the murders was on a Wednesday night then, despite his disclaimers. They studied him for a moment in the little room with its single window and its thin plasterboard walls. They were close enough to hear each other's breathing, and Lucy realised that Tony Pickard's, excited by the thrill of the hunt, was louder and more uneven than that of their quarry. From somewhere down a corridor, they heard the sound of a girl's loud, coarse laughter, followed by words they could not distinguish and a more general burst of hilarity. It made their own little drama seem even more bizarre. She said quietly, "The first killing, that of November the third, was on Saturday night, like the third. Were you also too tired to go out on that night, do you think?"

"I don't know. I might have chosen not to go out. We don't all have to be chasing girls around the town, you know."

"An unfortunate choice of words, Mr Devaney, in the circumstances." She looked into the animated, pliant face and realised in a disconcerting flash who this man reminded her of. Lucy was something of a film buff and attended the local cinema club whenever she could. They had recently run a Charles Laughton season, and she knew now that Devaney's blubbery lips and twitching, mobile face reminded her of the young Laughton, who had been educated not ten miles from Brunton at Stonyhurst.

To disguise the keenness of her scrutiny of that face, she affected a weariness she did not feel as she said, "You're telling us that you cannot account for your whereabouts at the time of any one of the three murders which have now been attributed to the Leopard. Is that correct, Mr Devaney?"

"Yes. There's no reason why I should be able to, is there?" The full lips set in a sullen, challenging pout.

Tony Pickard said, "No. And equally, there's no reason why we should remove you from our list of men who had the opportunity to murder these women." He paused, studied his man for a moment, and then said, "How do you get on with women, Michael?"

There was an immediate shift from sullenness to unease. "Well enough. Not that it's anything to do with you."

"Oh, but it is, Michael. You've just admitted that you can offer no proof of where you were on the nights when three women were strangled. In the light of that, how you get on with women generally is very much our concern."

"I told you. Well enough."

"You don't have a regular girlfriend, do you?"

"No."

"Or a boyfriend?"

A flash of hatred from that mobile face. "No. And you've no bloody right to imply that I—"

"Fair enough question, Michael, in these enlightened times. Ours not to distinguish between sexual proclivities, nowadays. Feel resentful towards women, though, do you?"

"Resentful? No! And why the hell you should ask—"

"I'll tell you why, shall I, Michael?" Pickard was swift as a poacher springing his trap upon an unsuspecting rabbit. "Because you've got a caution for hitting a woman. Because you've already got a track record of violence against women! That's why! So that when someone starts killing women, we search out people like you, who've proved in the past that they don't like them!"

"I don't know why you should say that. I've—"

"Oh, but you do know, Michael. I'm quite sure you do. But let me prod that reluctant memory of yours, with just two words. Rosie Woodhouse!"

They could see that it was the name he had expected, that he had hoped against hope they wouldn't be able to produce. Tony Pickard had gone for him hard, and Lucy reckoned that was fair enough. No doubt the young DC's technique owed much to Peach, though it seemed without the humour that was always at the edge of the DI's harshest interrogations. She watched Devaney's fleshy face crumple, thought for a moment that he was going to weep. She said quietly, "We have to raise this, Michael. If you give it a moment's thought, you will see that."

He would not look at her. He fixed his eyes upon the papers on his desk and said, "I was nineteen. It was ten years ago."

"So tell us about it, please."

His narrow shoulders shrugged hopelessly. "I don't know where to begin. It had been going on for months."

"What had, Michael?"

"The taunting. She was the worst." He shifted uneasily on his seat, realised that he would have to fill in more detail. "I worked in a local government office, then. It was at County Hall, in Chester. They teased me about girls, about the fact that I didn't have one. Then the girls would pretend to be attracted to me, but laugh in my face when I asked them out. Then they made out that I had a thing going on with one of the caretakers, an older man."

"Which you hadn't."

"No, of course I hadn't. If you'd just seen him! Anyway, they kept that going for several weeks, then turned to pretending that I was bisexual, that I had an insatiable appetite for sex. Rosie Woodhouse was the worst of them. She'd rub herself against me and then accuse me of assaulting her. That day she was wearing a short skirt. She came and sat on my knee and squirmed about. Put her arms round my neck and hugged me against her. Then she leapt off and said

141

I'd groped her. Said she was going to have me for sexual harassment."

"And you hit her."

"Yes. I snatched up the nearest thing to hand, which happened to be a stapler, and hit her with it. I just wanted to stop her tongue, to bring an end to the coarse things she was saying and the others were all laughing at!"

"And she ended up in hospital."

"Yes. In Casualty. I cut her eyebrow badly. It bled a lot." Whatever the rights and wrongs of that situation ten years ago, it was still vividly with him. His pain and resentment had come out in his account; once he had begun it, he had scarcely needed prompting. Now that it was over, he plunged his face briefly into his hands at the recollection, then, after a few seconds, raised it tearless to face them.

Lucy said coolly, "Whatever the reasons, Michael, the fact is that you hit her. She could easily have lost an eye."

Tony Pickard said, "And how many women have you hit since then, Michael?"

"None. I've kept away from them." He was staring down at his desk again now.

"Interesting. As I said earlier, you don't like them, do you?"

A shrug of the narrow shoulders. Michael Devaney was retreating into his own world now. They had thrown the worst they could at him, and he had accounted for himself, after a fashion. Let them make what they wanted of it.

Tony Pickard glanced sideways into the dark green eyes of his DS, received a tiny nod from her. He said to the man on the other side of the narrow desk, "If you can give us any more convincing account of your whereabouts on the three nights we've mentioned, we want to hear it, so contact us. Meanwhile, don't leave the area without telling us where you're going."

Lucy Blake studied the intense profile beside her as Tony drove the Mondeo back to the station. Eventually she said,

"Don't broadcast it among the boys, but there are times when I don't much like women."

Pickard kept his eyes on the road, digested this for a moment before he said, "You believed all that?"

"I think it was probably substantially true. He's the kind who would invite teasing, even now, and he must have been worse ten years ago. That sort of teasing soon becomes a kind of bullying."

"I'd like to hear Rosie Woodhouse's account of those months."

"She resolutely refused to bring charges. Said it was a joke that had got out of hand. She'd have got compensation easily enough, but she evidently didn't want it publicised."

"She could have lost an eye. And whatever the reasons, he obviously doesn't like women. He more or less admitted that, in the end."

They were silent for the rest of the short drive, each mulling over the possibility that Michael Devaney might have turned his resentment into a war against the whole sex.

Fourteen

Years ago, this had been a busy little place. Crowds had gathered at the railway station every morning, searching for seats on the train that ran from Hellifield to Manchester, through the busy mill towns of Brunton and Bolton and a multitude of smaller villages like this one.

The line was still there and trains still ran upon it. But there were fewer of them, and they hastened through this place now, for the station had long since ceased to function. But its buildings had not been demolished, and on this night their shadows cast a Gothic outline against the slim, sharp, crescent moon and a sky dappled with stars. It was a clear night; clear enough to make the orange glow from the lights of Bolton, three miles away over the hill, seem brighter and much nearer than they were.

The man who stood patiently within the station shadows was well wrapped against the cold. He wore a navy roll-necked sweater over a vest and a thick shirt; his lower limbs were encased in thermal underpants and heavy trousers. He had thick grey socks and rubber-soled shoes upon his feet: he had considered wearing his boots tonight, for warmth, but he knew his shoes were quieter. They were more anonymous, too, if he should happen to leave a print. He had a thick black coat on top of all these, a cap pulled tight about his ears, and even a woollen scarf about his lower face.

And the hands he occasionally flapped silently across his chest during his vigil wore a brand-new pair of thick leather gardening gloves.

The little cinema, like the station, had long been closed. What life there was in the village revolved mostly around the pub these days, but the final drinks for this night had been served twenty minutes earlier. The watcher saw the last men come out of the Fighting Cock, then reel unsteadily away as the cold night air hit their brains and turned their legs to cork. Four of them clumsily prevailed upon the fifth member of their group to leave his car in the park behind the pub rather than attempt to drive it home.

There was some rowdy leave-taking, a couple of shushes, much laughter as they departed in different directions. Surprisingly quickly, it was all over, and silence stole softly back into the village, as the noise of revelry became more distant and then disappeared altogether. The lights were still on in the pub, but they were the only ones he could see from where he stood.

The moment was nearly at hand, and he felt the excitement which was now familiar rising within him. He had feared that she might come out whilst those men were still around the place. He would have abandoned his plan, if she had: there was always another night. Even another woman and another place, if this was too dangerous after all.

But he knew now that it was going to be all right. The friendly, enveloping silence had dropped upon the place; the darkness which was his friend seemed thicker than ever without the noise.

He heard the barmaid calling her goodnights to the owner and his wife as they worked on with the business of clearing the tables and washing the glasses. She stood for a moment outside the pub, looking up and down the road. Then she shrugged and set off in the direction he knew she must take. That was the benefit of proper research, he told himself, as he slipped into place twenty yards behind her on his silent rubber soles.

Sally Cartwright told herself that she was not really nervous. For a few nights after the third girl had been killed in Brunton, her husband had picked her up twenty

145

minutes after closing time in the car; it only meant leaving the sleeping children for five minutes, he assured her. Then, as the weeks slipped away and the Leopard dropped out of the headlines, his resolution had faltered. She would find Ken dozing in front of the telly, she was sure, apologetic as he started awake and realised that she was already in the house.

Well, there was no real danger, was there? The killings had been over at Brunton and beyond; almost certainly the Leopard lived twenty miles or more from here. Anyway, she was only 600 yards from home: Ken had measured it. And she wasn't really afraid of the dark, she told herself, as she passed beyond the last street light and turned on to the lane towards home.

All the same, she lengthened her stride, walking so fast through the crisp night air that she was almost running, panting a little as she made hard for the bend that would reveal the friendly lights of home.

It was her breathing that stopped her hearing the man until he was right at her elbow. She opened her mouth to scream but he called out that there was no need to be afraid, said that he would show her something to reassure her about him. Then, as she hesitated and he thrust one hand beneath the breast of his coat to produce it, she saw the gardening glove on his other hand, and screamed.

It was but a single cry, the last sound she would ever make. Then the rough leather of the gloves was at her throat, the strong thumbs within them were pressing hard upon her windpipe. She died in twenty seconds, the horror bulbous in her wide eyes as she looked up at the head above those dreadful hands. Her last sight on earth was his blazing, exultant face.

He put her body down beside the gate into a field which marked the only break in the long black hedge. Then he walked swiftly, rhythmically back towards the derelict station and his car. He would not run; part of the pleasure was the perfect, unhurried execution of the deed. He was out of the lane and back on the wider road before he met anyone. He called a goodnight to a late dog-walker on the other side of the road, was pleased to hear how steady his voice was.

The car engine purred softly alive with the first touch of the starter. He eased it away from the shadows of the station, passed unhurriedly through the outskirts of Bolton and on to the A666, which would take him towards home. He was careful not to speed: it would be ironic indeed to be stopped by a police patrol for such a petty offence, after what he had just completed. ·

Later on, he turned down a side road which led him to the Leeds and Liverpool canal. He put the stones he had taken from underneath the front seat of the car into the gardening gloves and cast them with a soft splash into oblivion. Then he climbed unhurriedly back into the driver's seat and made for home. Careful preparation and cool execution: those were the secrets of success.

He was growing quite attached to the ridiculous label the press had given him. The Lancashire Leopard had struck again.

Fifteen

Superintendent Tucker was having a trying day. He had feared he would have, as soon as he heard of the Leopard's fourth strike, but that didn't make it any better. He had been forced to cancel his golf and come in to the station on a Saturday morning. He had endured a difficult session with the Chief Constable and the Head of the Serious Crime Squad, in which his weak grasp of the detail of the case had been made very obvious.

And now one of the media conferences he regarded as his greatest strength was going wrong.

He had little or nothing to offer the news-hawks, many of whom were as irritated as he was to be here on a Saturday. And his *bête noir*, Alf Houldsworth of the local *Evening Dispatch*, was laconically translating his every answer into a lurid tabloid headline. Audibly, to the sound of cheap laughter from the rows of chairs behind him.

"We are told that police patrols have been doubled. Was the body of this latest victim of the Lancashire Leopard found by one of them?"

Tucker took a deep breath. "No. Mrs Cartwright was unfortunately found by her husband. He was alarmed when she did not arrive home as expected and went out hoping to meet her. He discovered her body by the roadside in the lane where they lived."

148

"HOPEFUL HUSBAND FINDS HORROR IN HEDGE," intoned Houldsworth.

"And have you any clearer ideas on the Leopard's identity as a result of this latest outrage?"

"Our Scenes of Crime team is still at the site. As yet, I am not able to relay any of the findings to you."

"POLICE PLODDERS PERPLEXED. LANCASHIRE LEOPARD LAUGHING," Alf summarised helpfully.

"One of the excuses you have offered for your failure to arrest this man is your contention that he left little behind at the scenes of his first three killings. Has he revealed any more of himself in this latest one?"

Tucker coughed nervously, trying not to look at Houldsworth. "It is too early to say yet whether the killer has left behind anything more significant than on previous occasions."

"CAREFUL KILLER CONFOUNDS DUMB DETEC-TIVES," suggested Houldsworth, making a note of the fact on his pad.

"Over fifty years ago, all the males in this town were fingerprinted in the search for a child murderer. As a result, the killer was identified and eventually hanged. Should you not now be beginning a similar exercise?"

"That would be a massive exercise. A massive invasion of people's privacy. We are not considering it at present."

"CID'S OBSTINATE OSTRICHES FAIL TO FACE FACTS," said Houldsworth happily.

Tucker glared at him, then returned to his questioner. "In the case you mention, where a child was taken from the hospital and brutally killed, the police were certain that the killer was a local man. Modern criminals are more mobile. We cannot be certain that the Leopard is a Brunton man."

"MOBILE MANGLER MAKES MAYHEM AND MOCKS," said Alf. He lit another cigarette. This was taxing work, but rewarding. Tucker was getting redder and redder.

"Surely with all the resources of modern science, the

149

killer must be leaving something around that you can pick up on?"

Tucker was tempted to suggest vaguely that they had something this time, just to call off the pack. But he caught the single glittering eye of Houldsworth through his cloud of smoke and thought better of it. "A full team is still at the site, as I say. Certain items will no doubt be removed for forensic examination. And we await the results of the post-mortem examination." He looked at the sea of unresponsive faces and said, desperately and unwisely, "We have even had dogs at the scene."

"FORENSIC FARCE. LEOPARD LAUGHS AT LAB-RADORS," said Houldsworth, reacting to his responsive audience.

Tucker had had enough. He had nothing to offer them, no titbit of progress he could reserve for the end, in the hope that it might receive favourable emphasis. He rose and said, "Our recommendation is that women should not go out unaccompanied in the hours of darkness. You may rest assured that as soon as there is progress, I shall inform you of it."

He had tried to make his last sentence sound portentous, but the effect was spoiled by a scraping of chairs, as his experienced audience recognised the end of the briefing. He turned and marched towards the door behind him, stumbling over the bottom step of the platform in his haste to be away.

Alf Houldsworth sat and watched this departure thoughtfully. "TORMENTED TUCKER TELLS TALE OF RETRIBUTION, TURNS TAIL, TRIPS AND TOOLS OFF," he said with alliterative relish. He produced a small hip flask and happily toasted the thought.

Sunday, February 3rd

"It's good of you to see me on a Sunday," said DI Peach.

"It's flattering that you should want to see me at all, a seasoned policeman like you!" said Dr Hamish Wishart

150

dryly. "It's usually old hands like you who are the most cynical about forensic psychology."

"I like to keep an open mind. And anyway, I'm desperate!"

The two men grinned at each other. Wishart had agreed to meet him in the College Arms, a pub which on weekdays would have been crowded with students, but at this Sunday lunchtime was a quiet place. The narrow Manchester streets which had once provided its local clientele had long since been cleared to make way for the tall university buildings which accommodated the students of the new century.

Peach said, "I looked in on the scene of the crime on my way over here. I don't think the Leopard will have left any more of himself behind than he did at the first three places. We've got a man who thinks he spoke to him, but it was away from any street lights and he didn't see much. Youngish and over six feet tall, he thinks. They nearly always overestimate the height, when it's a violent criminal."

"On the other side of Bolton, wasn't it?"

"Yes. About three miles the other side."

"And you'd like me to think aloud about this, you say?"

Peach sighed. "Yes. Be as speculative as you like. You've an audience of one today, and I won't quote you elsewhere if you prove to be wide of the mark."

Wishart grinned, stroking his sandy beard with that unconscious gesture which he seemed to find an aid to thought. Perhaps that was why he'd grown it, thought Peach; perhaps that was why there were more beards among intellectuals than in the circles in which he usually moved. Wishart said, "I can put up various hypotheses which you won't be able to knock down today; you'll have to test them in the field first. Let's start by pinpointing the geographical context of these murders." He produced a rudimentary but neatly sketched map from his pocket and completed it by putting in the exact location of this fourth and latest of the Leopard's killings.

151

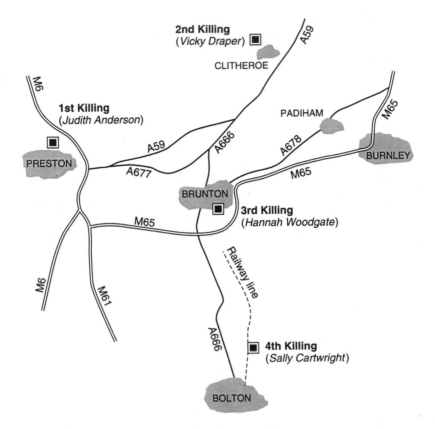

"I drew this after you'd phoned me this morning. Now, would you say that the killer had a detailed knowledge of the place where each murder took place?"

"Yes. I think he knew each area well to start with, knew it might be the kind of place where he would find a woman on her own late at night."

"And we agreed the other day that he was a planner. That he probably researched the opportunities, perhaps even the individual women he killed, before the actual night of the crime."

"Yes. I'm certain of it. The first woman he killed, on

152

the outskirts of Preston, was Judith Anderson, a twenty-six-year-old married woman teacher who had been visiting her sick mother. She had walked back to her own home at around the same time on the five nights which preceded her death. I think that he had decided upon the area, knew that it was quiet enough for the kind of killing he planned. I think he then selected a particular victim, probably watching her on previous nights, noting both her route and the particular place on that route where he might kill her with the least chance of detection."

"And the same with the second one?"

"Yes. That was on the outskirts of Clitheroe, well out beyond any street lighting – similar to Friday night's killing in many respects. A forty-one-year-old unmarried civil servant, Vicky Draper, who had a single drink in the pub there with her friends after evening class. Their routine this time was weekly rather than nightly, but just as regular. My guess would be that chummy had watched what happened on previous weeks and was there waiting for her, because again he's chosen the best spot, the one furthest removed from houses. This woman was one of only two in the group who walked home, and the other lived within a hundred yards of the pub."

"And the third?"

Peach thought hard. "We thought at first that Hannah Woodgate was an opportunist effort. But now I don't think so. The girl was at Manchester University, as you probably know. But she had the habit of attending the Saturday night dances at King George's Hall in Brunton, as a lot of the local girls do. I think the Leopard was expecting his victim to be there that night, and without a boyfriend to walk her home. And again he chose his spot, by a group of allotments, a deserted place in a built-up area. It was a short cut to the girl's home which she habitually used. At first we thought that argued that the girl's killer must be someone known to her, since he knew so much of her habits. Now I think it fits the Leopard's pattern of careful preparation."

153

"Right. And Friday night's killing follows a similar pattern?"

"Yes. It's a replication in many respects of the second killing, the one near Clitheroe. Sally Cartwright was thirty-six. An attractive brunette, as the papers are already saying. But a respectable woman, mother of two boys. Her husband was made redundant last year and had to take a job on much lower pay. She was supplementing that by working as a barmaid at the local pub, the Fighting Cock, three nights a week."

Wishart nodded. "So she would leave at the same time each night. Our man could have researched that, could have singled her out as his next victim."

"I'm certain he did. He could have either waited for her where he killed her, or followed her from the pub until she reached the quiet lane where she lived. She was killed within two hundred yards of her home: as with the others, we've found no traces of a vehicle being parked near the spot."

"Right." Wishart smiled his satisfaction at the logic of this, as if he were making a suggestion about some abstract problem rather than the brutal deaths of four women. "I think we're looking for a local man. Criminals have the same limitations as the rest of us, and the most serious one is knowledge. They need to be familiar with the ground to operate effectively. This fellow has detailed knowledge of the places where he's killed. He's a Lancastrian, or he has lived here for some considerable time. The papers have been full of speculation about the Leopard driving in from well outside the area, probably coming up or down the M6 or over the M62 from Yorkshire. I say he's a local, very probably from north-east Lancashire. Want me to go out on a limb?"

"You know I do."

"Well, look at this map. We now have four killings: one ten miles to the west of Brunton; a second thirteen miles to the north; a third in the town itself; and now a fourth, twelve miles to the south."

Wishart was quivering with excitement; Peach felt like a

student who must not let him down. "You're saying that the Leopard is based in Brunton?"

"I'm suggesting exactly that. We've only had four murders yet, thank God, so we haven't a lot of material to support the idea. But if you look at the patterns of previous serial killers, you will find that they usually operate around a central point. John Francis Duffy, who committed a series of murders and rapes in North London between 1982 and 1986 and was eventually found guilty of two murders and five rapes, operated from a base at the centre of the sites of his crimes. The police in Birmingham originally thought that the series of vicious rapes which took place there in 1987 and 1988 were the work of one man. They eventually proved to be the work of two men, not one, each operating in the area he knew well around his home."

"All right. The Leopard's a Brunton man."

"Probably. Certainly a man with a detailed knowledge of the area, who seems to be operating outwards from a central point. Someone who lives or works in the town."

Peach said, "We'll go through the people we've already interviewed from the town. The people who can't alibi themselves for any of these deaths." His mind flew back to the case that is a nightmare for all policemen, the Yorkshire Ripper. Peter Sutcliffe, the man eventually arrested and convicted, had been interviewed by officers on at least five occasions, but had each time been released without exciting much suspicion. Three different police forces had been involved in the search, had entered Sutcliffe's name on their files – and missed the connection. They had central computers now, which were supposed to rule out such cock-ups, but there was still the human factor, when you were sifting thousands of possibilities. Had some copper already talked to the Leopard, and let him slip through the net?

Wishart pulled at his bitter, wondering how to break more bad news to this determined little workaholic he had grown to like and respect. There wasn't any easy way. He said, "I think your man has been studying previous serial killers.

155

That he is determined to avoid the mistakes that eventually confounded them."

Peach took a large swallow of his own pint, replicating the action of the wiry little man on the other side of the small round table – as if the two of them were on strings with their limbs attached to each other, he thought wryly. He tried to savour the ale, and failed. "That's something I've been feeling for the last week. But what makes you say it?"

"The fact that he plans so carefully, leaving the very minimum to chance: it's often been when a man has killed on impulse that he has eventually been caught. The fact that he leaves so little of himself behind: no semen; no saliva; so far, not a thread of his clothing or a hair of his head: this is a man who is aware of DNA and its dangers to him, and of the whole battery of forensic weapons in crime-solving. The fact that he gives so little away with his modus operandi: even his strangling is as near anonymous as it could be. The same method, swift and ruthless, each time. The same kind of heavy-duty gardening gloves or motor-cycling gauntlets on each occasion. I think your man has probably studied other men who have raped and/or killed a series of women, with a view to learning from the mistakes which eventually led to their capture."

Peach stared bleakly and unseeingly at the far wall of the quiet pub room. "He'll trip himself up eventually, they always do. But the Ripper killed thirteen. I want to stop this bastard at four." There was real passion in his voice, ringing out oddly in that inappropriate setting. There was also a thing Wishart had not heard from him before: a tinge of desperation.

"Then let's see what else we can offer," Wishart said. "A locally based man, not travelling in from outside, who has studied previous serial killers and is determined not to be caught as they are. There's another peculiarity. I took away what you told me about the first three women and I've listened to what you've just told me about the one who died on Friday night. There's one thing which is unusual about them as victims. They're all what, for

156

want of a better word, I'll call highly respectable women. Am I right?"

"Yes. The first one was a twenty-nine-year-old school-teacher with two children. The second was a single woman in her early forties who'd been attending an evening class and was a highly respected member of her village community. The third was a nineteen-year-old student who had a regular boyfriend at university, whom everyone, young and old, thought was a smashing girl, who certainly didn't sleep around. Friday night's victim was a woman with two kids who was working part-time in the pub to help out a husband who'd had to move to an inferior job."

"No prostitutes; no thieves; no women with known criminal associates. All popular and respected people in their communities."

"Yes. Murder investigations often turn up some pretty dodgy habits among the victims, and nearly always a few people around them who felt they had it coming to them. This one is unusual in that we haven't had that. It's made it even more difficult to get leads."

"But I would be right in saying that in terms of simple opportunity, it would be easier for your killer to go for prostitutes?"

"Certainly. They're the most vulnerable women of all."

"Yet your man has avoided them. He has had the opportunity, but deliberately turned aside from it. So we can rule out any warped moral crusade to kill 'sinful' women, of the kind a lot of previous serial killers like Peter Sutcliffe have used to drive themselves on. I won't speculate on whether your man has any kind of grudge against 'respectable' women, because his chosen victims are too diverse to admit of any definite pattern. But it's my belief that when he moves again – as he will if he's not arrested – it won't be against a prostitute or someone passing her favours around."

Peach nodded glumly. "We've stepped up policing around all the red-light areas in the Lancashire towns. But I think you're right."

"I don't say you can call off all protection for prostitutes. It's rather that you should attempt to protect women living out more normal patterns of life. He seems to be concentrating on more successful women, in the sense of people who are happily coping with life. None of his four victims is a loser, or someone who's missed out on life. No prostitutes. No drug addicts. No women living in squats or derelict buildings, who would surely be easier targets than the ones he has chosen."

Peach nodded thoughtfully. "We can warn the women you call 'respectable', certainly. The problem will be doing it without scaring the pants off them, so that they don't go out of the house at all. Because without an army, we can't protect them with any certainty."

"I don't think you can issue any public warnings to particular sets of women. The Leopard would merely note them, digest them, and adjust his tactics. Probably go for different targets. You need to concentrate on what he's telling you about himself, and I'm afraid he's giving you very little."

"Do you think he will live alone?"

"In a psychological sense, certainly. Even if he is living with a wife or a partner, he is essentially alone. He may be the kind of husband who lives a separate life in his own part of the house, but we don't always see that from the outside. His crimes are a narrowing experience, not a broadening one. He will be becoming ever more excited by this secret life he lives at night, until it becomes the only really important part of his existence. He may, however, be meticulous in that public part of his being which we can see, because he realises what an important cover it is for what he sees as his real life."

"We've combed the ranks of the local unemployed, the known odd-bods and loners pretty thoroughly, without turning anything up."

Hamish Wishart stroked again at the neat, pointed beard. "I think it's probable your man has a job, perhaps quite a responsible one. He's a schemer, who probably enjoys designing his crimes. And he's rigorous in his own perverted form of self-discipline. He executes his carefully planned killings with the minimum of fuss. Most killers of his kind exhibit a wish to taunt the police or society in general, and I don't think this man is any exception. But so far, he's not indulging in the notes or phone calls which might enable you to find him. He knows how to kill women so as to leave as little of himself as possible behind, and he seems to have studied the methods and the downfalls of previous serial killers."

"A professional man?"

"Possibly. One who is used to discipline, and sees its values in this section of his life which is now all-important to him. As we've said, he enjoys planning and exhibits a degree of expertise in the way he kills, and that might find some reflection in his job."

"A lawyer? A doctor? Since the delightful Doctor Shipman saw off upwards of a hundred people around Manchester, we're always ready to consider medics."

"Lawyers and doctors are both possibilities. Someone who is used to discipline and timing in his ordinary daily life. Policemen are possibilities, of course. And schoolteachers; they're used to timetables and planning, though they might find it more difficult to conceal a secret life in their everyday dealings with people."

Peach wasn't sure from the academic's quizzical smile how strong he thought these possibilities were. Policemen would certainly have the knowledge and the discipline, he thought grimly. And they weren't all such disastrous planners as Tommy Bloody Tucker. He stared into his empty glass. "What the hell's driving the bugger?" he said, to himself rather than Wishart.

"That's a good question. Not sex, certainly. Probably not even sadism – a sadist would be torturing his victims before they died. It's interesting you should mention the infamous Doctor Shipman. What attracted him to killing seemed to be the feeling of power it gave him. The power over life and death: the power to take away someone's life is the ultimate power, and it's denied to anyone except absolute despots. I think it's that feeling of power which is the attraction for your man. That and making fools of the police and society in general."

Peach stood up. "Thank you for your help. If you should have any further thoughts—"

"I'll be in touch right away. I wish you good luck."

"We bloody need it," said Peach, with gloomy conviction.

"I think you do. Because this man is going to get more confident, if he feels you're not getting near to him. I think he's going to want to feel again that power over life and death, and that need to demonstrate how clever he is. I'm afraid he's going to kill again, quite soon."

Sixteen

W inter drops more heavily upon the country than upon the town. The people who live beneath the long flank of Longridge Fell are more conscious of the passing seasons than those in the nearby towns of Preston and Brunton. They can see the steep end of Pendle Hill, often looking much nearer to them than its ten miles on the map. And Pendle, with its head moving in and out of the low cloud, is a constant reminder of the changes in the weather of the Ribble Valley.

Agnes Blake, busying herself with her daughter Lucy in the kitchen of the low stone cottage, was pleased that Pendle rose clear and sharp against the blue sky at three o'clock on this winter afternoon. She always felt that the village looked at its best in the sunshine, even the low orange light of this winter sun, which would soon be setting, away to the west over the invisible Blackpool. She would not have admitted it to Lucy, but it was important to her that the village and her house within it should look at their best today. Agnes knew her daughter well enough to know that she would not have brought any man to Sunday tea with her mother if he was not rather important to her.

So she was glad that the snowdrops were out in the small front garden which she kept so neat and tidy, the way her dead husband had planted it and would have wanted it kept. It would have been nice to have the crocuses adding a cheerful outburst of colour beside the porch, but snowdrops were all you could really expect in early February. There

161

would be a frost again tonight, but the snowdrops wouldn't mind that.

"What time did you say he'd be here?" she asked Lucy for the second time. She wanted the man to see the cottage with the low sun still mellowing its stone frontage.

"Percy said he couldn't promise, but he'd make it as near to four o'clock as he could. He was at the station this morning and then he had to go over to Manchester to see one of the university professors who's helping us."

She was hoping to transfer a little vicarious status to her man by the mention of a university associate, but all Agnes said was, "Funny name, Percy. You didn't meet people called that much, even when I was a lass."

"Percy's not his real name, Mum. It's just that everyone calls him that."

"Even you?"

"Even me. He seems to like it. Perhaps it's the alliteration. Percy Peach drops off the tongue quite nicely."

Agnes thought, I bet she thinks I don't know what alliteration is, but I do. She's nervous. Well, it's understandable. When I brought my Bill home to the house all those years ago, I was nervous. Everyone knew you were courting, when you did that. No one seemed to speak of courting, nowadays. Probably because they dropped into bed so casually with each other, these youngsters. She didn't think Lucy did that, but you didn't really know what went on, when they got their own places and left home. "What's his real name, then?" she said.

"Do you know, Mum, I can't really remember? His initials are D. C. S. I've seen them on official forms often enough, but I've quite forgotten what they stand for. Everyone just calls him Percy, from the superintendent in charge of CID to the newest detective constable."

Agnes sniffed. Those initials seemed vaguely familiar to her, but it couldn't have anything to do with this man. "It's a rum do, when even his girlfriend doesn't know his proper name. And he's got a moustache, you told me. Bit like Clark Gable, would you say?"

Lucy giggled nervously. Mum expected everyone's ideal lover to walk straight out of *Gone With the Wind*. She thought of saying she was no Vivien Leigh, but that would only provoke a stout-hearted mother's defence of the superiority of her fair skin and chestnut hair. And she wasn't going to tell her that Percy was more like a small version of the fat one in Laurel and Hardy.

She went into the front room and put a little more coal on the fire which blazed cheerfully in the low brick grate, moving the brass fire-irons so that they caught the reflection of the flames. Glancing to the gate and the lane beyond, she saw no sign of Percy. For the first time in years, she began to study the two landscape paintings which had been on the parlour wall for as long as she could remember, becoming as much a part of the setting as the wallpaper or the curtains.

And then, at last, he was there, opening the gate, scarcely ten minutes after the time he had said, and her mother was snatching off her pinafore and raising her hand to her hair as she took a last look in the hall mirror. Two experienced women, whose agitation about this moment had been building for at least an hour, thought Lucy. What a ridiculous business life was.

If Percy Peach was nervous, he certainly did not show it. He marched confidently up the twenty yards of garden path with that bouncing, aggressive walk which was something of a trademark. "You must be Lucy's mother," he said on the doorstep. He took her hand in both of his and shook it firmly. "I'd have known that, even in a crowd."

And then he bestowed upon her what he considered the friendliest and least threatening of his hundred smiles.

He refused a welcoming cup of tea, sniffed appreciatively at the baking he could smell, and seated himself in an armchair by the fire in the parlour. "What a charming room!" he said. Something in Lucy's face beside her mother warned him not to lay things on too thickly. "Charming" was not a Percy Peach word, and Lucy had recognised that as well as he. He was glad when they left him to go and make the final preparations for tea.

Lucy peered at him through a crack in the door. Percy was sitting bolt upright with his eyes shut, wondering what he should say when her mother reappeared. Like many policemen, who are used to coming straight to the point with an erring public, Percy had no small talk, and little use for it in others. It was his large talk Lucy feared; like that of Henry Higgins in *Pygmalion*, it might get him into trouble in delicate social situations. Of which this was certainly one.

Things were not much better when she went into the kitchen. "He's not tall enough for a policeman," whispered Agnes Blake, as if he might after all be an impostor who must be exposed.

"They've relaxed the height regulations nowadays," her daughter whispered back. "He's five feet nine – he looks shorter because he's got broad shoulders. He's a detective inspector." As if that made a difference. As if your height could decrease as you went up the ranks, until the Commissioner of the Metropolitan Police might be a midget.

Agnes took a tray of scones out of the oven, slid a knife under each to deposit them on the wire grid to cool. This man looked too old to be courting, and to mothers their daughters are always teenagers. "Are you sure he's only thirty-six?" she whispered.

"Of course I am! What do you want him to do, put his birth certificate on the table beside his plate? He looks older because he's bald, that's all. I can assure you, everything is in good condition!" It was difficult being indignant in a whisper. Ridiculous was more the word.

Agnes glanced sharply sideways at her daughter. "There's no need for smut, our Lucy! Does he eat tongue?"

"I don't know: I've never tried it on him. Anyway, it doesn't matter if he doesn't – you've got lots of alternatives. There's enough to feed at least six."

Lucy was glad when they could stop whispering and go

back into the lounge, donning their smiles at the door like air hostesses coming out of the galley. Percy put his smile on to greet them, the passenger who was trying hard not to be a difficult traveller.

But now that Lucy had warned him off the easy compliments with that earlier look, he did not know what to say. He wanted to say something nice about her daughter to this pleasant lady who was obviously so proud of her, but he couldn't think of the right thing. Because the mind was the wayward instrument that it is, all he could think of was the vision of Lucy before the full-length mirror in her new green scanties. The fact that he'd rather give her a good seeing to than do anything else in this world hardly seemed the kind of light conversational gambit to offer to her mother. It didn't mean that he didn't love and cherish her for all kinds of other reasons, of course, but that might be difficult to convey if he started from the bedroom image on which his imagination seemed to have jammed. "The . . . the snowdrops. Very nice," he stuttered.

"Harbingers of spring," said Lucy, and he realised that she was enjoying his discomfort.

When they began the meal, he could only think of the formidable mother-in-law he had been so happy to discard years earlier. He had not thought of her for a long time now, yet here she was vividly before him, imprisoning his tongue as her long-gone criticisms echoed in his ears and her one-piece bosom loomed in his mind's eye. Agnes Blake could hardly have been more different, and yet he found himself watching his table manners, not looking at either of the women at the table when he spoke, picking his way through the conversation as carefully as if he were conducting it with chopsticks.

Lucy was amused at his predicament. She had not seen him like this before: to watch the formidable flood-tide of Percy Peach's word-flow stemmed at source was a new experience. It made her fonder of him, as a lover's vulnerability will, but she enjoyed it too much to end it.

165

And Agnes Blake was almost as stilted as he was, blushing at his compliments to her food, spilling scones on to the tablecloth as she urged him to take another.

The solution came from an unexpected quarter. When they left the table with their final cups of tea and went to sit in comfort in the parlour, Agnes said rather desperately, "Lucy says that your real name isn't Percy. That she's seen your initials on things but can't remember—"

"D. C. S. That's right, Mrs Blake. I was christened Denis Charles Scott Peach. Not after a saint, I'm afraid. But after—"

"After Denis Charles Scott Compton! I'm right, aren't I?" Agnes clapped her hands together in spontaneous delight.

"Well, yes, you are. My Dad was a cricket fan, you see, and the great Denis Compton was his favourite cricketer. But you're the first woman I've ever known who recognised the initials."

"Your parents couldn't have chosen a better model! Always played his cricket with a smile, Denis, never forgot that it was a game to be enjoyed. Three thousand eight hundred and sixteen runs he made, you know, in one season! Eighteen centuries. And every one a gem. He couldn't have bored you if he'd tried, couldn't Denis! Did you ever see him play?"

Percy smiled. "No, he'd stopped playing well before I was born, I'm afraid, Mrs Blake."

Agnes nodded. "That damned knee! Stopped him early, you know, when he could have gone on giving pleasure for years. And of course he lost the best years of his career to the war."

And so these two northern people who had so wanted to be relaxed and friendly with each other were brought together by a dead southern cricketer who had danced down the wicket half a century before, who lived on brightly in the sharp memory of a woman who had queued outside Old Trafford to see him when she was fifteen, and in the names chosen for a baby born long after he had ceased to play.

Agnes brought him the picture of her dead husband in his whites, a big man, tired but happy, staring at the camera with a shy smile and his sweater over his shoulder. "That's Bill when he'd taken six for forty-four against Blackpool. The paper said that even Rohan Kanhai had to treat him with respect."

She showed him her long row of cricket books, and was delighted to find that Percy had most of them on his shelves; she insisted on lending him a Neville Cardus and a John Arlott to take away with him. "Those are the two who paint a real picture. The two who are able to show you how cricket is a part of life, not something on its own," she said.

Lucy had not seen her mother so animated for years – not since before Dad died, she thought sadly. When she tried to get into the conversation, she was banished by Agnes as a pretentious non-expert. "You never did understand, our Lucy, so don't get in our way now. Stick to your netball, you were good at that!"

And she pushed back the chairs to demonstrate Denis Compton's unique leg-glance, played when the ball was almost past him, relying for its execution on dazzling footwork and timing. Percy tried to imitate it, and she corrected his posture, making him hit the invisible ball impossibly late, so that he lost his balance and they fell laughing together on to the sofa.

Agnes's cup ran over when she found that Percy had played in the Lancashire League, the greatest of all the leagues, in her view. "You're never *that* Peach?" she gasped happily. "I used to check your scores in the *Evening Dispatch*." She looked at him shyly. "It was your initials, you see, the D. C. S. And then the way they described you dancing down the wicket to the slow bowlers, that made me think of Denis too, you see. So I used to follow your scores each week."

Then he had to tell her about fielding against the magnificent Vivien Richards, who had played as professional for Rishton and made him see what greatness was. And

167

Agnes told them about the "three Ws" of West Indian cricket – Weekes, Walcott and Worrell, who had all played league cricket in Lancashire in the fifties, the first two in her favourite Lancashire League. And showed them pictures, and distinguished each from each by her enthusiastic descriptions of how they looked and how they batted.

At nine o'clock, she was still telling them just how good Ray Lindwall had been when he'd pro'd for Nelson. Lucy, who had been a delighted spectator for over two hours, brought in a pot of tea to top the gins and tonics she'd been dispatched to make earlier. "You'll have to let him get off, Mum. We've an early start tomorrow and a busy week ahead of us."

It was the first time that evening that either of them had thought about the Leopard.

She saw him off with a chaste kiss on the doorstep. "She's all right, your mum," Percy whispered in her ear.

The mother in question was putting her photographs away when Lucy went back into the house. She set the big one of her dead Bill carefully back on the sideboard and looked at it for a couple of seconds before she turned round to her daughter. "You're not such a bad picker, after all, our Lucy," she said with a smile. "He's all right, your Percy Peach."

Seventeen

S uperintendent Tucker wanted to hold Peach personally responsible for the Leopard's fourth murder and give him a severe dressing down. At the same time, he wished to dangle the carrot of promotion before him and claim credit for fostering his case. Tucker thought this would be a very difficult combination. A better man would have realised it was impossible.

"A fourth innocent woman dead. It's not good enough, Peach! I've got you double the resources a murder inquiry normally carries, and yet you appear to be quite baffled."

Peach was seized by an urge to scream at this hypocritical windbag; to tell him exactly how much he cared about these murders; how he lay awake at night, the innocence of the victims and the suffering among those left behind revolving in his mind; how he was determined above all else, above anything he had wanted in his whole professional life, to put away this man who was sneering at the efforts of his team, and planning more deaths among those whom the police were there to protect.

Instead he said, "Yes, sir. 'Baffled' is what the *Mail* says this morning, so it must be true." Tucker peered at him suspiciously. "Actually, sir, it mentions you by name, so I wondered if you'd actually told them you were baffled. Just here, sir, underneath the bit about outbursts of hot air and flatulent excuses." He thrust the most offensive of the morning's Leopard articles across the desk at his chief, pinpointing the offending passage with an immaculately groomed nail.

169

Tucker was almost seduced into reading the copy. Then he waved it angrily away and said, "I don't care what the gutter press is saying about our activities. What do they know about it, anyway?"

"What, indeed, sir? I agree with you absolutely about the gutter press. I prefer the broadsheets myself . . . though I have to say they are scarcely more complimentary this morning. "'Will no man rid us of this Turbulent Tucker?' is the *Guardian*'s line. I suppose it's nice for you to be compared to Thomas à Becket, but it doesn't really seem to be your saintliness the writer's dwelling upon. Of course, he won't know you as well as we do."

"I told you, I'm not interested in the tittle-tattle of the fourth estate. I'm interested in arresting this wretched Leopard fellow. Nothing more and nothing less. And quickly. We live and die by our results, Peach." He jutted his jaw in his most Napoleonic pose.

Silly sod's got constipation again, Peach thought. It was better to ridicule him than to indulge in outbursts of fruitless temper. "Been out to the scene of the latest crime, have you, sir?"

Tucker's gaze into the brighter future of his vision became a glare at his inspector. "You know I don't interfere with my team. My job is to secure the resources, to keep the overview of the situation, to keep the public apprised of our efforts."

And as a result, the public is told that the police are baffled and the man in charge of the case is a wanker, thought Peach. Even the British press chances upon the truth sometimes. He said, "I called at the site yesterday, on my way to Manchester. She was a respectable married woman with two kids, on her way home from work. Sally Cartwright. Died just before midnight, by the Leopard's usual method. He seems to have left no more of himself behind than he did at the scenes of the three previous killings."

He was curious to know what Tucker would say to this. Even a pillock like this must have some view. But all his

170

superintendent said was "Manchester? On a Sunday? What were you going to Manchester for?"

"I went for a chat with Dr Wishart, sir."

"Wishart? Dr Wishart?"

Perhaps Alzheimer's was claiming the old fool for her own at last, Peach mused. "Of Manchester University, sir. The forensic psychologist who came over to speak to us on Thursday."

"Oh, him! I didn't think you'd be wasting any more time on him. I certainly wasn't very impressed with your Dr Wishart. Bit of a charlatan, if you ask me! I'm surprised you thought it worthwhile to ask him over here in the first place. Waste of the team's valuable time."

"I thought you believed it was a good idea at the time, sir," said Peach, with as much mildness as he could muster.

"Oh, I think your memory's letting you down there, Peach. I think you'll find I was sceptical about the idea from the start."

"I see, sir. I apologise for the misapprehension. It was just that the Chief Constable was pretty enthusiastic about it and I naturally thought that you were part of his thinking. But I should have known you well enough to know that you'd take an independent line! If I get the chance, I'll let the CC know that you think forensic psychology's a right load of old codswallop. I'm sure he'll be most interested to know that such independence of mind is a feature of—"

"You'll do nothing of the sort, Peach! That would be overstating my view completely. I have an open mind on these things."

"Yes, sir. I see, sir. I often tell the lads and lasses on the team what an open mind you have." That's if "open" is synonymous with "vacant", thought Peach, with firmly crossed fingers.

"Anyway, what did this so-called professor have to tell those of us at the cutting edge of investigation from his ivory tower?" sneered Tucker. That was putting the fellow in his place, he thought. He was not sure at that moment whether he meant Wishart or Peach.

"Some interesting things, sir, I thought. But I won't waste your time with them, now I know your views."

"What did he say, Peach?"

The clenched teeth and the forced delivery were danger signs, Peach observed. Unless the constipation was worse than usual. "Well, sir, he thought the killer was probably a Brunton man, operating outwards from a Brunton base."

"Well, I'm with him there. That seems fair enough." Tucker had begun the process of reversal. He did not even look embarrassed.

"That the Leopard is killing not from any perverted sense of justice, like those men who seek out prostitutes and drug addicts. All his victims are respectable women."

"That might be helpful, I suppose."

"That he's a planner, who enjoys plotting and researching his crimes. That he's probably driven by a sense of power. The ultimate power, over life and death, that's what fascinates him about his killing."

Tucker's look of puzzlement increased. These were deep waters, too deep for him. Deprived of a reaction, Peach prepared to drop in his ace of trumps. "Hamish Wishart thought our killer might well be a professional man, rather than someone from the underworld of crime. Interesting idea, that. I thought perhaps you should keep a wary eye on your colleagues in the Lodge, sir, just in case it should prove that—"

"Don't be ridiculous, Peach! And I'll thank you to keep your wild theories out of my personal—"

"Not mine, sir. The theories of the man brought in to help us with his professional analysis of the situation."

"Well, it's ridiculous to suggest the Leopard could be a member of the Masons."

"I see, sir. Dr Wishart just thought it might be a doctor, or a lawyer, or a schoolteacher. Or even a policeman."

"A policeman?"

The Lancashire Leopard

"A possibility, sir, that was all he said. Because this is someone used to discipline in his working life, we thought. Someone organised, who brings the planning he is used to in his daily work to bear on his murders."

Tucker was still shaken by Peach's mischievous image of his lodge members as serial killers. "You're speculating much too far. Your killer will be found among the lower classes, I'm sure."

"The lower classes, sir. I see." Peach savoured that faintly old-fashioned phrase for a moment.

"Yes. You and I know from the wealth of our experience that most serious crime comes from people who already have a record. My advice is to scrutinise your files again. I shouldn't be surprised if you've already interviewed a candidate who would conform to the pattern I've outlined for you."

Pattern? thought Peach. More an assembly of vague prejudices than any pattern. "Well, there is one man, sir, I suppose. Fellow who's done time for GBH and came out last September, just over a month before the Leopard killings began. Who used to beat his wife and had started to hit his daughter before he went inside, but never laid a finger on his son. Unsavoury character by the name of Terry Plant. He'd fit your pattern, I suppose."

"Well, then. Has he been interviewed? Has he been questioned in connection with the Leopard killings?"

"Yes, sir. Matter of fact, he was even found threatening a woman with a baseball bat, only last week." And all this has been reported fully to you, in a file you've never bothered to read, you lazy wanker. You've asked for what's coming in a minute, you idle bugger.

"Well then. Why aren't you questioning him at this very minute about the murder of Sally Cartwright, instead of annoying me?"

"Because he was safely under lock and key in Preston Prison at the time, sir. Awaiting trial on a charge of armed robbery."

* * *

173

No one who worked with him would have suspected it, and he himself would certainly never have admitted it, but Percy Peach sometimes felt quite lonely. Not in his private life: the little leisure that the Leopard had left him at the moment was amply filled by the lively mind and livelier curves of Lucy Blake.

But sometimes DI Peach, outwardly so supreme in his confidence, felt a professional loneliness. He missed the exchanges about a case that he should have had with his superintendent, in which two experienced professionals exchanged views openly and productively about their current cases. The Leopard was stretching Peach's resilience and energies, his whole professional existence, further than they had ever been stretched in his career, and he felt the need of a sympathetic senior colleague off whom he might bounce ideas, and even gain a little of the reassurance he could never admit he needed.

He talked to DI Parkinson, his opposite number in the Serious Crime Squad, whose resources were being used to bolster the Brunton CID team, but the two men had never worked together before. Although they exchanged information freely and usefully as the list of possible killers grew ever longer, there were limits to what each would confide to the other of his thoughts and his increasing desperation. Neither wanted to voice his more outlandish speculations, when he knew they might eventually be made to look ridiculous. For example, when Peach passed on Hamish Wishart's idea that the killer might be a professional man, possibly even a policeman, he did so with studious neutrality, without any comment from himself on what he thought of the idea.

In the afternoon after his fruitless exchange with Tucker, Peach called together three of the officers who had worked most closely with him on the Leopard case for an exchange of views. He could not admit, even to himself, that it was an attempt to clarify his own thinking on the plethora of information that was pouring into the ever-open maws of the computers, a substitute for the kind of informal exchange he should really be having with an older officer who had seen it all before.

"I can't call the whole team in," he said awkwardly, as they arranged their chairs in his office, "because they're far too busy checking and rechecking people who might have had the opportunity to kill Sally Cartwright last Friday night. But I thought it might help us if we exchanged a few thoughts about the Leopard. Before he kills a fifth woman," he concluded bitterly.

It's as if the killer's campaign was a personal war against him, thought Lucy Blake. She said supportively, "I think we'd all find that useful."

DC Tony Pickard tried not to sound sycophantic as he said earnestly, "I'd certainly welcome it. We all seem to be working our socks off, but going round in circles."

Brendan Murphy nodded his fresh face and his head of rather unruly brown hair. "Tony and I haven't been DCs for that long. It's our first involvement in this kind of case."

"It's the first involvement for all of us with anyone like this bloody Leopard!" said Peach, with a touch of his normal acerbity. "That's one of our problems. Even the splendid leadership we're getting from Wanker Willy upstairs isn't much help with a serial killer who seems to be playing games with us."

DS Blake said, "Are you able to tell us anything useful about your meeting with the forensic psychologist yesterday, or does that remain confidential?"

Peach smiled. "I'll summarise exactly what he felt – what *we* felt, for the most part, when we'd discussed the facts. The Leopard works and probably lives in Brunton. He researches his murders carefully and almost certainly enjoys the planning. He is a loner, but not a dropout or one of our unemployed; he may not even have a criminal record. He may well be a professional person: a doctor, a lawyer, a teacher, even a policeman."

J. M. Gregson

Pickard grinned. "Does Dr Wishart expect us to entertain that as a serious proposition?"

Peach did not smile. "It's a possibility, based on the facts available to him. I haven't ruled it out myself. This man seems to be familiar with our procedures and to have some knowledge of forensics. He's left less of himself behind than any killer I've encountered, and he's done that four times. That isn't by accident. Of course, anyone with an interest in crime could have acquired all the knowledge he's using by simple research. Maybe because of my own prejudices, I think it's highly unlikely the Leopard is a policeman. But I haven't ruled it out."

DC Murphy said, "Perhaps we should check the activities of the men who've been chucked out of the police in the last few years."

"That's already being done. Not just those we've got rid of, but those with a Brunton background who've left the force of their own free will over the last five years." Peach sighed: another list; another set of men to be traced and interviewed. But this list would overlap with others, and some of the men would already have been seen on other grounds. Sometimes the overlaps themselves could be significant, making the man a suspect on several counts.

Pickard said, "That's an excellent idea. Someone who's left the service, for whatever reason, might well have a grudge against the police and enjoy making fools of us."

"That's probably one part of the Leopard's motivation. But a minor part. You don't kill four women just to make the police look silly. Usually sex, often in some perverted form, is the driving force for serial killers of women. But this man hasn't raped or even assaulted any of his victims. It seems to be the exercise of power over life and death which is the fascination for him."

Lucy Blake said, "The analysis of a diseased mind isn't really our province, is it? We need something more tangible."

"Which he isn't giving us. At least I came away from

176

Hamish Wishart feeling rather clearer about the kind of man we were looking for. But I agree we're going to need something more definite before we can find our killer. Which has got to be soon: Wishart thinks the more he gets away with, the more frequently he's going to kill, and I agree with that."

Tony Pickard said, "He seems to be extraordinarily lucky in isolating his victims in lonely places. We're told that last Friday's victim even managed to scream without attracting attention to her killer. And isn't there a report that he was seen after he'd killed the woman?"

"Yes. We think he was seen last Friday, after he'd killed Sally Cartwright. But only across the road in the darkness, by a man walking his dog. He didn't even think of the Leopard. If it was our man who passed him, he was perfectly in control of himself: he even called a goodnight through the darkness. Then he presumably collected his vehicle and made his escape."

Murphy said, "Do you think it may be one of the people we've already interviewed? All the ones we've really fancied for the crimes have been Brunton-based."

Peach sighed. "That's one of the reasons why I've brought you in here: I want your views. I need hardly remind you how many times Peter Sutcliffe had been interviewed and discarded before someone eventually realised he was the Yorkshire Ripper. I want this bastard before he gets beyond four victims."

Lucy Blake said with a bleak smile, "Tony and I put a lot of time in on Terry Plant. At least we can eliminate him, since he was in custody at the time."

"As I had occasion to remind Tommy Bloody Tucker this morning." Peach allowed himself a brief smile at the recollection of his exit line and Tucker's astonished face. He turned to Brendan Murphy. "You interviewed the black boy with me. What's the score there?"

"Clyde Northcott? What he said about the cocaine rocks held up. He was a user only, not a supplier. The drugs squad arrested his dealer behind the Ugly Heifer pub last Tuesday night. But Northcott's not been cleared for the first three murders yet. And he has no alibi for last Friday night. Not after ten o'clock, when he left some of his biking mates – even they think he's a bit of a loner, by the way. He could have got over to Bolton on that fast bike of his with time to spare."

Peach nodded. Another visit. Another attempt to put the frighteners on a man who in all probability had nothing to hide, who would probably think he was being victimised because of his colour. But as long as that phrase "in all probability" remained attached to him, he would need to be checked. He said, "One of the question marks against Clyde Northcott is that although I'd say he has no difficulty attracting women, he doesn't seem interested in them. He has no regular girlfriend, now or in the recent past. Yet that girl who was giving the party, Tracey Wallace, was plainly very taken with him. It was she who corroborated his story about the bust-up at the end of it. Lucy, you haven't seen this lad yet, and neither has Tony. Pay him a visit, and give us your impressions, please."

Pickard was more concerned with another suspect. "The bloke Northcott fought at the party that night, Paul Dutton. The National Front bloke, whom I interviewed with you about the fight. He's been charged with causing an affray and actual bodily harm. But he's not in custody, of course, so he could have killed Sally Cartwright. He says he was at an NF meeting last Friday, and drinking afterwards. But there are no witnesses to this, as yet."

Peach nodded. Prejudiced or not, he would dearly like their man to be the insufferable Dutton, but things rarely worked out to the satisfaction of policemen like that. "Brendan, he hasn't seen you before. Take someone out with you. Uniform, if you like – that could scare him more than most young thugs – and give him a grilling. And don't let him kid you that he's merely an oaf: he is an oaf, but not merely, and that's dangerous. He's cleverer than he likes to let on, in some things. He might well enjoy plotting violence. Wouldn't you say so, Tony?"

Pickard nodded, then grinned. "There were times during the course of his interview with DI Peach when I thought he was going to be a victim, though."

"So long as he thought that and opened his big mouth, I don't mind. Who else is near the top of the list?"

Lucy Blake said, "Michael Devaney. Tony and I went to see him on Thursday. He'd been reported as odd by three different women – not that that means very much, with the town in its present state of mass hysteria. He's certainly odd, and a loner. He's the Community Liaison Officer on the new estate, and he's in many respects his own boss, with no one directly in his line of work to report to."

Pickard said thoughtfully, "Devaney conforms to most of the criteria you've just outlined. He's used to organising his own time; he knows Brunton and the surrounding area well; he seems to enjoy planning, given the job he does; and he's a loner. I don't know whether the power over life and death would be an attraction for him, but he must get frustrated by the lack of power in the job he has. Everyone pays lip-service to good community relations, but no one wants to do anything or spend anything on implementing his schemes."

Lucy thought of those malleable, unformed, almost child-ish features, that air of vulnerability that Devaney had carried with him like a garment. She said almost reluctantly, "He has a record of violence against women. Or against one woman. Ten years ago, he hit a twenty-two-year-old woman so hard that she needed eight stitches over her eye."

"Was he charged?"

"No. The woman worked in an office with him. She refused to press charges; it never came to court. She admitted she'd taunted him for months before the incident. She seems to have been the worst of a group of young women who poked fun at him." Lucy could see those blubbery lips and watery, sensitive eyes. At nineteen, ten years ago, Michael

179

Devaney would have been a pitiable target for the cruel teasing he had described. She said, "For what it's worth, I believe his story about that incident."

Peach looked at her for a moment, then nodded. "Two important things from our point of view, though. First, the violence seems to have been unconnected with any sexual assault. Secondly, that sort of treatment might well have left him with a permanent fear of girls, a permanent wish to exercise the sort of control he could only exert in a one-to-one physical struggle."

Brendan Murphy, who had never seen Devaney, said thoughtfully, "The ultimate power over life and death. The power to end an individual female life," echoing the thought that had been put to them a few minutes earlier about what excited the Leopard.

There was a moment's reflective silence before Tony Pickard added, "We asked him where he'd been on the night when Hannah Woodgate died. He said he was in bed with a cold he thought was developing into 'flu. But there's no record of any time off work, before or after the death. He doesn't have a permanent girlfriend. Or a boyfriend."

Peach looked at the three grave faces before him. "It sounds like a persuasive case. But no more persuasive than half a dozen others. Still, our Community Liaison Officer Michael Devaney will need to be checked as to his whereabouts on Friday night, along with all the others."

The old nightmare was before him again: that a man they had already interviewed in connection with the case might have slipped through the net and killed another woman. "It's in hand," said Lucy Blake. "Two of the uniformed lads were due to see him at work this morning."

The phone on Peach's desk shrilled, as if in answer to a cue. He listened with a grave face, then put the phone down slowly. He couldn't keep the excitement out of his voice as he relayed what might be nothing, or might be a breakthrough. "That was DI Parkinson of the Serious Crime Unit. Your uniformed boys weren't able to talk to their man. It seems that Michael Devaney has disappeared."

The Leopard felt very relaxed on that Monday night. He found that he thought of himself as the Leopard now. That was the real him. When he had started his career as a killer, his secret life had been the smaller part of him. Now that secret part was the real him, and the things he did during the day were a meaningless ritual; a necessary ritual, it is true, but important only as the cover for the real him, the dangerous him, who existed so vitally in the hours of darkness.

The Lancashire Leopard.

It was three days now since the fourth killing, and he was sure that he had got away with it as completely as the first three. He had thought that they might pick something up from his brief sighting by that elderly man with the dog, but nothing had come of it. The man couldn't possibly have seen enough through the night to give any useful description. And he had made the usual mistake that amateurs did and over-estimated his height: he had described the man who passed on the other side of the road as "well over six feet in height". Thank you so much, punter, for misleading the fuzz.

It gave him an extra little thrill that this victim had emitted a single sharp scream before she was silenced for ever. That had added to the excitement and fear at the time, and to the exhilaration when he found that he had got away with it. But he wouldn't be allowing a repeat performance. You wouldn't always get away with it. And the Leopard was careful, wasn't he? That was his trademark.

The press and the media were already gunning for that fool Tucker. And the dissatisfaction was spreading outwards. People in the town were openly saying how inefficient and how stupid the police were: he had heard them yesterday, in the supermarkets and the newspaper shops, when he had patiently been gathering the Sunday papers,

181

never more than two at any one outlet, to read the reactions to his latest escapade. A team of over sixty, with their battery of computers and their vaunted forensic science, all being made to look equally foolish.

Soon, they would be shown to be even more witless. For he was ready for the latest and boldest of all his killings. It was only three days tonight since the last one. A lesser man than the Leopard would lie low for a time. But the Leopard had no need of such caution. He had been preparing for this death over several weeks now, had been working out the details even while he was rehearsing the Sally Cartwright death in the shadows of that deserted station outside Bolton, waiting to check the times when that silly woman left the pub to walk home.

He thought best in the darkness. This fifth killing would be the most daring of all his crimes. In his mind's eye, his plan was complete. There would need to be a degree of improvisation at the time, but that would just stretch him a little further. They hadn't seen the full extent of his talents yet.

He didn't need the television that night. He put out the light and sat in the darkness, revolving his plan over and over again in his head, until the phases clicked like clockwork into position, one after the other. Other, lesser men might have become either anxious or bored with the repetition.

The Leopard simply became more confident.

Eighteen

M ichael Devaney was located in a small semi-detached house in Wolverhampton. Why he was there was not clear in the message to Brunton CID from their counterparts in the Midlands. Probably he had not yet been questioned. But he had been arrested and taken to the nick at Wolverhampton: the bird which had flown from Lancashire was not to be allowed a chance to migrate further.

DI Peach held a terse conversation with a detective sergeant with a thick Black Country accent. It concluded with, "Keep him there. I'll come and interview him myself." If this should be the Leopard, Peach wanted it kept as quiet as possible, until he had a confession and the man was locked away securely. If the rumour got out, the press and television boys would besiege Wolverhampton police station. With the money the tabloids were offering for any whisper of the Lancashire Leopard, even policemen could be tempted. Anonymous "spokesmen" from the police service had already milked some handsome sums from the ample coffers of United News and News International in the first years of the new century. And there was no bigger story available than the first news of the arrest of the Leopard.

Peach deployed his troops for the day, then pointed his car towards the M6 and the Midlands. Three hours alone behind the wheel to wonder whether this might be their man at last; three hours to wonder what else they could do, if Michael Devaney was not the Leopard.

*   *   *

Whilst Peach sped southwards, Brendan Murphy was preparing to go out and check on Paul Dutton, the man who
had assaulted the biker Clyde Northcott as he tried to leave
Tracey Wallace's party. In Peach's absence, he sought the
advice of DS Blake as to who should accompany him.

"That's easy," said Lucy. "I'll come with you myself."

"I thought you were going out with Tony Pickard to see
the black boy?"

"I am. But not until this afternoon. Tony has a dental
appointment: even the Leopard has to wait when a filling
is lost."

She wondered why young Murphy's face had fallen at her
offer. Perhaps he just didn't like working with women. She
still met that, but less than she had eight years ago when
she had joined the police as a callow eighteen-year-old.
Perhaps he just didn't want rank with him, didn't want his
interviewing techniques scrutinised by a detective sergeant,
when Peach had said he might take one of the uniform boys
with him. Perhaps he would have preferred an admiring, or at
any rate largely silent, companion. Tough titty, Brendan!

Paul Dutton worked in the office of the local brewery.
He wore a white shirt and a dark blue tie, like the most
conformist of bankers. He had discarded his jacket before
they came. As he took them into the small room just off
the reception area which he had secured for this meeting, he
rolled up the sleeves of his immaculate shirt carefully. On
his right forearm this revealed a new tattoo of a Union Jack
with the National Front logo above it; on his left forearm
a crudely sketched female face leered, possibly Boadicea,
more likely Margaret Thatcher.

Lucy said, "I'm Detective Sergeant Blake, and this is
Detective Constable Murphy."

Dutton nodded at her, but only so that he could studiously
ignore the man at her side, whose Irish name he had registered with a sneer of contempt. He folded his massive arms,
trying hard to capture the hard-man image he created in his
leisure hours, looking like a bricklayer's hod-carrier thrust

incongruously into executive clothes. "This isn't convenient, you know. Having the police following me about. If it's about that fight with the wog, I've been charged and I've nothing more to say until it comes to court."

Lucy Blake eyed him with distaste. "I'm glad to hear it. I hear you've already said enough to ensure the right verdict is reached. We're here about something more important altogether."

Dutton glanced nervously at the door on his left, as if to reassure himself that it was shut. "This is harassment, this is. It's about this bloody Leopard, isn't it? I told the uniformed pig, I was at a Front meeting on Friday night." He dropped fewer aitches and was generally better-spoken here at work than he had been at the station when Peach and Pickard saw him, so that the words like "wog" and "pig" fell oddly from his lips.

Brendan Murphy said, "You weren't at a National Front meeting at the time in question, Mr Dutton, and you know that as well as we do. If I were you, I'd be desperately trying to come up with someone to confirm my whereabouts between ten and twelve p.m."

"Boozing, wasn't I? After we'd spent two hours planning to bring the country to its senses in our meeting, we were entitled to a drink."

"Where?"

"The Bull's Head on Northgate. Six of us, there were. Landlord will vouch for us, we always end up there." He smiled triumphantly at the eager faces in front of him.

Lucy said quietly, "And why didn't you say this before, Mr Dutton?"

"Didn't feel like it, did I? Don't take kindly to pigs, do I? Especially Irish pigs. Thickest of all, the Micks are!" He stared truculently at Murphy, challenging him to react.

Brendan was on his feet in an instant, leaning forward to pluck away the ham-like hands as they clasped protectively over the head of the sitting man.

"Easy, DC Murphy!" said Lucy sharply. Then as the DC's

lean body eased slowly back on to his chair beside her, she hissed, "This man's not worth it, and you know it."

Paul Dutton dropped his arms from their protective posture, grinned his triumph at the heavily breathing Murphy. Then he turned to DS Blake, his face twisting into a leer. "Don't like being fucked about by Gaelic thickos, do I? Bloody Sunday was a good idea, if you ask me. Now with you, my dear, I might be altogether more co-operative. It would be a different thing entirely. I might even let you take down my particulars, if you allowed me to handle yours."

Lucy Blake stared back into his face for a moment, to show that she was in no danger of losing control, as her companion almost had. Then she said dryly, "I can see why you don't have a girlfriend, Mr Dutton. And why you must be a suspect for the Leopard killings."

"Not any longer, lady. You'll find I can prove that I was nowhere near this bloody barmaid last Friday night."

Lucy had an uneasy feeling he could do just that. She ought to have been glad to have another man eliminated from the list. In this case, she thought she would make an exception.

Brendan Murphy leaned across the table until he could see the apprehension on the coarse, meaty features. His brown eyes bored into the widening grey ones of his adversary from no more than a foot. "We'll check this out, Dutton. It had better be right, or we'll be straight back here, without the kid gloves, without any cover-up for your employers."

Lucy Blake said coolly, "What time did you leave the Bull's Head, Mr Dutton?"

He pulled his shirt back down over the tattoos on his huge forearms, signifying his belief that this was almost over. "About half past eleven, I should think. Check it with the landlord. If he can't remember, I've five mates who can. And just in case you're planning on more harassment, I didn't drive. I walked home. Always do, when I've had a skinful."

Lucy was glad to get out into the open air. She sat in the

driver's seat of the police car, making no attempt to start it. "You almost hit that man in there," she said eventually.

"Well, the bugger was taking us for a ride. He was taunting us, when he might be the Leopard, for all we know!"

"If you're going to risk your career, don't do it for trash like that. You know damn well you'll have to resist far more provocation than that; must have already done so, to be in CID at all."

"Yes. I . . . I don't know how he got to me like that. You probably don't believe me, but I've never been as close to hitting anyone as that. Not while I've been in the police."

"I should hope not." She started the engine. "It won't go any further, so long as there's no repetition. But let it be a warning to you, Brendan. We're all under strain, with this Leopard on the prowl and the public baying for blood. But you can't afford to have a short fuse, especially with scum like that, who'll be delighted to play it for all it's worth."

"It won't happen again." Brendan Murphy gazed straight ahead through the windscreen, watching the pedestrians in the town centre, resolutely refusing to look at the young woman alongside him.

Percy would have handled Paul Dutton better than either of them, thought Lucy, as they drove the short distance back to the Murder Room at CID. Even when Dutton had in effect set them up, Percy would have put him on the back foot, somehow – even if he'd had to fall back on the old standby of wasting police time, he'd have made it seem serious, made it seem as if Dutton was making the mistakes.

And like all great artists, Percy would have made it seem effortless.

Peach took one of the local DCs into the interview room with him at Wolverhampton, with instructions not to interfere. He found Michael Devaney a predictably pathetic figure.

The Brunton Community Liaison Officer looked as if he had been crying at some time during the morning. His face had the grey marks of old tears and his thick lips shuddered with the uneven intakes of his breath. When he was brought into the room and Peach ordered him brusquely to sit down, he cowered away from them on the upright chair, as if he feared physical violence. His appearance and his movements proclaimed that this was a man at the end of his resources.

It could all be an act, Peach supposed. Or it could be perfectly genuine. Perhaps this pathetic creature was a Jekyll and Hyde, finding himself a different identity when he walked alone by night and imposed himself upon defenceless women. He wouldn't be the first multiple killer to seem inadequate for the demands of the everyday world, unable to cope with mankind in the mass.

"You should be at work in Brunton, not rotting in Wolverhampton nick. How come, Mr Devaney?"

"The Lancashire Leopard. You think it's me, don't you?"

"I didn't. I'm more inclined to think it might be, now. Innocent men don't need to run away."

The mobile features twitched the pain behind them. "I couldn't stand it any more." The words took Peach back to his first days as a copper, when one of his duties had been the finding and return of runaway children. They had often spoken these words, often looked as helpless as this. But this man was twenty-nine.

"Why did you run away, Michael?"

"I read in my Sunday newspaper about the woman the Leopard killed on Friday night. And someone pushed another paper through my letter box, the *News of the World*. That had a more lurid account, and a big picture of the place where the woman was found. There was a gate into a field. And someone had drawn a figure of a man into the picture, just in outline, and put my name on it. I couldn't stand it any longer. I went to my mother's house. She moved down here to be nearer to my sister."

The words were delivered in a monotone, with the speaker staring fixedly at the desk, as if he feared that any eye contact would halt the explanation he wanted to spit out. Peach said,

"Been on at you before about the Leopard, have they, your neighbours?"

"Yes. I see them whispering behind my back. The women. It was them who brought your people in to me last week, the girl with red hair and the man with the fierce eyes."

"We'd have been round to see you, anyway, Michael. We've been checking on any men who live alone. You're one of hundreds."

He looked into the inspector's round, impassive face for the first time. Peach saw in the watery blue eyes a desperate desire to please him, succeeded swiftly by the doubt that told Devaney to beware of anything men like this said to him. He said, "They shout things after me, the worst of them."

Peach sighed. "It happens, in cases like this. Some people get frightened. Others just see a chance to hound someone in a worse position than themselves. You won't be the only one who's suffering."

Devaney saw the logic of this. He nodded slowly for a moment. Then his pliant features shuddered, like the surface of water under a wind. "I can't stand it. I'm sorry, but I can't."

And I can't offer you any protection, thought Peach. I can't spare men to protect a pathetic creature like this from bullying, not with the Leopard prowling about and choosing his next prey. He said gently, "You make it worse if you react to it, Michael. Try to treat them with contempt." But he knew that this man wasn't capable of doing that. He said, "I have to ask you, for our records. Where were you last Friday night, Mr Devaney?"

"I was at home. I am most nights. I don't go out much – especially since, you know . . ."

"Since the Leopard. I know. But you must have realised that the quickest way to excite suspicion was to make a sudden exit from Brunton, without telling anyone where you were going?"

"I see that now, when you put it like that. I didn't think, at the time. I just wanted to get out." He looked up: another

189

thought had hit him for the first time with full force. "Will I lose my job?"

"That's not in my hands. I shouldn't think so."

"I left a message on the answer-machine at the town hall."

"I see. Well, I don't think you should go back, just yet. Take a week off and stay at your mother's. I'll get someone to ring from the station and say you're ill, when I get back to Brunton. Go to a doctor down here, and get something to calm your nerves."

Peach paused at the desk of the Custody Sergeant on his way out. "No charge. Sorry you've been bothered. Let sonny boy out and send him home to his mother, will you, please?"

These Midlanders had only seen Percy Peach for twenty minutes. They must think he was a soft touch, he thought, as he climbed back sadly into his car.

Clyde Northcott had been pulled off his work at the bench at the electrical manufacturing factory to meet two officers from Brunton CID. The news excited much curiosity and not a little excitement as it ran round his fellow-workers.

For the powerful young six-footer was a loner and by common consent "a mad bastard". He was also very black, and, deep within the psyche of Brunton men and women who would have vehemently denied that they had even a hint of racial prejudice, that added a little *frisson* of the strange. And strange quickly became sinister, when the town was agog for sightings of the Leopard.

Neither DS Blake nor DC Pickard had talked to Northcott before. Having seen the opponent who had attacked him with a knife earlier in the day, Lucy Blake found the contrast between the two men interesting. Northcott was as still and watchful as Dutton had been active and aggressive. At the station, Percy Peach had caught him on the back foot, fearing charges of drug supply and actual bodily harm, and had characteristically kept him there even when no charges

190

matcrialised. Now Northcott had recovered his poise; his stillness combined with his handsome ebony face gave him a certain dignity as they sat together in the room that had been assigned to them in the office section of the works for this meeting. Lucy Blake found it also made him seem impenetrable.

She introduced herself and Tony Pickard and said, "Your information about the cocaine supplier was accurate. An arrest has been made."

"I know. At the Ugly Heifer on Tuesday."

"Your name will not be connected with that arrest. There is no way anyone involved in the supply is going to find out where the information came from."

He nodded a curt acknowledgement. "I've told you all I know about that. What else do you want?"

Tony Pickard said, "We want to know where were you last Friday night."

Northcott eyed him coolly. "Still on about the Lancashire Leopard? I haven't killed any women."

"Where were you?"

"You're not going to do me any good at work, are you? Coming here and pulling me off the bench to answer questions I've already dealt with."

Lucy Blake said, "We can't choose our times. Answer the question, please."

"I was with my friends. I usually am on a Friday night."

Pickard said, "Then we'll have a few names. A few details about times and places. Then we'll be on our way, quiet as mice. We'll do some checking, of course."

Northcott eyed them evenly, looking for a moment as if he might refuse to answer. Lucy was glad she had not Brendan Murphy but Tony Pickard beside her, as calm as the man on the other side of the table, not likely to lose his cool even if the subject refused his co-operation. The silence seemed to stretch abnormally before the lips above the small rectangle of trimmed beard said abruptly, "Darren Green, Martin Attwood, Jason Murray. They're

191

J. M. Gregson

all Yamaha owners. And they're all white. You might believe *them*!"

Lucy said, "We believed you, when you told us about the fight you were involved in, didn't we? We believed your tale about the drugs, when the evidence was against you. No one's saying we don't believe you now. But we have to check. You're right, it is the Leopard who's brought us here. There are checks like this being carried out all over Brunton, all over a larger area outside the town. If you were a woman, you'd want us to check."

Clyde looked for a moment into the flushed, animated face, with its greenish eyes under the nimbus of red-brown hair, which was such a contrast to his own resolutely impassive features. "All right. So long as it isn't just me. I can give you other names, if you want them."

Tony Pickard grinned, trying to ease away the tension. "Three should be quite sufficient. Where did this meeting take place?"

Northcott gave no answering smile. "At Darren Green's house. His parents were out. We had a few cans of lager and a bit of a laugh. We were planning where to go on Sunday. They let me do an initial plan, because I enjoy it. Then we all discuss it."

"And where did you decide to go?"

"Up to Ingleton. Then on to the Lake District, and over the Kirkstone Pass. We always set off early, about seven o'clock, to avoid the crowds. And come back early. It's great up there, on a frosty winter's day." For the first time, against his will, enthusiasm forced its way into the previously studiously neutral voice.

So they had ridden directly away from Bolton, where the fourth murder had been committed some thirty-one hours earlier. But there might be nothing significant in that. Lucy Blake said as casually as she could, "What time did your meeting break up on Friday?"

He switched his dark eyes back to her. "Half past ten. Darren's parents were due home from the cinema. We

192

broke up and went off to the pub for a last couple of drinks."

"And you were in the pub until what time?"

If he was tempted to lie, his stone-like calm did not reveal it. He said, "I wasn't. I don't drink much. I didn't go with the others to the pub. I'd had a couple of cans while we were talking in the house, and that was all I wanted."

"So you went straight home?"

His dark brown eyes looked directly into her green ones as he said slowly, "No. I went for a ride on the Yamaha. I often do, late at night. I like it when the roads are quiet. It was after midnight when I got home."

"And where did you go?"

"Along the M65 to Nelson. Then north, along the A682, picking up the A59 near Gisburn, and back home along that, by-passing Clitheroe." He paused, as if waiting for a reaction. "I was home at about twelve thirty."

Tony Pickard said, "And is there anyone who can confirm either the route or the time for us?"

"No. But you wouldn't expect that. I'm a bit of a loner, as you might have gathered."

"So is the Leopard, in all probability."

If Tony Pickard hoped to nettle him, he didn't succeed. Clyde Northcott looked from one to the other of the two intense, observant faces, then permitted himself his first, mirthless smile. "I expect he is. But then you believe my story, don't you? Just the same as if I was white."

Nineteen

S t Paul's revelation came to him on the road to Damascus. Percy Peach's was altogether more prosaic. It came to him in a crowded service station car park beside the northbound carriageway of the M6.

When the Detective Inspector joined the motorway at Junction 11, he found the notoriously overcrowded lanes as busy as he might have expected. He had thought that having dismissed Michael Devaney as a possibility for the Leopard, he might spend the hours of his drive back north in a review of other possibilities. In the event, he found that the driving, even with the power and automatic gearbox of his Scorpio, was taxing enough to require all his attention and concentration.

In an indirect way, it was the driving which was in the end his salvation. As they moved past Stafford and the traffic thinned a little, he settled back and prepared to enjoy a better cruising speed. Only ten miles above the legal limit, he reflected: even senior policemen had to maintain a steady eighty if they were not to be confined to the inside lane among the pantechnicons. But in a few minutes, he found himself struggling to keep awake, and realised that he had now been driving in crowded conditions for over four hours, with only the scarcely relaxing forty minutes he had spent at Wolverhampton nick as a break.

Cup of black coffee, strong as possible, then twenty minutes' rest. That was the formula. That way you began driving again just as the caffeine kicked into your system.

194

He concentrated grimly until he reached the welcome haven of Keele Services. Peach queued for his coffee, resisted a doughnut and found the beverage considerably more drinkable than the Brunton nick version of coffee. They should have an Egon Ronay guide to police station coffee, he thought; Brunton might make one star on a good day. Might as well put that down to Tommy Bloody Tucker, as he blamed him for everything else.

Back in the car park, he found it easier to rest in the comfortable leather seat of the Scorpio than he had expected. Must be getting old. For the first time, he admitted to himself that the Leopard had actually been disturbing his sleep patterns at nights. The sod was getting to him. He shut the killings resolutely out of his mind, even succeeded in dozing for a few minutes.

And that was when the revelation came to him. He awoke with the idea complete in his mind, as clear as a mountain against a sharp blue winter sky. His recent interviews of suspects, his exchanges with Hamish Wishart, his discussions with his own team, all flashed before him in succession; each face, each idea, it seemed even each word, was as lucid as if it was being spoken now in this warm cubicle of car. And everything confirmed the revelation.

It was dark by the time DS Blake and DC Pickard got back to the Murder Room at Brunton CID.

There were very few people there. With a new Leopard murder still screaming for investigation, most officers were out in the town checking various leads, working through the lists of men who had not already been cleared for one of the previous three killings.

"I'll stand you tea and a bun before we check our messages," offered Lucy Blake. It was already after five o'clock and they might well have seized an early getaway while the opportunity was there, but she somehow fancied a natter. When every alley seemed to turn into a blind one, it felt as if you weren't doing your duty if you went home without an exchange of ideas.

"You're on, Sarge," said Tony Pickard promptly. "Two minutes in the little boys' room, and I'm yours in the canteen. Mine's a flapjack, by the way."

Lucy had half expected him to refuse, to make some excuse to get away. She wondered idly as she paid for the tea and two flapjacks if Tony was trying to impress a DS with his diligence, if he would have gone off home if it had been a fellow DC who had asked him. She didn't really think so: Tony was new to the team, like Brendan Murphy, but she had worked quite a bit with him over the last few weeks, and he didn't strike her as a promotion creeper.

It seemed they would be the only two in the canteen. She took the tray to the far end of the big room, well away from the counter, so that any discussion they had should be a private one. You had to inculcate an appropriate caution in young officers, she thought, from the eminence of her twenty-six years. Well, nearly twenty-seven, as she told her mother; she must be at least four years older than Tony Pickard!

As soon as Tony came into the canteen, she was struck by the change in his appearance. His face was strained and grey, and he was looking back over his shoulder to make certain he was not observed. He was carrying a small sports bag. He set it down carefully on the chair beside him as he sat down, where it could not be seen by anyone coming unexpectedly into the room.

"What on earth's the matter?" she asked.

He answered her with another question. "Have you seen Brendan Murphy?" His voice, emerging as little more than a hoarse whisper, edged the query with melodrama.

Lucy smiled, attempting to remove the tension. "No, I expect he's gone home, unless he's out in the town somewhere. Were you afraid he'd pinch your flapjack?" She pushed his tea and plate towards him, but he scarcely noticed the gesture. Lucy bit into her flapjack and waited

196

to see what was troubling him: she had never seen Tony as agitated as this before; he had been calmness personified with Clyde Northcott an hour earlier.

He stared down at his steaming cup without registering its presence. Presently he looked up at her, caught her small white teeth biting into her flapjack, and gave a small, nervous smile. He picked up his own slice and bit into it thoughtfully. Then he put both hands round his steaming cup, in a gesture which recalled to her the town's dropouts, living in derelict buildings and conserving whatever tiny morsels of warmth they were offered in the winter cold.

"You'd better spit it out," said Lucy. "A trouble shared is a trouble halved, they say. Whoever 'they' might be."

He looked at her again with that little, shaken, half-smile. "Don't take this the wrong way, but how much do you know about Brendan?" he said.

"Rather less than you do, I should think. You've worked with him more than anyone else on the team. He joined the CID section only about a fortnight before you."

"He never lived in the section house with the rest of us. I did, until I got my own place." Pickard was staring ahead of him, past Lucy, apparently voicing thoughts as they came to him.

"No, he wouldn't need to. He's Brunton born and bred, is Brendan, despite his Irish name. I think he still lives at home with his parents."

"No, he doesn't. He's got his own house. I've been there several times."

Lucy sighed. "Stop warming your hands and drink that tea before it gets cold; I've finished mine. You'd better tell me exactly what's worrying you. It needn't go any further, if you don't want it to."

Pickard looked at her, attempted a smile, drank the tea as meekly as if he had been a child. He stared ahead for a moment before he seemed to come to a decision. "All right. You remember Percy Peach put out this idea that the

Leopard might just be a policeman, and I thought it was rather a joke?"

"I remember that Percy passed on the suggestion from Dr Wishart, the forensic psychologist, that our man might be a lawyer, or a doctor, or a teacher, or just possibly a policeman. As I remember it, Percy said that he couldn't believe it himself, but was passing it on for what it was worth."

If Tony registered her prickly defence of her man, he did not show it. "It would make sense though, wouldn't it? Explain why the Leopard seems to be perpetually one step ahead of us."

"I suppose it would be one explanation, yes. There are others. Tony, you'd better come out with what you're thinking. I shouldn't need to tell you that there's no case for sheltering a friend, in something as serious as this."

"No." He looked round wildly at the deserted canteen, then stared down at his empty plate. In a second or two, he said dully, "All right. I think it's possible Brendan Murphy might be the Leopard."

Lucy Blake glanced round automatically to make sure they were not overheard. She felt her own pulses pounding at the suggestion, told herself that it was important for her man-management that she should not ridicule this startling idea. This man had never thrown outlandish suggestions out before, had behaved quietly and responsibly earlier in the afternoon when Clyde Northcott might have riled him. She said, "How long have you been thinking that, Tony?"

"For about ten minutes. Since I went into the locker room."

"So something suddenly put the idea in your head. What was it?"

For a moment, he looked as if he would draw back, would refuse to talk even when he had gone so far. Then, with a sigh which seemed to be wrung from deep within him, he said, "Brendan's locker is next to mine. I noticed the door wasn't quite shut. So I opened it to slam it shut – they lock automatically. That's when I saw these. They were on the shelf at the top of his locker."

He slid the sports bag on to the table between them, but did not extract the contents. Instead, he carefully held back the sides to allow her to see inside it. She realised immediately why he was so careful that no one else should see this.

She was gazing down at a pair of brand new thick leather gardening gloves.

Peach eased the Scorpio back on to the M6. He drove slowly at first, unable to believe the logic of his own thoughts, going over certain exchanges again and again in his mind to confirm them. Then, as the idea took firm root, he speeded up the car. It was almost dark already, and the traffic would thicken as he got near Manchester.

He wondered whether to take the M56, risking the rush-hour traffic round Manchester and Bolton, then decided to stick to the M6. He would race north, joining the A59 near Preston; he could be in the Brunton CID within twenty minutes from there, with luck.

He was impatient now, anxious to be back with his colleagues, to test his notion against their perceptions. He wouldn't bother with Tommy Bloody Tucker, of course. Nor even with DI Parkinson of the Serious Crime Squad. There was no point in that: Parkinson was competent enough, but he didn't know the people involved. He would speak to Lucy Blake first, on her own. She was his DS, after all, so no one could cavil at that. He needed to convince himself that there wasn't a perfectly sensible explanation of this after all, that he wasn't going to make a monumental fool of himself by going public on it.

The time seemed to be racing past, whilst he was held in a hiatus of inaction. Yet when he glanced down the needle on his speedo was approaching ninety. He made himself slow to a steady eighty. It took a real effort of will.

*   *   *

DS Blake stared for long seconds at the gardening gloves, then motioned silently to Tony Pickard to close the bag.

He said dully, "They're only a pair of gardening gloves, I suppose."

"New ones. The kind everyone says the Leopard uses." Lucy felt like a reluctant prosecuting counsel.

"The kind sold in their thousands every week. That's probably why the Leopard chose to use them."

"Yes, but we have to investigate them, don't we?" She was gentle but insistent.

He nodded, then said reluctantly, "I don't think they're the kind of gloves Brendan would be buying for any innocent reason."

She looked at him sharply, then said, "You've been to his house. Does it have a garden?"

"A small one, yes. Mainly at the back."

"Well, then. Perhaps Brendan's about to tackle some winter work." She smiled, as if by relaxing her tension she could make the bag and its contents go away.

Tony Pickard could not relax. He said, "I considered that. He's no gardener, Brendan. The place is a bit of a wilderness."

"That's it, then. He's made a resolution to do something about it. He's going to tidy the place up."

Still Tony Pickard could not smile. He shook his head bleakly. "In February? The weeds would have to be coming in through the windows, before Brendan was moved to tackle them. Besides, what chance do we get to garden, whilst this Leopard business is on? No time during the week and precious little at the weekend, at present."

It was true enough. She thought of putting other innocent solutions to him, such as that Brendan Murphy had bought the gloves not for himself, but for his parents, or a friend, though she knew that Tony would have considered these things for himself. But she knew that what she had said at the outset was true: they were going to have to investigate this. You couldn't afford to ignore any leads, however strange the directions in which they pointed.

She wished Percy was here, ready with a decision, whether it was to deride the notion or to spring into swift action. But she knew what he would have said: you're paid as a DS to take responsibility, to act on your own initiative when it's appropriate. There won't always be DIs around to take the responsibility. She could almost hear him saying it, though he would probably have put it more trenchantly.

And there was a tiny part of her which said that this crazy thought of Tony's might just be true, and that she could bring in the Leopard, on her own. Well, with Tony Pickard's help, of course. She would give him all due credit, if the incredible idea she had drawn from him turned out in the end to be justified.

She said tersely, "Where was Brendan last Friday night? If he was on duty, that would stop this idea at source, before we go any further with it."

"He was off duty when Sally Cartwright was killed. I know from my own rota. And I've thought about the first three, in the last few minutes. Brendan was off on all the nights concerned."

"All right. We'll check it out. Do you know where he is now?"

"Maybe at home? He's not in the station."

"Right. No time like the present. Let's go and confront him with those gloves."

Tony looked aghast at the thought of confronting his friend and colleague. "Shouldn't we wait for Percy Peach to come back?"

She smiled. He seemed to be feeling the same urge she had to shrug this off on to higher-ranking shoulders, to let others take responsibility for investigating what might make them both laughing stocks around the station. She said, "We can't, Tony, can we? He probably won't be available until tomorrow morning. And if it is the Leopard we're talking about, we can't afford to leave it overnight, just in case . . . we can't take the risk. We'll go out there now."

"But just the two of us? Shouldn't we take someone else with us? Or at least let them know we're going?"

"Do you feel we need reinforcements?"

He frowned. "No. I can handle Brendan. And at least . . . well . . ."

"At least there will only be the two of us involved, when this proves to be an almighty farce? Yes. I'm glad you've thought of that, too. I've agreed this warrants investigation, but I'm no more anxious than you to let others in on it if it proves to be a wild goose chase."

"I'm sure it will. But you're right, we can't leave it. I've tried Brendan on my radio in case he's out in the town, but I haven't picked him up. Mind you, it's been on the blink all day."

"Try mine. I'll be with you in a minute."

She made a swift visit to the ladies' locker room, then joined Tony in CID. He looked both uncomfortable and disappointed as he gave her back her radio. "No luck. Brendan must be at home. He'd probably be out of range there, even if it was switched on. Sarge, are you sure you want to tackle him head-on like this? Perhaps we should sleep on it, buttonhole him when he comes in tomorrow, let him—"

"You know that isn't on. Come on. The sooner it's over with, the better, as far as I'm concerned!" She turned for the door without another look at him.

They passed out of the station, swift and silent as conspirators. Lucy, all thoughts of picking up her messages swept away in the thrill of the chase, was glad that she didn't have to drive. In the front passenger seat of Tony Pickard's Mondeo, she folded her arms and indulged her vision of radioing back to the station with the news that they had arrested the Leopard.

Twenty

P each made good progress until he was within three miles of the point where he was to leave the M6. There, where the northbound M61 from Manchester joins the longer motorway, there was trouble.

The back of one of the huge juggernauts speeding north had caught the cab of a much smaller lorry, sending it spinning across the hard shoulder and through the barrier at the side. There did not seem to be any serious injury, but two lanes of the M6 were shut, and a four-mile jam had built up within ten minutes. Peach tried to be philosophical as the single lane of cars inched forward. He watched the drivers rubber-necking as they passed the scene of the mishap, and marvelled once again at the public's taste for the macabre.

If they knew what he knew, they would really be excited. Or thought he knew: he corrected himself. What had seemed so certain, so logical, sixty miles back seemed more outlandish as he neared the place where he would have to do something about it. During one of the many minutes whilst he was stationary, waiting for the vehicles in front to filter into the one lane available for them, he rang Lucy Blake on her personal mobile phone.

There was no reply. She must still be at work, then – she always switched her personal phone off when she was working. The traffic ground to a halt again in front of him, giving him time for reflection. He was glad that he had this personal relationship with his DS. He would be able to talk to Lucy completely off the record before he went public on

203

this. She would tell him in no uncertain terms if she thought he was going to make a fool of himself.

He smiled at the thought of her flushed, excited face as she argued with him.

It was after six now, and the Brunton evening rush hour was tailing off. Tony Pickard drove without haste, as if he was suddenly anxious not to reach the house of the man who for the last five months had been his friend.

Lucy thought he was probably rehearsing what might happen when they got there, how he might best confront Brendan Murphy with their astonishing theory. She tried the same thing herself, but she couldn't get near to imagining how the conversation might go. Murphy would laugh in their faces, she was sure of that. But then he would be bound to do that, even if he was the Leopard. After his laughter, she couldn't think what would happen.

They ran out of town and into country; with the side of her head against the window, she got her first glimpse of stars against the black void of the night. Brendan Murphy lived on the edge of the small town of Padiham, some eight miles from Brunton. Far away from any of his colleagues in CID, thought Lucy. In a place where a man might be dangerously alone with his own thoughts, where he might develop his own strange plans.

Tony Pickard spoke for the first time since they had left the station. "Do you remember the map Percy Peach showed us of the Leopard's murders?" he said.

His voice seemed oddly clear in the warm car, as if the momentous nature of their mission was sharpening their senses. Lucy said, "Yes. The one showing the geographical distribution of the killings."

"Yes. It's just struck me. They were neatly distributed, weren't they? The first one was west of Brunton, on the outskirts of Preston; the second was pretty well north, near Clitheroe; the third was in Brunton itself; and the fourth one, last Friday, was due south."

"Yes. Wishart thought that implied the killer was Brunton-oriented, moving his killings around the central point of the town. What of it?"

"Well, the Leopard seems to have a passion for neatness. And the only direction from Brunton where there hasn't been a killing, the one necessary to complete the pattern, is due east, out towards the Pennines."

Lucy Blake saw his point, though she rather wished he hadn't made it. "Yes. Where we're heading now. Where Brendan Murphy lives."

Peach drove into the Brunton Police Station car park to find it almost deserted. He sat for a moment in the darkness, gathering his resources, preparing for what he must now do. Then he got out and marched into the station with his normal bouncy gait. No need to betray any sign of uncertainty to those you worked with; you had an image to sustain.

There was no sign of Lucy Blake, though he had seen her blue Corsa in the car park. He tried her mobile again, but there was still no reply. She must be working – out in the town somewhere, probably. He tried her on her radio, but there was no reply on that either. For the first time, Percy felt a pang of anxiety.

He went into the reception area, spoke to the station sergeant: the man on the desk tended to know where most people were. "Have you seen Brendan Murphy?" he said. "I need to speak to him, urgently."

It was only seven o'clock when Tony Pickard turned the Mondeo carefully into the road where Brendan Murphy lived. But it might have been the middle of the night, for all the activity there was around the place.

Pickard knew exactly where Murphy lived, or they might have had difficulty finding the place. The road was unpaved, with no street lights. They bumped gently over large potholes as he drove past the silent house. He parked forty yards past it, so that anyone peering between the curtains from the unlit frontage would have thought the car was visiting one of the other houses.

"What do we do now?" said Tony.

"Turn the car round, ready for a quick getaway if we're embarrassed," said Lucy tersely. "Brendan may still be in there. He might be at the back of the place. Check that. But don't confront him; I want to be there for that." She wondered if her speech betrayed her tension.

Tony Pickard slid out of the driver's seat, drew himself to his full height, and stood for a moment looking at the building. Then he walked up the path to the front of the silent house. It was semi-detached, built in the 1930s, pebble-dashed in a style long departed. Builders had not allowed for garages in those days, and the house was separated from the adjoining pair only by a narrow passageway, allowing pedestrian access to the rear. Pickard hesitated for a moment before the front door, then disappeared into the shadows as he took this route to the back of the house.

Lucy controlled an absurd wish to run after him, to keep the two of them together in this unfamiliar environment, where the darkness and the silence suddenly seemed to threaten rational thought. She wondered whether she should try to radio in to CID, to report their position and warn that help might be needed. But she could not do that without stating why they were here and what they were about, and her mind shrank from that. If this was as preposterous a quest as she still felt it would be, the fewer people who knew about it the better.

Why was Tony taking so long? He had only to check whether there were lights on at the back of the house to know whether Murphy was there. She had told him not to go beyond that. She couldn't radio him without risking blowing his cover, but she would do it, if he wasn't back in another minute.

Peach radioed Brendan Murphy and had him back in the station within minutes. They had a terse exchange in Peach's

206

office, away from the few people who were logging information in the Murder Room.

No one seemed to know where DS Blake had got to: the popular view was that she must be off duty by now. Yet there was still no reply from either her personal phone or her police radio. Murphy hadn't seen her since he had interviewed Paul Dutton with her in the morning. He said, "I lost my cool a bit with that bugger, when I shouldn't have done. He was so bloody arrogant that—"

"Never mind Paul Dutton. Where the hell is DS Blake? And where the hell is Tony Pickard?"

"They went out to see Clyde Northcott at the electrical works this afternoon. But that was hours ago, now."

Peach took the steps two at a time as he raced down to the car park, with Murphy following more sedately, despite his youth. Lucy Blake's Corsa was still there; Pickard's Mondeo was not. Peach stood with his arms on the top of his black Scorpio and his head thrust down upon them for a moment, forcing himself to think when he wanted the release of action. He looked up, seemed for a moment surprised to find Murphy beside him. "You live out at Padiham, don't you, Brendan?"

"Yes. It's just a—"

"That's east from here, isn't it?"

"Yes. Almost due east, I think, but—"

"Get in!"

He had the engine started and the car moving even as the big DC's buttocks hit the seat. Murphy only got the door shut just in time to avoid the brick pillar at the exit.

"Where the hell have you been?" Lucy Blake let out her tension in the abruptness of her question to the returning Pickard as he slid into the driver's seat of the Mondeo beside her.

"Sorry, Sarge. He's not there."

"Right. We wait." She was determined to give the orders,

to take charge of a situation she felt was in danger of passing out of her control.

"He might not be back for hours. There is something we can do, though. If you approve, that is."

She glanced sharply sideways at him. All she could see was a dark profile, staring ahead. "Well?"

"There's a window I can force at the back. The frame is old and worn. Brendan's house maintenance is about as effective as his gardening!"

It was meant to be a little joke, reducing the tension. But neither of them laughed. It took Lucy's mind back to those stark new gardening gloves, which had started all this.

"You want to break in? To a colleague's house?"

"A colleague who might be the Leopard. Correction: a colleague who *is* the Leopard. I know I'm right, and I'm sure there'll be evidence in there. Maybe notes about his planning, newspaper cuttings about the murders, that sort of thing. We might need that evidence, to make a case against him: he's sure to deny it, and he's left nothing of himself at the scenes of the crimes."

And if you find nothing, it will help to destroy the theory you're now so cocksure about, thought Lucy. "All right. But what do I do if he turns up while you're in there?"

"He won't. Or rather he might, but he won't come to the front. These places have garages at the back, with an unpaved track down to them. I've checked and his car isn't in there. That's another reason why I was so long."

The fact that the whole exchange was conducted in whispers seemed to increase the tension. Lucy thought for a moment, then said as calmly as she could, "All right. I'll go round to the back and keep watch. I'll radio you if there's any sign of him returning. But don't be in there longer than ten minutes. I don't want you conducting a full house search."

She slid out of the warmth of the car, pulled her coat more tightly about her in the biting cold. She could see the frost sparkling already on the grass of the field opposite the houses. Best get this over and done with, as quickly as possible.

Peach drove fast, switching the Scorpio's headlights on full whenever he had the chance, watching the ribbon of dark road leaping towards and under him like a rally-driver on a night assignment. The big man beside him brushed back his unruly brown hair and watched anxiously as the familiar landmarks flashed past. Brendan Murphy had never known Percy Peach drive like this.

He was even more disturbed when he heard the terse statement of the DI's accusation. He stuttered out some sort of denial, some assertion that this could not possibly be true.

There followed a staccato summary of Peach's thinking, punctuated by pauses as he flung the big car round long bends and their progress became even more hectic. It was a strange setting for an even stranger theory. Murphy crouched in his seat and tried to come to terms with it.

Brendan put a cautionary hand on his driver's forearm as the thirty limit sign leapt at them out of the darkness, beside the customary notice that told him they were running into Padiham. He had never neared his own house with such trepidation.

Lucy Blake found Brendan Murphy's garage without much difficulty. It stood like a dark box against the night, looking larger than it was because of the unbroken outline of its roof and the absence of larger buildings to give it any perspective.

There was no moon, but the pale light of the stars reflected from the single small window in the side. She peered automatically through this; she could see nothing of the interior save that there was no car within it, as Tony Pickard had reported. She moved into the shadow between the back wall of Murphy's house and the garage on the other side of the unpaved track which skirted it,

209

J. M. Gregson

providing access to three other garages behind the short row of houses.

She wondered how she would explain her presence here if any of the other residents discovered her. She would have to flash her warrant card and say she was on police business. At least the public generally felt less threatened by women than men in these circumstances. She tried not to think of those other women, the four who had died swiftly and silently at the hands of the Lancashire Leopard.

It was a fairly still night, but it had the biting cold of early February in the foothills of the Pennines. What little wind there was came from the north-east, funnelling down this gap between the garages and the houses, coming straight from Siberia and feeling as if it did. She glanced at her watch, registering the time: ten minutes here was going to seem much longer.

After five, she extracted her radio from the pocket of her coat with fingers that were clumsy with the cold. Tony must be inside by now: there could be no harm in asking what he had found. And she would exhort him to rejoin her as swiftly as possible: she did not fancy being here if Brendan Murphy should come home.

The radio was dead. She could not understand that: it had been working perfectly earlier in the day. Perhaps the battery was down. Or maybe it was just a connection. With her hands shivering with the cold, she managed to ease the battery compartment open. She stared dumb and uncomprehending at the small, empty recess. There was no battery there.

It was at that moment that she heard a slight sound on the other side of the wall and the wooden gate in the wall opened with a tiny squeak of its hinges. Her relief leaped to her lips. "Well? Did you find what you were looking for? Or are we—"

Out of the blackness, the Leopard was abruptly upon her, a black balaclava enclosing his head, the rough leather of the gardening gloves snatching at her throat. She caught the whites of the eyes, then the centres of them blazing with madness as she was borne down, as she felt the strength she had no way of countering above her.

She forced herself to fight. She must keep those questing hands at all costs from her throat. She punched instinctively with her small fists at the face above the hands, then remembered that her only hope was to go for the groin. She turned her shoulder into the centre of this black shape which seemed so huge, so irresistible, threw her weight on to her left leg, brought her right knee up with all the force she could muster into the genitals of her attacker.

But this man was as trained in personal combat as she was. He anticipated her move and brought his thigh up to frustrate it. She provoked a grunt, no more. Not even a muttered curse came through the darkness. And the Leopard was immensely more powerful than she was. Even as she attempted to scream, the coarse leather of the glove was over her mouth, the palm of it was pushing her head inexorably backwards, exposing the throat she knew she must protect.

She went on fighting as he bore her down, knowing now that she must lose. Her resistance was translated into the wish to leave some mark of herself upon him, some scar from her nails upon his face, which might suggest to those left behind who it was that had done this to her.

He pushed aside her hands, held her wrists, brought his own knee up violently in a parody of what she had tried to do, hitting her stomach with it like a mallet, knocking the wind from her in a single gasp of pain and despair. And then those hands were at her throat, seeming huge in the thick leather of the gloves, seeming to have a strength which was more than human. Lucy felt herself thrust down, passing into oblivion, wanting to plead for a last prayer and without the voice to do so.

And then, suddenly, at the moment when consciousness was passing from her, the pressure was released, the hands of the Leopard were torn away from her throat. She saw nothing in those first few seconds of her release. But she heard Percy's voice, in a curse more terrible, more pain-filled, than any sound she had ever heard. Then strong hands were holding the Leopard against the wall, pinioning his arms to his side. And Peach's hand was wrenching the balaclava from Tony Pickard's head.

And Brendan Murphy was yelling the words of arrest into Pickard's face, repeating the familiar, formal phrases about harming his defence if he did not mention when questioned something which he might later rely on in court.

It was almost an hour before the last of the three police cars left the quiet road, the sirens which had announced their arrival long since stilled, their blue lights no longer flashing with the urgency which had proclaimed their presence outside the small semi-detached house.

Tony Pickard had made no great protestations of innocence, had submitted with a dazed air to the handcuffs before he was bundled into the back of the car between the two burly men in uniform. Perhaps, as with other serial killers before him, there was a kind of relief for him in being caught. But he gave no sign of that; he looked merely dazed that what he had planned and executed so carefully had failed after all.

Lucy Blake had a bruise on the left-hand side of her throat and a certain hoarseness of speech to remind her of how near she had been to death. She looked shamefacedly at Brendan Murphy. "I never really believed him, you know, when he said you were the Leopard."

"No? But you thought you'd better come out here and investigate me, just in case!"

She shook her head wearily, stopped the movement abruptly as it hurt her throat. "We were supposed to be investigating any lead, however bizarre. I wanted you to defend yourself to us and dispose of the idea, before it went any further. And he was very persuasive with those gardening gloves."

"I don't know how the hell he expected to get away with it."

Peach looked at him sharply. "Don't you, Brendan? You haven't thought it through, then. He produced the gardening gloves and pretended they'd come from your locker. He removed the batteries from Lucy's radio. He persuaded Lucy that you might be – just might be – the Leopard and got her out here to check on you. He'd have killed her, left her, and been away from the scene long before her body was found."

"But why try to frame me?"

Peach shook his head slowly. "I don't think he was. Lucy's body would have been found here and you'd have had to explain yourself. No doubt he'd have had extra pleasure if you'd had any difficulty in proving you were elsewhere at the time. But all he was really interested in was another killing – a bolder one than ever, with a policewoman as victim – with nothing at all to direct suspicion towards him. I've no doubt Tony Pickard would have been back at Brunton nick within half an hour, probably pretending he'd been there all the time. Don't forget that in all probability the body wouldn't have been found until tomorrow morning, if he'd dumped it by the side of your garage. By then, no one could have been very precise about the time of death."

Lucy Blake shivered. She didn't like being talked about as "the body": it had been far too near the truth for comfort. "He was bloody clever: he made me think I was making most of the decisions. And he must have taken the batteries out of my radio back at the station." She looked suspiciously at Percy. "How long have you suspected Tony Pickard?"

Peach grinned ruefully. "Since about three o'clock this afternoon. It came to me in a flash."

"What did?"

"When we put our heads together about the Leopard yesterday, he mentioned that we'd been told that the last victim, Sally Cartwright, screamed before she died. But we hadn't. No one had mentioned that. Not even the man walking his dog who thought he spoke to the killer afterwards mentioned any scream. The only person alive

213

who could have heard that scream was the Leopard himself."

"And how did you know that he'd be out at Brendan's place?"

"I didn't. I was desperate, once I found that he'd taken you off in his Mondeo. The only thing I could think of was that the next murder was likely to be east of Brunton, to complete the geographical pattern – we thought the Leopard was a planner, who enjoyed that planning and his own perverted logic. I knew that Brendan lived pretty well due east, that Tony Pickard would have known Padiham well from visiting Brendan – and that it was quite a remote spot. I've been here too, you know!"

"And so have I, now," said Lucy Blake grimly. "I think I might need to come back some other time, to exorcise the demons. Some bright summer's afternoon, perhaps."

They left Brendan Murphy in his own house. Peach drove slowly on the way back into Brunton, glad to have something to do with the hands he found suddenly wanted to tremble. When they had travelled a good two miles of the way, he managed to say, "Tha wer't a daft prat tonight, lass."

Lucy smiled for the first time in hours. She liked it when he thee'd and thou'd her. "Ay. A gret gobbin, my Dad would have said. Tha'll need to take better care of me, Percy Peach."

He was still too shaken by the narrowness of her escape to continue in light-hearted vein. "And you'll need to take better care of yourself, won't you?"

She nodded a little, watching familiar Brunton landmarks appear as they reached the outskirts of the grimy old cotton town. "We got the Leopard, though, didn't we?"

"Ay, lass, we did that." Percy allowed himself a small sigh of satisfaction. Then another thought clouded his horizon. "And I've no doubt Tommy Bloody Tucker will get his promotion out of it."

Percy Peach felt suddenly very weary.